ANALOG II

ANALOG II

Edited by
JOHN W. CAMPBELL

DOUBLEDAY & COMPANY, INC.
GARDEN CITY, NEW YORK

"The Weather Man" by Theodore L. Thomas, "Junior Achievement" by William M. Lee, "Ethical Quotient" by John T. Phillifent,
and "The Circuit Riders" by R. C. FitzPatrick, reprinted by permission of the authors.

"Novice" by James H. Schmitz, reprinted by permission of the author and the author's agents, Scott Meredith Literary Agency, Inc.

"Good Indian" by Mack Reynolds, reprinted by permission of the
author and the author's agents, Scott Meredith Literary Agency, Inc.

"Philosopher's Stone" by Christopher Anvil, reprinted by permission
of the author and the author's agents, Scott Meredith Literary
Agency, Inc.

"Blind Man's Lantern" by Allen Kim Lang, reprinted by permission
of the author and the author's agents, Paul R. Reynolds & Son.

CONTENTS

TO
Leslyn
Who not only pretty much had to read it
but will also have to live a good bit of it
or something very much like it.

PREFACE

This is the second volume of stories taken from Condé Nast's science-fiction magazine, *Analog*—a sort of sampler of what the field of science fiction can do, and the fun it can have doing it.

We start with "The Weather Man," by Theodore L. Thomas—an answer to the ancient complaint that "everybody talks about it but nobody does anything about it." One of the problems of a good science-fiction writer is to try to present not only the things that can be, and will be, done—but the reasons why those things may not be so darned nice and easy when we do have them worked out. I've been editing science fiction now for over twenty-five years; for all those years I've wanted stories about weather control, because it's so thoroughly fascinating a problem and a possibility. Ted Thomas is a patent lawyer, and knows something of the complications that follow a nice, simple, technological achievement; Thomas is the first one to do a weather-control story that seemed to me to express both the scope and the immediacy of weather control.

Weather control is a typical science-fiction theme, in that the purely technical side of weather control is going to be as minor a factor in its use (and misuse!) as it is in the field of nuclear energy. Thomas brings out the fact that the weather controllers would be the absolute controllers of the politics of the Earth; no dictator, no intransigent population could stand against the men who could give them drought, floods, or thirty feet of snowfall.

An atomic bomb is a club—a war ax. But weather control can be a garrote, a hangman's noose, or slow poison.

But not even Thomas attempted to handle the really insoluble problem of weather control. In Florida, the citrus growers need rain to keep the fresh-water table of the sandy peninsula high enough to prevent salt water seeping in and killing their trees. And the immense resort industry, of course, wants nothing but clear, sunny, balmy weather. The one thing they'll agree on perfectly is that it must *never* be cold! But if farmers want rain and resorts want all sunshine . . . what should a weather controller do?

And then there are the ski resorts that want snow and sun at least ten months a year; usually, the ski-lift owners live next door to the summer-camp operators, too—and *they* want sun and warm weather ten months of the year.

The province of science fiction is both the ridiculous and the sublime. On the ridiculous side, we have "Good Indian" to offer. Mack Reynolds is a foreign correspondent by profession, and science fiction is a way for him to express some things he's not quite able to say in overseas dispatches . . . some things that are thoroughly ridiculous but which politics and diplomacy treat with the most pompous solemnity.

Just to set the record straight, incidentally—the Seminole Indians *are* still officially at war with the United States.

Basically the thing the reader pays the author to do for him—whether it be a murder mystery, a book of essays, science fiction, or a serious novel—is to think some problem through with more attention to detail than the reader has time to. Or think it through to some surprising or off-beat conclusion. The essence of originality in fiction is much the same as it is in inventions of the scientific kind; a careful and detailed consideration of relevant factors leading to an unexpected result.

Allen Kim Lang certainly did this in "Blind Man's

Lantern." The delightful—and, once understood, highly cogent—idea of Aaron and Martha Stoltzfoos, Amish folk, riding their horse-drawn wagon from the hold of an interstellar liner, to set up their farm on some remote planet of an alien star—that is one of the better concepts of this or any other year!

To a very large extent, philosophy has been the intellectual framework on which some impassioned man has built an ideology and carried his ideology to a crusade. Looking back on history, we can usually say, "It was a very painful and difficult time, but it all worked out for the best." Poul Anderson pointed out a while back that that aspect of having "worked out for the best" is the inescapable consequence of the viewpoint of the people who descended from the victors. Suppose Hannibal had conquered Rome? The glory of Rome—which was largely tinsel, supported by slaves and entertained by the deaths of thousands in public spectacles of sadism—would never have been. It was more than a millennium later that Venice became the first commercial empire . . . but Carthage was headed that way before Rome destroyed it. We might have skipped a thousand years of blood-soaked history.

Of course, we—the individuals we are—wouldn't have been born. It certainly did "work out for the best" for *us!* No other history could have produced us, naturally!

But philosophy has always seemed the mumblings of inept men with long beards; the crusade based on a new ideology doesn't seem at all like a philosophy. Well, neither does the inexpressible howling, shrieking fire demon riding the tail of a space rocket taking off seem related to the quietly smoking, slender column that stood there so peacefully a moment before. "An ideology" or "a crusade" is simply "a philosophy" after someone has pushed the igniter button. The philosophy is the structure and the engine; emotion supplies the fuel—and the take-off can neither be predicted nor controlled. Once the igniter has been fired, only the destruct button can stop the flight of a rocket. Or of a philosophy-turned-crusade.

One of the advantages of science fiction is that it can launch a paper rocket, in a fictional trajectory, thirty years before the first Sputnik circles Earth. It gives us a chance to do some of our thinking before, instead of after, the philosophy has become a campaign. Those who were startled by the introduction of space flight and atomic energy in World War II either hadn't been reading science fiction, considered it sheer nonsense, or read it and thought we were just kidding.

For your information: We were not kidding in the 1930s when we said the rocket ships and space flight and atomic energy were coming, and coming soon.

We aren't kidding now when we say new philosophies are coming. New approaches to living, developing from new techniques both of objective science—weather control for instance—and, equally, new techniques of subjective science. Of psychology and sociology. There are totally ununderstood talents human beings have manifested down through the ages—and which we cannot, today, either understand, find a place for in our present picture of the Universe, or apply.

In that general department, you'll find "Novice," by James H. Schmitz, "Ethical Quotient," by John T. Phillifent, and a curious little story of a kind of invasion-of-privacy, "The Circuit Riders," by R. C. FitzPatrick.

After you've finished it, and appreciated in full just how "wonderful, wonderful lucky she was"—consider whether you, as a citizen of the city, would have voted for the installation of the deAngelis boards when it was proposed. Would you have wanted those damnable contraptions monitoring your emotions every hour of every day? Would you have rejected the things when they were suggested . . . ?

Science fiction can help evaluate the coming problems before the fever of the Crusade gets started. It can, even, take some of the propaganda value out of the Crusaders' shrieks when they do start!

John W. Campbell,
Mountainside, N.J.
June 17, 1963

THE WEATHER MAN

by Theodore L. Thomas

". . . And the name 'Weather Bureau' continued to be used, although the organization itself was somewhat changed in form. Thus the Weather Congress consisted of three arms. First was the political arm, the Weather Council. Second was the scientific arm, the Weather Advisors. Third was the operating arm, the Weather Bureau. All three arms were relatively independent, and each . . ."
THE COLUMBIA ENCYCLOPEDIA, 32nd Edition
Columbia University Press

Jonathan H. Wilburn opened his eyes and immediately felt the tension in the day. He lay there, puzzled, seeking the source of it. It was the start of just another day in Palermo. The street noises were normal, his apartment was quiet, and he felt good. That was it. He felt good, very good, full of vigor and strong of mind, and with the feeling that he was ready for anything that might happen.

In one movement he threw back the cover and rolled to his feet alongside the bed. Not bad for a man who had turned fifty last week. He stepped into the shower and dissolved his pajamas into a rich foam of cleansing lather. He dried and stood motionless in the center of his dressing room. The tension and the excitement were still with him.

He depilated and dressed, and as he slipped into his jacket it came to him.

Sometime during the night in his sleep he had made up his mind that the time had come for him to make a move. He was fifty years old, he had carefully built a good reputation, and he had come as far as he could in the normal course of events. It was now time to push, time to take a chance. To reach the top in politics you have to take a chance.

Wilburn finished slipping into his jacket. He bared his teeth at himself in the mirror. Now he knew why the day felt different. But knowing the reason did nothing to diminish the tension. He would live with it from now on; this he knew for a certainty. He would live and work on the tips of his toes, looking for a way to seize the god of luck and give him a good ringing out.

For a quarter of a century he had moved cautiously, planning each move, insuring its success before he committed himself to it. Slowly he had climbed through the tiers of politics, the House, the Senate, the United Nations, an ambassadorship, several emergency chairmanships, and finally, the most elite of all bodies, the Weather Congress. His reputation was made, he was known as a brilliant, affable diplomat, one with high skill at bringing about agreement among other hostile Councilmen. He had built a strong following among the two hundred members in the Weather Council. But in politics as in everything else, the higher one climbs, the tougher the advancement. Wilburn suddenly came to the realization that he had not made any advancements in four years. Then came his fiftieth birthday.

Jonathan Wilburn ate breakfast with his wife that morning. Harriet was a slim woman, quietly wise in her role of the wife of a member of the Council of the Weather Congress. In one quick glance she saw that her husband was tight as a wire, and she touched the Diner and placed coffee in front of him. While he sipped it she touched out a set of onion-flavored eggs and carefully hand-basted them with the pork sauce he loved so much; she did not trust the Diner to do it right. While she worked she chatted about the news in the morning paper. Wilburn ate his breakfast, part listening, part smiling and grunting responses, and part staring into space. He kissed her good-by then, and went out and stepped on a walk.

He rode the walk through the soft Sicilian air, and then became impatient with standing still. He stepped off the walk and strode alongside, and he felt pleased at the way his legs stretched. Off in the distance he could see the dome of the main Council building, and it brought his mind back to the problem at hand. But, even as he thought it, he knew it was nothing he could reason out in advance. This was something he would have to pick up on the spur of the moment. And he would have to stay alert to recognize it when it came.

Wilburn stepped back on the walk and rode it to the Council.

He entered the Great Hall by the north stairs and walked along the east wall toward the stairs to his office. A group of sight-seers were being guided across the Great Hall by a uniformed guide, and the guide was describing the wonders of the Hall. When the guide saw Wilburn coming, he interrupted his lecture to say, "And coming toward us from our left is Councilman Wilburn of an eastern United States District of whom you have all heard and who will play such an important part in the vote today to reduce the water available to northern Australia."

The sight-seers stopped, stumbling into one another at the unexpected appearance of such a celebrity. Wilburn smiled and waved at them, and this confounded them even more, but he did not stop to talk. He knew from the guide's remarks that none of his constituents were in the group; the guide would have contrived to warn him so that he could act accordingly. Wilburn smiled to himself—an officeholder had many advantages over a mere candidate for office.

Wilburn turned to the stairs and rode up with Councilman Georges DuBois, of middle Europe. DuBois said, "I heard him. Decided yet how you are to vote on this Australian situation, Jonathan?"

"I lean toward an aye, but I don't know. Do you?"

DuBois shook his head. "I feel the same. It is a thing we should do only with the greatest of caution. It is a terrible thing to make men suffer, and even worse to do it to women and children. I don't know."

They rode in silence to the top of the stairs, and just before they parted Wilburn said, "My wife stands with me in everything *I* do, George."

DuBois looked at him thoughtfully for a moment, and then said, "Yes, I understand you. The women there are as much to blame as the men, and deserve punishment as much. Yes, that will help me if I vote aye. I will see you in Council." They nodded good-by to each other in a wordless gesture of mutual respect and understanding. DuBois was one of the thoughtful Councilmen who knew better than most the fearful responsibility carried by the political arm of the Weather Congress.

Wilburn nodded to his staff as he passed through the outer office. Once at his desk he swiftly settled down to take care of the many chores. The small pile of papers stacked neatly in the center of his desk melted away as he picked up one after another, dictated the words that disposed of it, and dropped it on another pile.

He was just finishing when a gentle masculine voice said through the speaker, "Have you time to see a friend?"

Wilburn smiled, and got up to open the door of his office for Councilman Gardner Tongareva. The two men smiled and shook hands, and Tongareva settled back deep into one of Wilburn's chairs. He was a yellow-skinned man, a Polynesian, wrinkled and old and wise. His trousers were full and short, reminiscent of the sarong worn by his ancestors. His hair was white and his face was warm and kindly. Tongareva was one of those rare men whose mere presence brought smiles to the faces of his companions and peace to their hearts. He was a man of enormous influence in the Council solely by virtue of his personality.

His district was 15–30 degrees north latitude 150–165 degrees east longitude, the same fifteen-degree-on-a-side landed area of the Earth as the District of each of the other Councilmen. But in Tongareva's case the land was vanishingly small. The only land in the entire region was Marcus Island, one square mile in area, and supporting exactly four people. This was quite a contrast with the 100 million people living in Wilburn's District of 30–45 degrees north latitude 75–90 degrees west longitude. Yet time after time when the population-weighted votes of the two hundred Councilmen were counted, it was apparent that Tongareva had swayed a large percentage of the entire globe.

Wilburn leaned back in his chair and said to Tongareva, "Have you reached a decision yet about the Australian drought?"

Tongareva nodded. "Yes, I have. I believe we have no choice but to subject them to a year's drought. Naughty children must be spanked, and for two years these people have persisted in maintaining an uneven balance of trade. What is really involved here, Jonathan, is a challenge to the supreme authority of the Weather Congress over the peoples of the world. These people in Queensland and the Northern Territory are a hardy lot. They don't really believe that we can or will chastise them by controlling their weather to their detriment. They must be punished immediately or other sections of the world will begin acting up, too. At this time a simple drought to take away their lush prosperity for a year ought to serve. Later it might become necessary to make them suffer, and none of us wants that. Yes, Jonathan, my vote will be cast in favor of the Australian drought."

Wilburn nodded soberly. He saw now that the vote almost certainly would be in favor of punishment. Most of the Councilmen seemed to feel it was necessary, but were reluctant to cause suffering. But when Tongareva stated his position as he just had, the reluctance would be put aside. Wilburn said, "I agree with you, Gardner. You have put into words the thoughts of most of us in this matter. I will vote with you."

Tongareva said nothing, but he continued to stare sharply at Wilburn. It was not a discomfiting stare; nothing Tongareva did was ever discomfiting. Tongareva said, "You are a different man this morning, my good friend. Just as you have been still a different man for the last three weeks. You have resolved whatever it is that has been disturbing you, and I am pleased. No," he raised a hand as Wilburn was about to speak, "it is quite unnecessary to discuss it. When you want me, I will be there to help you." He stood up. "And now I must go to discuss the Australian situation with some of the others." He smiled and left before Wilburn could say anything.

Wilburn stared after him, awed at the enormous ability of Tongareva to understand what he had been going through. He shook his head and gathered himself and then went out into his waiting room to talk to the dozen people who were waiting to see him.

"I'm sorry to keep you waiting," he said to all of them, "but things are hectic around the Council this morning, as I guess you know. Please forgive me for not seeing each of you alone, but we will be summoned for Council business in a few minutes. I did not want to miss the chance to see all of you for a moment or two at least. Perhaps we can get together this afternoon or tomorrow morning."

And Wilburn moved around the room shaking hands and fixing in his mind the name of each visitor. Two of them were not constituents. They were lobbyists representing the northern Australian Districts, and they launched into a tirade against the taking of any punitive action against the Districts.

Wilburn held up his hand and said, "Gentlemen, this topic may not be discussed under these circumstances. I will listen to the arguments for and against on the floor of the Council, nowhere else. That is all." He smiled and began to pass on. The younger of the two seized his arm and turned him to face him, saying, "But Councilman you must listen. These poor people are being made to suffer for the acts of a few of their leaders. You cannot—"

Wilburn shrugged away from the restraining arm, stepped swiftly to the wall and pressed a button there. The lobbyist turned pale and said, "Oh, now, Councilman, I meant no harm. Please do not lodge a protest against me. Please—"

Two men in the uniform of the Weather Congress swept in the outer door. Wilburn's voice was calm and his face impassive, but his eyes glinted like ice crystals. He pointed and said to the guards, "This man grabbed my arm to try

to force me to listen to his arguments on Council business.
I lodge a protest against him."

It all happened so fast the rest of the visitors had difficulty recalling exactly what had happened. But the record-
ing tapes showed, and Wilburn knew that the lobbyist would
never again be allowed in the halls of the Weather Congress.
The two guards softly hustled him out of the room. The
other lobbyist said, "I am sorry, Councilman. I feel responsible for his conduct; he is new."

Wilburn nodded and started to speak, but a low musical
chime sounded repeatedly in the room. Wilburn said to the
visitors, "Please excuse me. I must go to the Council Floor
now. If you wish, you may watch the proceedings from the
Visitor's Auditorium. Thank you for coming up to see me,
and I hope we can talk more another time." He waved
and smiled and went back into his office.

Hurriedly he checked his staff to see that they were ready
for the day's business. All were in position, all knew their
roles in the coming debate. Wilburn then took the belt to the
Floor, walking the last hundred yards out in the public hall
where he could be seen. As he came to the main doors
several newspapermen asked permission to approach, but
he refused; he wanted to get to his desk early and start
work.

He went through the doors and down the short wide hall
that led to the Floor. He came out into the huge room and
went down the main aisle toward his desk. A few Councilmen were already there, and as the Recorder called off
Wilburn's name, they looked up and waved at him. He
waved back and continued on his way to his high-seniority
desk up front. He sat down and began flipping the buttons
and switches that put him in touch with everything that
was going on. Immediately a light glowed indicating that
one of the seated Councilmen wanted to talk to him. Coun-

cilman Hardy of 165–180 west longitude 30–45 south latitude—containing most of New Zealand—said to him, "Well,
Jonathan, have you talked with Tongareva yet?"

"Yes, George, I have."

"Going to vote the way he wants?"

"Yes, although I want to wait and hear what is said in
opposition before I finally make up my mind. Where do
you stand?"

There was a perceptible pause, then, "I will probably vote
against it, unless someone expresses the extreme reluctance
of the Council to vote for drought."

"Why don't you do it, George?"

"Maybe I will. Thank you, Jonathan." And he cut the
circuit.

Wilburn looked around the huge chamber, and as always, he became a little awed at what he saw. It was more
than the impressive array of the two hundred huge desks,
the raised President's chair, the great board that showed
the weather at the moment on every part of the Earth's surface, and the communications rooms set off from the main
room. There was an aura about this great chamber that was
felt by all the men and women who entered it, whether to
work in it or simply to visit. The fate of the Earth was
centered here, and had been for fifty years. From this chamber flowed the decisions that controlled the world.

The Weather Congress was the supreme body of Earth,
able to bend states, nations, continents, and hemispheres to
its will. What dictator, what country, could survive when
no drop of rain fell for a year? Or what dictator, what
country could survive when blanketed under fifty feet of
snow and ice? The Weather Congress could freeze the
Congo River or dry up the Amazon. It could flood the Sahara or Tierra del Fuego. It could thaw the tundra, and

raise and lower the levels of the oceans at will. And here, in this chamber, all the political decisions had been made, and the chamber seemed to acquire some of the feeling that had been expressed over the last half century, from the stormy early days, to the more settled and reflective present. It was a powerful chamber, and it made its power felt by those who sat in it.

A great many Councilmen had seated themselves. Another chime sounded, and the weather requests began to be relayed to the Councilmen. The Recorder read off the requests, and his voice reached each desk through a tiny speaker. At the same time the written request flashed on the big board. In this manner the Councilmen could busy themselves with other duties while keeping an eye on the requests.

The first request, as usual, came from the Lovers of the Lowly Cactus Plant, and they wanted less rainfall and more desolation in Death Valley to keep the Barrel Cactus from becoming extinct.

Wilburn rang Tongareva's desk and said, "How many have you talked to, Gardner?"

"About forty, Jonathan. I caught a large group having a cup of coffee."

"Have you talked to Maitland?"

There was a perceptible pause. Maitland seemed always to be against anything Wilburn stood for. His District was 60–75 west longitude 30–45 north latitude, adjoining Wilburn's and including New York City and Boston. Maitland always made it plain that he considered Wilburn unfit for the position of influence he held in the Council. "No," said Tongareva, and Wilburn could see him shake his great head, "no, I did not talk to Maitland."

Wilburn signed off, and listened and watched. The president of Bolivia complained that the region around Cochabamba was running a little too cool to suit his taste. The mayor of Avigait in Greenland stated that the corn crop was ten per cent lower this year due to an extra two inches of rainfall and too much cloud cover. Wilburn nodded; there was one that should be treated seriously, and he pushed a button on his desk marked "favorable" to insure that it would be considered by the entire Council.

His phone rang. It was a constituent asking him to address the Combined Rotary Club at their annual meeting October 27th next. The clear light flashed as Wilburn's staff, monitoring and checking everything, indicated that he was free on that day. "Why, thank you, yes," said Wilburn, accepting the invitation. "I shall be grateful for the chance to talk to your group." He knew he had made no address in that region for a year, and it was high time. Probably his staff had subtly set it up in the first place.

A farmer outside of Gatrun, Libya, wanted his neighbor's water cut back so that all their crops would be the same height.

Then a conference was called among half a dozen Councilmen to discuss the order of speeches on the Australian situation. While they worked this out, Wilburn noted a request from Ceylon to be allowed to go over from rice in the inland sections to wheat, with the attendant reduction in rainfall and average temperature. He pushed the "favorable" button.

It was decided that George DuBois, of Middle Europe, should introduce the drought resolution, with appropriately reluctant language.

One George Andrews of Holtville, California, wanted to see snow fall again before he died, which would be in a few weeks now, no matter that it was July. He could not leave the semitropical environment of Holtville.

Tongareva would second the resolution, and then they

would hear the Councilmen from the Australian Districts
present their reasons why the punishment should not be
instituted. After that they would play it by ear.

The seaport city of Stockholm requested an additional
fifteen centimeters of elevation for the Baltic Sea. Kobdo,
Mongolia, complained that there had been two disastrous
avalanches due to the extra snow burden. And it was there
that the hairs on the back of Wilburn's neck began to
prickle.

He stiffened in his seat and looked around to see the
source of the strange sensation. The floor bustled with activity, all of it normal. He stood up, but he could see nothing more. He saw Tongareva looking over at him. He
shrugged his shoulders and sat down and stared at the bar-
rage of lights on his desk. His skin almost crawled and the
adrenalin poured into his veins and he felt wildly exhilarated. What was it? He grabbed the edge of the desk and
closed his eyes and forced himself to think. He blanked out
all the activity around him and forced his mind to relax
and find the source of the stimulation. Australian problem?
No, not that. It was . . . it was something in the weather
requests. He opened his eyes, and pushed the playback button and watched the requests again.

One by one, more quickly now, they flashed on the miniature screen on his desk. Avalanches, Baltic Sea level, snow
in southern California, Ceylon's rice to wheat, the Libyan
farmer, the— Wait. He had it now, so he turned back to it
and read it very slowly.

George Andrews of Holtville, California, wanted to see
snow fall again before he died soon, and he would be unable
to leave the semitropical environment of southern California. The more Wilburn stared at it, the more it seemed to
have everything he needed. It had universal appeal: a dying

man with a final request. It would be difficult: snow in July
in southern California was unheard of; he wasn't even certain that it could be carried out. It was almost completely
irrational; the Council had never bothered with such requests in the past. The more Wilburn looked at it, the more
he became convinced he had found the proper cause on
which to risk his career. People the world over would be
behind him if he could bring it off. He remembered how it
had been in the tradition of American presidents to show an
occasional high concern over some unimportant individual.
If he failed, he would probably be finished in politics, but
that was the chance to take. And there was something about
that name George Andrews, something that set off a vague,
disturbing memory in the back of his mind, something that
had attracted him to the request in the first place. No matter. It was time for him to call up for action all the forces
he could muster.

He cut his entire staff into his circuit, and cut all others
out. He said, "I am considering supporting the George Andrews request." He paused to allow the statement to sink in,
smiling to himself at the shock to his staff; never had they
heard of anything so wild from him. "Check out everything
you can about George Andrews. Make certain that his request is bona fide and isn't some sort of trap for an innocent
Councilman like me. In particular, make certain that no
connection exists between George Andrews and Councilman Maitland. Check with Greenberg in the Advisors as to
the chances of coming up with a solution to the problem of
snow in July in southern California in an extremely re-
stricted region. Given that answer, check with the Bureau,
probably Hechmer—he's up on the sun right now—and see
what the chances are of carrying it out. This must be completed in . . . just a moment." Wilburn looked around
him. The weather requests had ended, and Councilman

Yardley had left his desk and was walking toward the front
of the Floor to assume his role as President. "You have
four hours to get all the information. Go, and good luck.
We will all need it this time." And Wilburn sat back. There
was no time to relax, however.

Calls had piled up while he had set the investigation in
motion. He began clearing them as President Yardley
called the Council to order, swiftly dispensed with the old
business, and then brought up the matter of the censure of
Australia. Wilburn kept an ear on the transactions on the
Floor as he continued to handle the incoming calls and
other demands on his time. The President stated the order
of the speeches for and against the drought resolution, and
the Council sat back to listen. Councilman DuBois made
his preliminary remarks, expressing the deep and abiding
regret that the Council found it necessary in this manner
to uphold the principles of the Weather Congress. It was a
good speech, thought Wilburn. There could be no doubt of
DuBois' sincerity, and when he solemnly stated the resolution itself, there were tears in his eyes, and his voice shook.
Then the first of the Councilmen from Australia got up to
argue against the resolution.

Wilburn pocketed the portable receiver, punched the
button that showed he was listening via receiver, and left
the floor. Many other Councilmen did the same, most of
them heading for the Councilmen's Closed Restaurant
where they could have a cup of coffee without having to deal
with constituents, the press, lobbyists, or any of a multitude
of organizations. They sipped their coffee and nibbled sweet
cakes and talked. The conversation was all on the coming
vote, and it was easy to see that opinion was hardening in
favor of the resolution. The Councilmen talked in low
voices so they could follow the trend of the arguments being

made back on the floor; each Councilman had his portable receiver with him and each listened through the bone microphone behind an ear. The talk grew louder as it became apparent that the Australian Councilman was advancing nothing more than the same old arguments, don't-cause-suffering and give-us-another-chance. The vote was now almost a certainty.

Wilburn wandered back to the floor and handled some more of the day's business at his desk. He went out for more coffee, and returned. He rose to make a brief speech in favor of the resolution, expressing regret for the necessity. Then, as the arguments pro and con began to draw toward the end, the information on George Andrews began to come in.

George Andrews was one hundred and twenty-six years old with a heart condition, and the doctors had given him six weeks to live. There was no discernible connection between Andrews and Councilman Maitland. Wilburn interrupted to ask, "Who checked on that?"

"Jack Parker," was the answer, and Wilburn heard a slight chuckle, which he forgave. Jack Parker was one of the keenest investigators in the business, and Wilburn noted to himself that the staff member who had thought of putting Parker on that particular investigation was due for a bonus. At least Wilburn could now make a decision without fear of walking into a political trap of some kind. But the report continued.

"As I guess you know, Andrews came very close to being one of the most famous men in the world a hundred years ago. For a while it looked like Andrews would get credit for inventing the sessile boats, but he was finally beaten by Hans Daggensnurf. There used to be a few people around who insisted that Andrews was the real inventor all along, and that dirty politics, shrewd lawyers, unethical corporations, and filthy money combined to make a goat out of him. The name 'sessile boats' was Andrews' name for the sun boats, and the name has stuck. But then, you could never have called them Daggensnurf boats."

Wilburn remembered now, awed that his subconscious mind should have somehow alerted him to the need to check out the name George Andrews. Andrews had been the George Seldon of the automobile industry, the William Kelly of the so-called Bessemer steel process. All were forgotten men; someone else reaped the immortality. In Andrews' case, he had, according to some, been the man who invented the sun boats, those marvelous devices that made the entire Weather Congress possible. Sliding on a thin film of gaseous carbon, the sessile boats safely traversed the hell of the sun's surface, moving from place to place to stir up the activity needed to produce the desired weather. Without the sessile boats there would be no Weather Bureau staffed by lean, hard-eyed men, working the sun to produce the results called for by the Weather Council. Yes, Wilburn was lucky indeed to have dragged out his piece of ancient history just when he needed it.

The report continued, "We checked with the Weather Advisors, particularly Bob Greenberg. He says there is a fair chance they can find a way to pull snow in southern California this time of year, but he's not guaranteeing anything. One of his people has the beginnings of a new theory that might just work, and our request might be the one to test it out. But he doesn't want to be quoted on any of this. He's got a personnel problem with the genius who would do the work if our request was official. I gathered he would like for us to push it through so he could settle things one way or the other with this bright-eyed genius."

Wilburn asked, "How about the Bureau?"

"Well, we talked to Hechmer as you suggested. It is his

tour on the sun right now, so he's in close touch. He says they've only got one Boat Master in the entire Bureau with enough guts and imagination, and he's having some kind of trouble at home. But Hechmer says if we come up with something special, he'll find a way to make his man produce."

Wilburn listened to many other details relating to the Andrews situation. His first assistant had added a feature of his own to the investigation, one which showed why he was such a highly paid member of Wilburn's staff. He had supervised a quiet opinion survey to find how Wilburn's constituents would react to his sponsoring a motion to grant Andrews' request. The result was predictable: If the request went through quickly and smoothly, and if the snow fell, Wilburn would be a wise, humane, and generous man. If acrimony developed in a debate and if snow did not fall, Wilburn would be a man who had blundered badly.

The report ended. Wilburn cleared his desk of all activity and took a quick look out at the floor. The debate was winding up. The Councilmen were visibly restless to get on to the voting, and it was now clear that the vote was overwhelmingly in favor of the resolution calling for a drought. Wilburn sat back to think.

But even as he sat back he knew the answer; there was really no need to make a decision here. He was going to do it. The only question was: How? And as he turned his mind to the timing of presenting his motion, he saw that here and now was the time. When better than right at the time the Council was finishing an unpleasant piece of business? He might be able to slip his motion through to help take the unpleasant taste from the mouths of the Councilmen. That was it. Wilburn sat back to wait the vote. In another ten minutes it started.

And in twenty minutes it was over. The vote in favor of the drought resolution was 192 to 8. The President lifted his gavel to adjourn the session, Wilburn stood up.

"Mr. President," he said, "we have just had to carry out a necessary but unpleasant duty. I now wish to move that the Council carry out an unnecessary but pleasant duty. I respectfully direct the attention of the honorable members to Weather Request Number 18, today's date."

He paused while the members, looking puzzled, punched the button on their desks that would play back for them the Andrews' request. Wilburn waited until he saw most of the faces turned toward him in disbelief. Then he said, "I just said that our duty in this matter was unnecessary, but in a larger sense we have never had a more necessary duty in conscience to see that justice . . ." And Wilburn stated his case for Andrews. He briefly traced the history of George Andrews' career, and the debt owed him by the human race, a debt that had never been paid. As he talked, Wilburn smiled to himself at the phone calls he knew were racing from desk to desk on the Floor. "What's got into Jonathan?" "Has Wilburn lost his mind?" "Watch yourself on this one; he's up to something."

Wilburn stated the difficulty of knowing for certain whether the request was even within the realm of technological possibility. Only the Weather Advisors could tell. And even if it were possible, the Bureau might not be able to carry it out. But such considerations should not stop the Council from trying. And he concluded with an impassioned plea for this act of grace to show the world that the Council was made up of men who never lost sight of the individual.

He sat down amidst silence. Then Tongareva rose, and with soft words and gentle manner he supported the resolution, emphasizing the warmth and humanity of the motion at a time when there would be many who thought the Council too harsh. He sat down, and Maitland rose to the Floor. To Wilburn's astonishment, Maitland, too, supported the resolution. But as Wilburn listened, he understood that Maitland supported the resolution only because he saw disaster in it for Wilburn. It took nerve for Maitland to do it. He could not know what Wilburn had in mind, but Maitland was willing to trust his judgment that a mistake had been made and to try to capitalize on it.

Wilburn answered all the incoming calls from his fellow Councilmen, all of whom wanted to know if Wilburn wanted them to rise in support of the motion. Some of these were his friends, others were those who owed him a favor. To all of them Wilburn urged support in the form of a brief supporting speech. For forty minutes Councilmen bobbed up, spoke for a moment, and then sat down. When the vote came, it was one of the few unanimous votes in the history of the Council. The Australian drought was forgotten, both on the floor and on the video screens of the world. All thoughts were turned to the little town of Holtville, California.

Wilburn heard the gavel adjourn the session, and he knew he was fully committed. His fate was in the hands of others; his work was done for now, possibly forever.

But after all, if one wants to reach the top in politics, one has to take a chance.

Anna Brackney wandered up the broad steps of the Weather Advisors Building half an hour early, as usual. At the top she stopped and looked out over the city of Stockholm. It was a pretty city, sturdy under its heavy roofs, sparkling under the early morning sun, and quiet and restful. Stockholm was a fine place for the Advisors. In fact it was such an excellent choice for the kind of work the Ad-

visors did, Anna wondered all over again how it was possible for men to have chosen it. She turned and went in.

The Maintenance Supervisor, Hjalmar Froding, directed
the Polishing Machine around the lobby. He saw Anna
Brackney and immediately guided the Machine to lay down
a tic-tac-toe pattern in wax on the floor, and then he bowed
to her. She stopped, put her finger in her mouth, and then
pointed to the upper right-hand square. The Machine put
an "O" on it, and then placed an "X" in the center square
for Froding. The game went on until Froding had three
"Xs" in a row, and the Machine triumphantly ran a straight
line through them. Hjalmar Froding bowed to Anna Brackney, and she bowed to him and went on her way. She ignored the escalator and walked up the stairs, feeling pleased
that she again was able to have Froding win in an unobvious
manner. Anna Brackney was fond of Froding; he seldom
spoke or smiled, and treated her as if she were the queen of
Sweden. It was too bad some of the other men around here
couldn't be guided as simply.

She had to pass through the main Weather Room on her
way to her office. A great globe of the world occupied the
center of the room, and it showed the weather at the moment on every part of the Earth. The globe was similar in
purpose to the map in the Weather Council, but it had a
few additional features. Every jet stream, density variation,
inversion, every front, isobar, isallobar, isotherm, precipita-
tion area, clouded area, and air mass showed on the globe.
The globe was a mass of shifting colors, undecipherable to
the untrained eye, making sense only to the mathemeteorologists who made up the technical staff of the Advisors. The
curved walls of the room were covered with the instruments
that made up the Weather Net, the senses of the Advisors.
The entire room looked like something out of a nightmare
with its seething globe and dancing lights and shimmering

dials. Anna walked through without noticing with the callousness of long proximity. She headed for the private wire
from the Weather Council to see if that strange request had
come in yet.

The guard in the Council Communications room saluted
and stepped aside for her. She went in and sat down and
began to flip through the night's messages from the Council.
She picked up the one that related to the imposition of a
drought in northern Australia, and read it. She snorted
when she finished, and said aloud to herself, "Nothing, no
problem at all. A child could figure out how to bring that
about." And on down the stack of messages she went.

She found it and read it carefully, and read it again. It
was just as the news flashes had reported: Snow in July on a
one-square-mile area in southern California. The latitude
and the longitude of the area were given, and that was all
there was to it. But Anna Brackney felt the excitement grow
within her. Here was the nastiest problem to confront the
Advisors in decades, one that probably could not be solved
by standard technics. She put her finger in her mouth. Here
was what she had been waiting for, the chance to prove
out her theory. Now all she had to do was convince Greenberg to give her the problem. She restacked the messages
and went to her office.

It was a small office measuring about eight by eight feet,
but Anna Brackney still thought it too big. Her desk was
in one corner facing one wall to give her the illusion of
being more cramped than she really was. Anna could not
stand the feeling of open spaces when she worked. There
was no window, no picture on any of the walls, nothing
distracting against the plain dark gray walls. Other Advisors had different ideas on the proper working environment. Some used bright splashes of color, others used wood-

land or ocean scenes, Greenberg had his walls covered with
a black and white maze, and Hiromaka's walls were covered with nudes. Anna shuddered with disgust as she
thought of it.

Instead of sitting at her desk, she stood in the middle of
the small room, thinking of how she could persuade Greenberg to assign the Andrews problem to her. This would be
hard. She knew that Greenberg did not like her, and she
knew it was only because he was a man and she was a
woman. None of the men liked her, and as a result her work
never received the credit it deserved. A woman in a man's
world was never allowed to be judged on the basis of her
work alone. But if she could get the Andrews problem, she
would show them. She would show them all.

But time was short. The Andrews problem had to be
solved immediately. Sometimes the Advisors' weather programs took weeks to put into operation, and if this turned
out to be one like that it would be too late. It had to be
worked on and solved now to see if there was enough time.
She spun on her heels and ran out of the office and down
the escalator to the wide steps at the front door of the building. She would waste no time. She would meet Greenberg
as he came in.

She had a ten-minute wait, and Greenberg was early at
that. Anna Brackney pounced on him as he reached the
top step. She said, "Dr. Greenberg, I am ready to start
work immediately on the Andrews problem. I feel—"

"You've been waiting for me?" he said.

"I feel I am best equipped to solve the Andrews problem since it will call for new procedures and . . ."

"What on Earth is the Andrews problem?"

She looked at him blankly and said, "Why that's the problem that came in during the night, and I want to be the one
who . . ."

"But you've nailed me out here on the steps before I've had a chance to go inside. How do I know what problems came in during the night? I haven't been upstairs yet."

"But you must know . . . you have heard of it, it's all on the news."

"There's a lot of junk on the news about our work, most of it untrue. Now why don't you wait until I get a look at it so I know what you're talking about."

They went up the escalator together in silence, he annoyed at being accosted in such a manner, and she annoyed at his obvious effort to put off doing what she wanted.

He started to go into his office first, but she said, "It's over in the Council Communications room, not in your office."

He started to retort, but thought better of it, and went on in and read the message. She said, "Now may I have it?"

"Look, damn it. This request is going to be treated like any other until we understand its ramifications. I am going to give it to Upton as I do all the others for a preliminary opinion and a recommendation as to assignment. After I have that recommendation I will decide what to do. Now don't bother me until Upton's had a look at it." He saw her mouth curve down and her eyes begin to fill. He had been through these crying sessions before, and he did not like them. "See you later," he said, and he all but ran to his office and locked the door. One thing nice at the Advisor Building. A locked door was inviolate. It meant the person inside did not want to be disturbed, and the caliber of the work was such that the wish was honored.

Anna Brackney raged back to her office. There it was again. A woman did not stand a chance around here; they refused to treat her like a man. Then she went and waited at Upton's office to explain the whole thing to him.

Upton was a portly man with an easy disposition and a mind like a razor. What's more, he understood the operation of a single-tracked mind. Anna had got out no more than half her tale of woe when he recognized that the only way to get her off his back for the day was to review the Andrews request. He sent for it, looked at it, whistled and sat down at a twenty-six-fifty computer. For half an hour he fed in data and sat back while the computer chewed and then spat out the results. The job grew, so he called in some help and soon there were three men working on the computers. In another three hours Upton swung around to Anna who had been standing behind him the entire time.

He said, "Do you have some ideas on this?"

She nodded.

"Care to tell me something about it?"

She hesitated, then said, "Well, I don't have it all yet. But I think it can be done by"—she paused and glanced at him shyly as if to see in advance whether or not he was laughing at her—"a vertical front."

Upton's jaw fell. "A ver . . . You mean a true front that is tipped perpendicular to the Earth's surface?"

She nodded, and put her finger in her mouth. Far from laughing, Upton stared at the floor for a moment, and then headed for Greenberg's office. He walked in without knocking and said to Greenberg, "There is a forty-six per cent chance of carrying out this Andrews mandate by conventional technics. And by the way, what's the matter with the Council? I've never known them to do such an idiotic thing before. What are they trying to do?"

Greenberg shook his head and said, "I don't know. I had a call asking about this from Wilburn. I've got the uncomfortable feeling that they're trying to see just what we *can* do here, sort of test us before they put some real big problem to us. They voted a drought for northern Australia yesterday, and maybe they are getting ready to put the real squeeze on some region and want to see what we can do first."

Upton said, "Drought in Australia? Well, they're getting a little tough, aren't they? That isn't like the good old easy-going Council that I know. Any difficulty with the Australian drought?"

"No. It was such a standard problem I didn't even bother to give it to you for screening. I turned it right over to Hiromaka. But there's something behind this Andrews thing, and I don't like it. We'd better find a way to carry it out."

Upton said, "Well, Brackney has an approach that's wild enough to work. Let's let her try to work out a solution, and then we can look it over and see if we feel it has a better chance to work than conventional technics."

Anna Brackney had been standing near the door. She came forward and said angrily, "What do you mean 'wild'. There's nothing wrong with it at all. You just don't want me to be the one that solves it, that's all. You just—"

"No, no, Anna," said Greenberg, "that isn't it. You'll be the one to work it out, so don't—"

"Good, I'll start right now," said Anna, and she turned and left.

The two men looked at each other. Upton shrugged his shoulders, and Greenberg raised his eyes to the ceiling, shook his head, and sighed.

Anna Brackney sat herself down in her corner and stared at the wall. It was ten minutes before she put her finger into her mouth, and another twenty minutes before she pulled out a pad and pencil and began scribbling notations. It went fast then. With her first equation set up on a small sheet of paper, she left her office to find a resident mathe-meteorologist; Anna refused to use the speaker at her desk to call one of them in.

The residents were all seated at desks in one large room, and when Anna entered they all bent over as if hard at work. Ignoring their behavior, Anna went up to the desk of Betty Jepson and placed the sheet of paper on it. Anna said without any preliminaries, "Run a regression analysis on this," and her finger traced out the equation in the form $y = a_1x_1 + a_2x_2 + \ldots + a_nx_n$, "noting that n equals 46 in this case. Take the observational data from the banks of Number Eighty-three computer. I want a fit better than ninety per cent." And she turned on her heels and returned to her office.

Half an hour later she was back with another equation for Charles Bankhead, then one for Joseph Pechio. With the pattern established, she asked for the aid of a full mathe-meteorologist, and Greenberg assigned Albert Kropa to her. Kropa listened to her somewhat disjointed description of what she was trying to do, and then wandered around looking over the shoulders of the residents to see what they were doing. Gradually he understood, and finally he raced to his own office and began turning out the polynomial relationships on his own.

Each equation demanded the full use of a sixteen-fifty computer and its staff under the direction of a resident, plus six hours of time to arrive at even a preliminary fit. As Anna and Kropa turned out more of the needed basic equations, it was apparent that too much time was being used in evolving each one individually. Anna broke off and spent two hours working out a method of programming a twenty-two thirty to explore the factors needed in each regression analysis. The computer began producing the required equations at the rate of one every ten minutes, so Anna and Kropa turned their attention to a method of correlating the flood of data that would descend on them when each analysis was complete. After half an hour it became apparent that they could not finish that phase of it before the data began coming in. They asked for and got two more full mathemeteorologists.

The four of them moved out to the Weather Room so they could be together as they worked. The correlating mathematics began to unfold, and all the remaining residents were called in to help with it. In another hour all the available sixteen-fifties were tied up, and Greenberg called on the University of Stockholm for the use of theirs. This held for twenty minutes, and then Greenberg called on half a dozen industrial computers in the city. But that wasn't enough. The net of computers began widening steadily out to the Continent, reaching in another two hours to the cities on the eastern seaboard of the United States. The overriding authority of the Advisors in the solving of a weather problem was absolute.

It became necessary for Upton to join the group, and when Greenberg himself took a chair at the large circle in the Weather Room there was a brief break in the work for some catcalls and some affectionately sarcastic remarks. Commitment of the Advisors was total.

Anna Brackney seemed not to notice. Her eyes were glazed and she spoke in crisp sharp sentences in contrast to her usual vague and slurred sentences. She seemed to know just a little in advance when a breakdown in the mounting flow of data was impending, and she stepped in and supplied the necessary continuity. It was fifteen hundred before Hiromaka noticed that none of them had eaten lunch. Greenberg sent for food, again at twenty-three hundred, and again at zero nine hundred.

Everyone looked terrible with sunken cheeks and rumpled clothes and great hollows under the eyes. But there

was fire in the eyes of all of them, even down to the newest
resident, a fire born of participation in the most complex
weather problem yet to confront the Advisors.

Upton took over the task of pulling together the mathematical models relating to the planet Earth. He kept under
his control the regression analysis results relating to such
variables as the various possible distances of Earth from
the sun; the rotational positions of the Earth relating to
the sun; the shape, position, density, variation, and charge
of both van Allen radiation belts; the velocity, temperature, direction, width, and mass of fourteen hundred jet
streams; the heat flow of the major ocean currents; the effect on air drift of each major land mass; the heat content
of the land masses; the Coriolis effect; and superimposed
over all these factors and many more, the effect of the ex-
isting and programmed weather playing over the face of
the entire Earth.

Greenberg took the sun and worked with the analysis
results on the movement of each sunspot; the sun's rota-
tions; fluctuating temperatures and pressures in the photosphere, reversing layer, chromosphere, and corona; spec-
trum variations; and the relative output from the carbon
cycle and the proton-proton chain.

Anna wandered everywhere, now looking over Upton's
shoulder, now on the phone to the computers in Washington, D. C., now guiding a resident on his next chore, now
inventing a new notational system to simplify feeding new-
ly-derived mathematical models into the computers. She
wandered as if in a dream, but when a question was asked
or when something slowed down, her responses were far
from dreamlike. Many a resident, several computer operators, and Upton himself felt the bite of one of her crisp
sentences pointing out what could have been a rather obvious blunder. As time wore on and the work grew more

frantic, the normally harsh lines on Anna's face softened, and she walked erect instead of with her usual slouch. Several of the mathemeteorologists, who formerly would not even have talked to her unless it was absolutely necessary, found themselves willingly turning to her for further guidance on their part of the problem.

The first partial solution was fully worked out for the first time at eleven hundred hours the next morning. It had only an eight-one per cent fit, but that was good for the first time out; more would be coming soon. But Upton found a flaw. "No good," he said. "This solution would also increase that proposed drought in Australia by a factor of twelve. That would be nice. We pull something like that and we'll all be back reading electric meters."

The remark struck a responsive chord in the group, and the laughter spread and grew more intense. In moments every person in the Advisors Building was convulsed with violent laughter as the long strain finally took its hysterical toll. It was several minutes before the eyes were wiped and the people settled down to work again. Greenberg said, "Well, that's where our danger will be. Not necessarily in Australia, but anywhere. We've got to make sure we don't get a drastic reaction somewhere."

Anna Brackney heard him and said, "DePinza is working on a definitive analysis to insure that there can be no undesirable reaction. He'll have it in an hour." She walked off, leaving Greenberg staring after her.

It was fifteen hundred when the final set of equations was completed. The fit was ninety-four per cent, and the check-out against DePinza's analysis was one hundred and two per cent. The residents and the mathemeteorologists gathered around the large table as Greenberg considered the results. They had finished none too soon. The procedure they had worked out called for sunside operations starting three hours after the beginning of the second shift, and that went on in four hours. Greenberg rubbed the heavy stubble on his face and said, "I don't know whether to let it go or not. We could report that our procedures are untried and ought not to be used all at once."

The eyes of the group turned to Anna Brackney, but she seemed supremely unconcerned. Upton voiced what was in everyone's mind. "There's a little bit of the heart of each one of us in there." He nodded to the equations. "Since they represent the very best that we can do, I don't see how we can report that they ought not to be used. Right now those equations represent the best Advisors output; in that sense they *are* the Advisors. Both we and the people who put us here have to stand or fall on our best efforts."

Greenberg nodded, and handed the two sheets of paper to a resident and said, "Break it down to the sunside procedures and then send it up to the Weather Bureau. I hope they don't have to sweat it out the way we did." He rubbed his face. "Well, that's what we get paid for."

The resident took the sheets and went off. The others drifted away until only Greenberg and Upton were left. Upton said, "This will be quite a feather in Anna Brackney's cap. I don't know where she pulled her inspiration from."

"I don't either," said Greenberg. "But if she sticks her finger in her mouth again, I may quit the business."

Upton chuckled. "If she brings this one off, we'd better all learn to stick our fingers in our mouths."

James Eden rolled out of his bunk and stood poised on the balls of his feet. Yes, there was a faint, barely discernible chatter in the deck. Eden shook his head; the sun was rough, and it was going to be a bad day. If Base had a chatter, then the sessile boats would be hard to manage. Never knew it to fail. Try something tricky and you had to work in the worst possible conditions; try something routine, and conditions were perfect. But that was what you had to expect in the Bureau. Even the textbooks talked about it—an offshoot of an old Finagle Law.

Eden depilated and dressed, wondering what the job ahead of him would be like. They were always the last to hear anything, yet they were the ones who had to do all the dirty work. The whole Weather Congress depended on the Bureau. The Council was nothing more than a bunch of rich old fat politicians who scratched each other's backs and spent their days cooking up Big Deals. The Advisors were a bunch of nuts who sat on their duffs and read out loud all the stuff the computers figured out. But the Bureau was something else again, a fine body of dedicated men who did a job so that the planet Earth could flourish. It was good to be in the Weather Bureau—and there it was again.

Eden could not keep his thoughts away from the problem that had been nagging at him during this entire tour. He rubbed his forehead and wondered again at the perversity of women. Rebecca, black-haired and black-eyed, with warm white skin, waited for him when his tour was over, but only if he left the Bureau. He could see her now, close to him, looking deep into his eyes, the soft palm of her hand pressed against his cheek, saying, "I will not share you with any person or any thing, even your beloved Bureau. I want a complete husband. You must decide." With other women he could have laughed and picked them up and swung them around and quickly jogged them out of the mood, but not Rebecca, not Rebecca of the long black hair. Damn it!

He swung around and stepped out of his tiny cabin and headed for the mess hall. There were half a dozen men al-

ready there when he entered, and they were talking and
laughing. But they stopped what they were doing and looked
at him and hailed him as he came in through the door. "Hey,
Jim." "About time you were rolling out." "Good to see you,
boy."

Eden recognized the symptoms. They were tense, and
they were talking and laughing too loud. They were relieved to have him join them. They needed somebody to
lean on, and Eden pitied them a little for it. Now they would
not have to make such an effort to appear normal. The
others had felt the chatter in the deck, too.

Eden sat down and said, "Morning. Anything on the
Board yet about the shift's work?"

The others shook their heads, and Pisca said, "Not a
word. They always wait and tell us last. Everybody on the
planet knows what's going on, but not us. All we get are
rumors until it's time to go out and do it."

"Well," said Eden, "communication with the Bureau is
not the easiest thing in the world, don't forget. We can't
expect to hear everything as soon as it happens. But I sort
of agree with you anyway; seems to me they could keep us
posted better as things develop back on Earth."

They nodded, and then applied themselves to the breakfast. They chatted over coffee until a soft chime sounded
throughout Base. They rose. It was time for the briefing,
and they headed for the briefing room up at the top of the
Base. Commander Hechmer was there when they walked
in and took their seats. Eden watched carefully as he found
a seat and sat down. In the past he had sometimes wondered if Hechmer had taken particular notice of him—an
extra glance, closer attention when he asked a question,
talking more to him than to the others at a briefing, little
things, but important nevertheless.

Commander John H. Hechmer was a legend in the Weather Bureau at the age of forty-five years. It was he who had evolved and perfected the Pinpoint Stream technic in which a thin stream of protons could be extracted from the 4,560-degree level in a sunspot and directed against any chosen sunside part of Earth. In the days when Hechmer was the Senior Boat Master in the Bureau, great strides had been made in weather control. A fineness and detail of weather patterns on Earth had become possible that had astonished all the experts. Hechmer had even guided the Advisors, showing them the broadened scope of the Bureau's abilities. His handling of a sunboat had never been matched, and it was one of the goals in Eden's career—if he chose to stay with it—to be thought of as the man who most nearly approximated Hechmer.

Eden watched, and finally when Hechmer looked up from the table it seemed to Eden that his eyes swept the group to rest for an instant on Eden, and then they moved on. It was as if Hechmer wanted to assure himself that Eden was there. Eden could not be sure of this, but the possibility of it made him sit straighter in his chair.

Hechmer said, "Here is Phase One of the next shift's operation as received from the Advisors." He flashed the requisite portion of the page on the upright panel behind him. It took Eden one quick glance to see that it represented a substantial departure from customary procedure. Immediately he began to slump down in his seat as he lost himself in the problem of studying out how to handle it. He did not notice that Hechmer saw his instant grasp of the problem. It was a moment or two before several low whistles announced that the others had grasped it, too.

Hechmer sat quietly while they studied over the page. All of them were now thinking out how the report had to be modified to place it in useful condition for the Bureau

to use. The Advisors always prided themselves on stating
their solutions in clear and explicit terminology. But as a
practical matter their solutions were totally unusable as received for they did not mention many of the sun conditions
that the Bureau had to cope with. These are accomplish-
ments not explained by mathematics. It was one of the quiet
jokes of the Bureau to listen to the talk of an Advisor about
the thoroughness of his solution and about the lack of thinking required by the Bureau, and then to ask the Advisor
what he knew about "reversing granulation." No one except a working member of the Bureau could experience
that strange upwelling sometimes found in the lower regions of the reversing layer.

The silence grew long. Eden's forehead was wrinkled
with concentration as he tried to find some way to break
into the problem. He finally saw a possible entry, and he
pulled over a pad and began trying for a method of breakdown. Hechmer began to polish his own figures while the
rest stared at the page on the wall as if hypnotized. It was
ten minutes before another of the men finally began to make
notes.

Eden sat back and looked over what he had written. With
growing excitement he realized that his possible answer had
never been tried before. As he looked at it more closely,
though, he realized that it might not ever be done; it was a
radical approach, calling for Boat performance not mentioned in the Boat specifications.

Hechmer said, "Gentlemen, we must begin. To start
things off, here is my proposed answer. Pick it apart if
you can."

Eden looked up at it. It was different, too, but it differed
in that it called for the use of every single Boat on the sun,
a thing never before needed. Hechmer's answer was to

carry out the mission by sheer weight of numbers, and by this means to dig from the various levels in the sun's atmosphere the total of the streams and sheets needed to bring about the desired weather on Earth. But as he looked at it Eden began to see flaws. The streams, being taken from different parts of the sun's surface would strike the Earth and its environs at angles slightly different from those that were called for. Hechmer's answer might work, but it did not seem to have as good a chance as Eden's answer.

Hechmer said, "The main feature wrong with this plan is the wide scattering of the impinging streams. Can you think of any way to overcome that?"

Eden could not, but his mind was more occupied with his own plan. If he could be certain that the Boats could stand submersion in the sun's surface for the required length of time, there would be few problems. Oh, communication might be more difficult, but with only one Boat down there would be a much reduced need for communication; the Boat would succeed or not, and no instructions from anywhere else could help.

One of the other men was beginning to suggest the unfeasible modification of having all the Boats work closer together, a grave mistake since the Boats could not control their toruses with sufficient nicety. Eden interrupted him without thinking. "Here is a possible answer." And he dropped his page on the desk.

Hechmer continued to look at the man who had been talking, waiting politely for him to finish. The man avoided an embarrassing situation by saying, "Let's see what Jim has to offer before we go on with this one."

Hechmer slipped Eden's page into the viewer, and they all studied it. It had the advantage at least of being readily understandable, and they all began talking at once, most of them saying that it couldn't be done. "You'll lose the

Boat." "Yes, and the men in it, don't forget." "Won't work even if the Boat holds up." "You can't get a Boat that deep."

Eden carefully watched Hechmer's face while he studied the plan. He saw Hechmer's eyes widen, and then narrow again, and Hechmer realized that Eden was watching him closely. For a moment the room faded from Hechmer's mind, replaced by another similar room, many years ago, when a younger and rasher Hechmer sat and anxiously watched his superior eye a new kind of plan. Hechmer said, without taking his eyes from the projected page, "Assuming the Boat can get down there, why won't this plan work?"

"Well," said the man who had stated it wouldn't work, "the streams and sheets won't necessarily emerge in the direction. . . ." But as he talked he noticed that the energy of the sunspot's field was channeled to serve as a focusing lens, and his words faded.

Hechmer nodded approval, "Glad you saw it. Anybody else? Any flaws in it once the Boat gets down and stays long enough?" The men worried at it, but could find nothing wrong, given the stated assumption. Hechmer continued, "All right, now why won't a Boat stand that kind of submersion."

One answered, "The sessile effect is not as great on the top. Burn right through."

Eden popped out, "No. Double the carbon feed to the top torus. That'll do it."

They argued for half an hour. Eden and two others defending the concept, and in the end there was no more opposition. They all worked at polishing the plan to take out as much risk as possible. By the time they finished there really was no decision for Hechmer to make. The group of Boat captains had accepted the plan, and it went with-

out saying that Eden's Boat would be the deep Boat. There
was a bare half an hour to the start of the shift, so they went
to get ready.

Eden struggled into the lead suit, muttering the same
curses every Boatman since the first had muttered. The
Boats had ample shielding, and the suits were to provide
protection only if a leak allowed in some stray radiation. But on the sun it seemed highly unlikely that a leak
would allow in only a little radiation. It seemed much more
likely that a leak would allow in so much of the sun's atmosphere that the men in the Boat would never know what hit
them. A lead suit then would be like trying to dam a vol-
cano with a feather. Nevertheless, lead suits were man-
datory.

Entering the Boat from Base was always a tricky
maneuver. The torus above the joining lock was not a permanent part of the lock, and if it moved, the full gravitational field of the sun could pull at the man, pulling his
entire body down into his shoes. Eden slipped through and
made the rounds of the Boat on the standard captain's
inspection before he went to his chair and began the start-
up procedure.

He noted the continuing roughness of the sun. First he
checked the carbon supply, the material which vaporized
and then in the form of a thin film protected the entire
Boat from the searing heat of the sun's surface. The Boats
rode the layer of vaporized carbon the way a drop of water
rides a layer of vaporized water on a red-hot plate; this
was the sessile effect. Next he checked the over-head torus.
Here in a circular path there traveled a few ounces of protons at a velocity approaching that of light. At these velocities the few ounces of protons weighed incalculable tons
and thus offset the enormous gravitational attraction of

the sun itself. The same magnetic tape that supplied the
field to maintain the protons in their heavy-mass state also
served to maintain a polarity the same as that of the adja-
cent sun's surface. Hence the torus and the sun's surface
repelled each other. Objects under the torus were sub-
jected to two gravitational fields, the one from the torus
almost, but not quite, canceling the sun's. As a result men
worked in the Boats and in the Base in a 1-G field.

Eden ran down the entire list checking off one by one
the various functioning parts of the Boat. His crew of four
worked with him, each responsible for a section of the
Boat. Five minutes before castoff the board was green, and
at zero time on the shift they shoved off.

The Boat felt good under his hands. It leaped and surged
as the sun's surface roiled and boiled, but he kept it steadily
headed outward, sliding ever downhill on its thin film of
carbon vapor.

"How do you ride?" he said into the intercom.

A chorus of "fines" came back, so Eden tipped the
Boat a little more to increase her speed. They were on a
tight schedule and they had distance to make. As always
Eden felt exhilarated as their speed increased, and he did
the thing he always did when he felt that way.

Carefully, he drew back one after another of the sound-
deadening panels on the bulkhead next to the pilot's seat.
As the eighth panel drew back he could hear it faintly,
and so he drew back the ninth panel slowly, and on the
tenth the roar filled the pilot's cubicle. Eden sat bathed in
a thunderous roar that washed over him, shaking his body
with its fury, and taking everything from his mind except
the need to fight and strain and hit back. This was the
direct naked roar of the sun itself that came in upon him,
the thunderous concatenation of a million fission bombs
detonating every infinitesimal portion of a second. Its

sound and fury were mind-staggering, and a man could only let a little of it in and keep his sanity. But that little was an awesome sound, cleansing, humbling, focusing a man's attention on the powers he controlled, warning him to mind his business.

This was a thing that Eden had never told to anyone, and no one had ever told him. It was his own secret, his own way of refreshing and replenishing whatever it was that made him the man he was. He supposed that he was the only one of the pilots that did this thing, and since on this one point he did not think clearly, it never occurred to him to wonder how it came about that the only movable sound-deadening panels in the entire Boat happened to be located right alongside the pilot's seat.

For half an hour Eden guided the Boat toward its first action point, easily coping with the usual roughness of the sun's surface. He checked the operation of the inertial guidance system exactly twice as often as was required by standard operating procedure to make sure that the extra bouncing did not affect its precise operation. As they approached the action point, Eden closed the sound-deadening panels and checked in with his crew. "Four minutes to operation. What color have you?"

Back came the answer from all four points, "All green, Master." Formalities aboard the sessile Boat had started. Each man watched his own program, his fingers on the keys and his feet on the pedals, waiting for the position light. It winked on.

Out went the torpedolike capsules, down into the bowels of the sun where the carbon-nitrogen cycle raged. At a temperature of three point five million degrees the ablation head disintegrated and released into the inferno a charge of heavy nitrogen. The heavy nitrogen, appearing as it did at the end of the carbon-nitrogen cycle, disrupted the

steady state conditions and produced a flood of helium
that served to dampen and cool the fusion reactions in the
entire region. The resultant thermal shock to the interior
caused an immediate collapse followed by an incredible
increase in pressure with the attendant temperature rise.
The vast explosion heaved its way to the surface and became a great prominence licking its way toward the Earth
and channeling huge masses of protons toward the pre-
selected site in the vicinity of the Earth. The initial phase of
the operation appeared successful.

The next hour passed in moving from site to site and
planting the proper charges, now to bring about a vast elec-
tron discharge at the correct angle, now to dampen a flare,
now to shift the location of a spot. On two occasions the
instruments showed that the detonations did not take place
at a sufficiently precise location to meet the unusual re-
quirements for accuracy, and so subsidiary detonations
had to be made. They were in constant, if difficult, communication with the other three Boats and with Base. None
of the Boats was specifically aware of it, but the beginnings
of the Australian drought were set in motion during the
second hour out.

There was no tension aboard Eden's Boat as the time for
the deep operation approached; they were all too busy.
When the time came Eden merely checked out over the
communication net and reduced the polarity of the magnetic field on the overhead torus. The Boat went down fast,
leaving the photosphere behind. Eden kept a careful check
on the temperature drop across the walls of the Boat as
they fell; when the sessile effect began to diminish, he
wanted to know about it. The interior walls began to heat
up sooner than he expected, and once they started, the
heat-up proceeded ever more rapidly. A quick check
showed that the rate of heating was faster than their rate

of descent; they could not reach the required depth without becoming overheated. The Boat would not withstand the temperatures that Eden had thought it would. "Too hot, too hot," he said aloud. He checked the depth; they had another half a mile to go. There was no use in even attempting to release the water where they were. It was half a mile deeper, or nothing. The plan was in jeopardy.

Eden did not really pause to make the decision. He simply drastically cut the power to the polarity-control generators to the torus, and the Boat fell like a stone toward the center of the sun. It dropped the half mile in forty seconds, the last few hundred yards in violent deceleration as Eden brought up the power level. The drop was so fast there was little additional heat-up. He hit the water releases and flung the Boat into the pattern that had been worked out, and in ten seconds the disruption was complete and a blast of Oxygen 15 was started on its way to Earth. The plan, at least, was consummated.

Eden brought up the torus power to a high level and the Boat began to rise to the relative safety of the surface. The time at the deeper level had been sufficiently short that the interior temperature of the Boat was at a tolerable 120 degrees F. The control panel showed no signs of trouble until they rose to within a thousand yards of the surface.

The steady rise slowed and drifted to a halt. The Boat sank a little and then bobbed up and down and finally found a level, and then it remained motionless. There was no way to strengthen the polarity in the torus. The instruments showed that full power flowed to the coils, and it was not enough. Eden began a check-out. He had barely started when a voice spoke in the intercom, "A portion of

our right outboard coil is inoperative, Master. Possibly
burned away, but I am checking further."

Eden turned his attention to the coils and soon saw the
telltale reduced output. He activated all the thermocouples
and other transducers in the vicinity of the coil, and in two
minutes he understood what had happened. The burn-out
had occurred at the point where the coil turned the corner.
The sessile effect there must have been slightly less effective than elsewhere. The unexpectedly great heat had
pushed past the film of carbon vapor and destroyed a
portion of the titanium-molybdenum alloy wires. Full
power to the coil was not enough now to increase the polarity sufficiently for the Boat to rise any farther.

Eden cut into the intercom and explained the situation
to the crew. A cheerful voice responded, "Glad to hear
that there is nothing seriously wrong then. It is just that
we cannot move up. Is that what you make of it, Master?"

"So far, yes. Anybody have any suggestions?"

"Yes, Master. I request a leave of absence."

"Granted," said Eden. "Now put in some time on this.
We've got to get up."

There was silence aboard the Boat, and the silence
stretched out to twenty minutes. Eden said, "I'll try to raise
Base."

For ten minutes Eden tried to reach the Base or another
Boat with his long-long wave-length radio. He was about
to give up when he heard a faint and garbled reply.
Through the noise he could just recognize the call of the
Boat mastered by Dobzhansky. He transmitted their situation, over and over, so that the other Boat could fill in missing parts of any one message. Then he listened and eventually learned that they understood and would notify Base.
But as they listened to the faint retransmission all sound

faded. A check of their position showed that they had drifted out of radio range, so Eden tipped the Boat and began a circle. Three quarters of the way around he picked up the signal again and listened. He heard nothing but routine communication.

One of his men said, "Fine thing. We can move in every direction with the greatest of ease except the one direction we want to go."

Base was now coming in through the other Boat, and Hechmer himself was speaking. All he had to say was, "Stand by while we see what we can do about this."

There was no levity aboard the Boat now. The Boat floated a thousand yards beneath the surface of the sun, and they began to realize that there was nothing anybody could do about it. A sharpened corner on a coil, and the Boat was helpless to return to the surface. Each man sat and stared at his instruments.

A dark-haired vision floated in front of Eden's panel, and in his mind's eye Eden could see the reproachful look on her face. This was what she meant, the black-haired Rebecca, when she said, "I will not share you with any thing." He understood, for now she would be sorry for him, trapped in a place where men had never been.

"Lost the Boat again, Master." The words jarred him. He tipped the Boat and began the circle again. The shadow of Rebecca was still on him, but suddenly he grew very annoyed. What was this? The worry of a woman to get in the way of his work? This was not for him; this was not for the Bureau. There could be no cloudiness of mind, no dichotomy of loyalty—and then he saw the way up.

As he completed the circle he checked the charts and found the nearest sunspot. It was an hour away. He came within radio range again and told Dobzhansky he was

heading for the sunspot and that he would come up to
the surface there. So saying he headed for it. By the most
careful operation they cut their time to the spot to fifty
minutes. The last ten minutes of time on the way they
spent in building the speed of the Boat to the maximum ob-
tainable. A thousand yards beneath the surface of the sun
they entered the magnetic discontinuity that defined the
sunspot.

They rode into it in a direction opposite to that of its
rotation, and the great coils of the Boat cut across the
lines of enormous magnetic force. The motion generated
power, and the additional power flowed to the torus, and
the Boat began to rise. It was a good spot, five thousand
miles wide, and still in its prime. The Boat rode against
the direction of its rotation and spiraled upward slowly as
it went. It took great patience to note the fact that the Boat
rose at all, but hour after hour they worked their way up
and finally broke out on the indistinct surface. They rode
the edges of the spot until Base came for them, and they
docked the Boat and went aboard.

Eden reported to Hechmer, and they made arrangements
to round off the relatively sharp corners on all coils. Most
important of all, the deep technic appeared to be a success;
it was added to the list of usable technics.

"Well," said Eden toward the end of the reporting session, stretching his tired muscles, "I see I'm due back on
shift again in an hour. That doesn't give me much time to
get rested up."

Then Hechmer said the thing that made Eden glad he
had decided to stay in the Bureau. "Hm-m-m, that's right,"
said Hechmer, glancing up at the chronometer, "tell you
what you do. You be an hour late getting back on duty."

George Andrews was very tired, and he had to work very

hard to draw air into his lungs. He lay propped up on a soft bed out under the hot California sun, and his fingers plucked at the thin cover that lay over him. He was on a hilltop. Then he noticed an odd cylindrical-shaped cloud that seemed to rise from the level of the ground and reach way up through the scattered alto-cumulous clouds that dotted the blue sky. George Andrews smiled, for he could see it coming clearly now. The vertical cylinder of frothy clouds moved toward him, and he felt the chill as the leading edge touched him. He threw back the cover when the flakes began to fall so the snow could fall on him. He turned his face up to it, and it felt cold and it felt good. But more than that, he felt content.

Here was the snow he had loved so much when he was a boy. And the fact that it was here at all showed him that men had not changed much after all, for this was a foolish thing. He had no trouble with the air now; he needed none. He lay under the blanket of snow, and it was a good blanket.

GOOD INDIAN

by Mack Reynolds

Mortimer Dowling opened one eye accusingly and said, "Miss Fullbright, I thought we had a standing agreement that I was never to be bothered while in conference."

Millie said, "Take your feet off the desk you'll scratch it. Am I or am I not your receptionist?"

"You am. Now go away. It was very drunk out last night."

"A receptionist recepts and . . ."

Mortimer Dowling opened the other eye, too, and interrupted. "No she doesn't," he said severely. "You don't do enough crossword puzzles. A *recept* is an idea formed by the repetition of similar percepts, as successive percepts of the same object. A receptionist does something else. I forget what. Go away. I'm tired."

". . . And when someone comes into my office asking for an appointment to see the Director of the Department of Indian Affairs, then it's my duty to so inform you."

He closed both eyes and snorted. "Don't be ridiculous."

"Three of them," Millie said definitely.

Mortimer Dowling said sleepily, "Three what? Why don't you go away? Go away and do a crossword puzzle or something."

"Three Indians to see you, sir," Millie said formally.

The head of the Department of Indian Affairs opened

both eyes again and said severely, "Miss Fullbright, I am in no mood for jest. You know very well that there is no such thing as three Indians. The last Indian died almost ten years ago. The President proclaimed a day of national mourning. I made a speech. It was all very sentimental. Are you going away or not?"

Her mouth tightened. "They say they're Indians. And they look like Indians. I've seen pictures of Indians."

Mortimer Dowling blinked. "You're serious?"

"Of course, I'm serious."

"Three men in the outer office, and they say they're Indians?" A certain tremor was coming into Mortimer Dowling's voice.

She nodded definitely.

"Good Heavens," said the Director of Indian Affairs. "For nearly fifteen years I've held this job, and my father before me. By the terms of the final Indian treaty there must always be a Department of Indian Affairs so long as the United States shall endure, the original idea being that the Indians would always have somewhere to go to find justice. It never occurred to those who compiled the treaty that the Indians would eventually blend into the rest of the population. The last bit of business conducted by the department was almost half a century ago. Miss Fullbright, do you realize what you're saying? *There's actually something for me to do!*"

"Yes, sir," said Millie, overwhelmed by it all. "What shall I tell them?"

Mortimer Dowling sat up straight behind his desk, businesslike. "Now, just what was it they wanted?"

"An appointment."

He thought about that. "Well, we should give them one, Miss Fullbright. Yes, indeed. An appointment."

Millie was impressed by the new aggressive mien of her superior. "Very good, sir," she said.

"Mark it down on the calendar, Miss Fullbright."

"Yes, sir. When do you wish to make this appointment, sir?"

He thought about that. Finally, decisively, "Now."

"Right now?"

"Right now. They might go away and not come back."

"Yes, sir."

There were three of them all right and they came in assorted sizes ranging from a six-footer pushing three hundred pounds to a five-footer pushing ninety pounds. The one in the middle averaged out neatly.

Mortimer Dowling shook hands with enthusiasm. "You have no idea how pleasant it is to meet you chaps," he said. "Our records show that the last full-blooded Indian died ten years ago. Where have you been keeping yourselves? Miss Fullbright, chairs for these gentlemen."

When they were seated, Mortimer Dowling looked them over happily. They were Indians all right, all right. You could see they were real Indians.

Mortimer Dowling said, "Yes, sir, a real pleasure. Now then, what can we do for you? The Department of Indian Affairs places its full resources at your disposal, gentlemen."

The one in the middle said, "We're Seminoles. We've come to sign a treaty."

Mortimer Dowling's face went blank. "Seminoles?" he said. "A treaty?"

They gave him one concerted nod, lapsed back into frozen-faced silence. Oh, they were Indians all right.

Mortimer Dowling cleared his throat. "Look here, the government of the United States cleared up all its Indian difficulties over a century ago. We signed final treaties with every tribe."

"Except the Seminoles," the one in the middle said. "We represent the Seminoles." He indicated his hefty companion to the right, "This is Charlie Horse and I'm Fuller Bull, and . . ."

"You're *what?*"

"Who, not what," the Indian said strictly. "I'm Fuller Bull."

"Oh," Mortimer Dowling said. "I thought you said— Never mind." He looked at the small one and tried to place the conversation back on a lighter level with a *bon mot.* "And I suppose this is Chicken Little."

"And this is Osceola the Eighteenth," Fuller Bull said. "We call him Junior."

Junior spoke up for the first time. "For your information, the three of us took our LL.D.s at Harvard. We carry powers of attorney for all fifty-five of the other surviving members of the Seminole tribe."

"*Fifty-five?*" Mortimer Dowling was astounded. "You mean there are fifty-five more of you?"

"Correct," Charlie Horse said. "And we've come to sign a treaty between the Seminole Nation and the United States of America."

Already Mortimer Dowling was beginning to feel a bead of very cold sweat forming on his forehead. He said anxiously, "Miss Fullbright. Please. The file on the Seminole Indian Nation."

"Yes, sir," Millie said. She scooted out. Came scooting back in mere moments, a thin file held in both hands. She put the file before him.

Mortimer Dowling renewed his information on the Seminoles quickly. Scanned paper after paper. Emitted

occasional grunts. Finally he looked up at them in satisfaction.

"Now," he said definitely, "I don't know what your game
is, but it won't work. More than a century ago, the whole
world went through a period of settling its difficulties
with its minorities. World opinion grew so strong that not
a major power on earth dared do otherwise. Why, even the
Sino-Soviet Complex freed its satellites—of course, by that
time there was nobody left in the satellites except good
commies, so they immediately applied for readmission.
However, that's beside the point. The point is that the
United States reviewed every dealing we had ever had with
every Indian tribe. Settling all the Indian questions beg-
gared the United States treasury, but we satisfied them
all—every tribe, every member of every tribe." He let his
eyes go ceilingward for a moment. "As I recall, the hardest to please were the Delawares. There were only three
hundred seventy-five of them left, and they got a million
dollars apiece."

"Peanuts," Charlie Horse said.

"I beg your pardon?"

"Peanuts," said Charlie Horse.

Mortimer Dowling thumped the papers before him with
an emphatic fingertip. "When we attempted to contact
the Seminoles we found there were none to contact. They
were all gone. The only ones we could find were along the
Tamiami Trail and at Silver Springs selling baby alliga-
tors and souvenirs made in Japan to the tourists. It turned
out they were all Armenians, making an honest living. No
Seminoles left."

"We went underground," Junior said.

Mortimer Dowling gaped at him. "What?" he said.

"We went underground," Junior told him. "We realized
that the longer we could put off our final settlement with

the government, the better off we'd be. Look at history. The great powers start off by butchering the aborigines of the countries they conquer. Then, as time goes by, their conscience begins to hurt and they make wards of those that are left. More time goes by and they begin to wax really sentimental. They seek out the very last survivors and load them with honors, with privileges, sometimes with positions superior even to their own citizens. Look at the British and the Tasmanians, the New Zealanders and the Maoris, the Swiss in Switzerland."

Millie cleared her throat. "What happened to the Swiss?"

"Finally there were so many more tourists in the country than Swiss that they began to thin out. Like the Chinese used to do, with invaders, only sort of in reverse. The tourist hordes interbred with the Swiss until finally you couldn't find a full-blooded one. The last man who could yodel died in Berne, twenty years ago."

Mortimer Dowling said severely, "Let's get back to the point."

"The point is," Charlie Horse said, "that the United States has no treaty with the Seminole Indian Nation. We didn't sign up when everybody else did. We realized the tribe would benefit more if we hid out, kept secret our existence, put off signing for a full century."

There was another bead of sweat on Mortimer Dowling's forehead.

He said weakly, "I assume you have proof, that you can prove that your fifty-eight Seminoles are all full-blooded Indians?"

Junior said, "We've planned this, remember, for a whole century. We've studied every aspect. There are no loopholes by which you can escape. The United States is the only nation on earth that has not settled its problems with all its minorities. You can imagine the impact of public opinion upon you, if this hits the world's headlines."

Mortimer Dowling said hoarsely, "I have before me,
the treaty we had prepared a hundred years ago. It offers
every Seminole one hundred thousand dollars to settle all
claims against the United States."

Fuller Bull chuckled his sarcasm. Junior and Charlie
Horse didn't even bother to do that.

Mortimer Dowling said, "I'll up it. I'll promise you the
same as the Delawares got. A million dollars apiece for
every man, woman and child in the tribe."

They gave him the oatmeal look.

Mortimer Dowling said desperately, "What do you
want?"

"Florida," said Junior.

"Florida!"

"Florida," Junior said. "We owned it originally and
we've never signed it away."

"Do you realize that half a billion people now live in
Florida? Do you realize how much money the citizens of
this country have invested in the Florida peninsula in the
past three centuries? Why the bridge to Havana alone—"

"We're going to make it a toll bridge," Fuller Bull said
with satisfaction.

"And we're going to confiscate every house, every
orange tree, every motel, in the State," Charlie Horse
added. "I get Miami."

"Miami?" Mortimer Dowling repeated, trying to hold on
to reality.

"That's my share," Charlie Horse told him.

"Good Heavens," Mortimer Dowling said.

"We're going to make every white man move out of the
State," Charlie Horse wound up, with satisfaction.

Mortimer Dowling blurted, "You'll never get away with this. It's impossible."

Fuller Bull said darkly, "If necessary, we'll take our case to the Reunited Nations."

"The RN?" Mortimer Dowling said in despair. "We wouldn't stand a chance. There's not a country in the RN that hasn't already cleared itself of every taint of colonialism and imperialism. Why, the very expressions have become bad words."

The three Seminoles were smug.

Mortimer Dowling looked at his watch. "See here, gentlemen, let's not be hasty about this."

"So who's being hasty?" Junior said. "We've waited a hundred years for this moment."

"Well, see here, we needn't rush into things. It's time for lunch. Will you gentlemen be my guests? Ha ha, on Uncle Sam, of course. Do you realize this will make quite a precedent? In my fifteen years as head of this department, I've never before had the occasion to submit an expense account."

The three Seminoles exchanged glances.

"Why not?" said Junior.

In the morning, Mortimer Dowling opened one bloodshot eye and said, "Miss Fullbright, please go away. I'm dying."

Millie said, "Take your feet off the desk. Aren't you ashamed of yourself?"

"No. Go away. I need rest."

"Just look at yourself," Millie said disgustedly. "The first time in fifteen years at this job you get something to do, and what happens? You blow up. Instead of trying to figure out an answer, you go get yourself stoned. Absolutely stoned."

Mortimer Dowling grunted. He pointed with his finger at an official looking document lying on the desk. "Do you see that, Miss Fullbright? One of the most brilliant pieces of work done by an American official in the past century."

"Heavens to Betsy, the treaty. And all three of their signatures on it. How in the world did you ever—"

Mortimer Dowling allowed himself a self-satisfied leer. "Miss Fullbright haven't you ever heard the old saying *The only good Indian is a dead—*"

Millie's hand went to her mouth. "Mr. *Dowling,* you mean . . . you put the slug on all three of those poor Seminoles? But . . . but how about the remaining fifty-five of them? You can't possibly kill them all!"

"Let me finish," Mortimer Dowling growled. "I was about to say, *The only good Indian is a dead drunk Indian.* If you think I'm hanging over, you should see Charlie Horse and his wisenheimer pals. Those redskins couldn't handle firewater back in the old days when the Dutch did them out of Manhattan with a handful of beads and a gallon of applejack and they *still* can't. Now, go away and do a cross-word puzzle, or something."

BLIND MAN'S LANTERN

by Allen Kim Lang

*Walking home in the dark from an evening spent in mis-
chief, a young man spied coming toward him down the
road a person with a lamp. When the wayfarers drew
abreast, the playboy saw that the other traveler was the
Blind Man from his village. "Blind Man," the youngster
shouted across the road, "what a fool you be! Why, old
No-Eyes, do you bear a lantern, you whose midnight is no
darker than his noonday?" The Blind Man lifted his lamp.
"It is not as a light for myself that I carry this, Boy," he
said, "it is to warn off you fools with eyes."*

—Hausa proverb

The Captain shook hands with the black-hatted Amishman while the woman stood aside, not concerning herself
with men's business. "It's been a pleasure to have you and
Fraa Stoltzfoos aboard, Aaron," the Captain said. "Ship's
stores are yours, my friend; if there's anything you need,
take it and welcome. You're a long way from the corner
grocery."

"My Martha and I have all that's needful," Aaron
Stoltzfoos said. "We have our plow, our seed, our land.
Captain, please tell your men, who treated us strangers

as honored guests, we thank them from our hearts. We'll not soon forget their kindness."

"I'll tell them," the Captain promised. Stoltzfoos hoisted himself to the wagon seat and reached a hand down to boost his wife up beside him. Martha Stoltzfoos sat, blushing a bit for having displayed an accidental inch of black stocking before the ship's officers. She smoothed down her black skirts and apron, patted the candle-snuffer *Kapp* into place over her prayer-covering, and tucked the wool cape around her arms and shoulders. The world outside, her husband said, was a cold one.

Now in the Stoltzfoos wagon was the final lot of homestead goods with which these two Amishers would battle the world of Murna. There was the plow and bags of seed, two crates of nervous chickens; a huge, round tabletop; an alcohol-burning laboratory incubator, bottles of agar-powder, and a pressure cooker that could can vegetables as readily as it could autoclave culture-media. There was a microscope designed to work by lamplight, as the worldly vanity of electric light would ill suit an Old Order bacteriologist like Martha Stoltzfoos. Walled in by all this gear was another passenger due to debark on Murna, snuffling and grunting with impatience. "*Sei schtill,* Wutzchen," Stoltzfoos crooned. "You'll be in your home pen soon enough."

The Captain raised his hand. The Engineer punched a button to tongue the landing ramp out to Murnan earth. Cold air rammed in from the outside winter. The four horses stomped their hoofs on the floor-plates, their breath spikes of steam. Wutzchen squealed dismay as the chill hit his nose.

"We're *reddi far geh,* Captain," Stoltzfoos said. "My woman and I invite you and your men to feast at our table when you're back in these parts, five years hence. We'll stuff you fat as sausages with onion soup and Pannhaas, Knepp and Ebbelkuche, shoo-fly pie and *scharifer* cider, if the folk here grow apples fit for squeezing."

"You'll have to set up planks outdoors to feed the lot I'll be bringing, Aaron," the Captain said. "Come five-years' springtime, when I bring your Amish neighbors out, I'll not forget to have in my pockets a toot of candy for the little Stoltzes I'll expect to see underfoot." Martha, whose English was rusty, blushed none the less. Aaron grinned as he slapped the reins over the rumps of his team. "Giddap!" The cart rumbled across the deck and down the ramp, onto the soil of Murna. Yonnie, the Ayrshire bull, tossed his head and sat as the rope tightened on his nose-band. He skidded stubbornly down the ramp till he felt cold earth against his rear. Accepting fate, Yonnie scrambled up and plodded after the wagon. As the Stoltzfooses and the last of their off-worldly goods topped a hillock, they both turned to wave at the ship's officers. Then, veiled by the dusty fall of snow, they disappeared.

"I don't envy them," the Engineer said, staring out into the wintery world.

"Hymie, were you born in a barn?" the Exec bellowed.

"Sorry, sir." The Engineer raised the landing ramp. Heaters hummed to thaw the hold's air. "I was thinking about how alone those two folks are now."

"Hardly alone," the Captain said. "There are four million Murnans, friendly people who consider a white skin no more than a personal idiosyncrasy. Aaron's what his folks call a *Chentelmaan,* too. He'll get along."

"Chentelmaan-schmentelmaan," the Engineer said. "Why'd he come half across Creation to scratch out a living with a horse-drawn plow?"

"He came out here for dirt," the Captain said. "Soil is

more than seedbed to the Amish. It feeds the Old Order
they're born to. Aaron and Martha Stoltzfoos would rather
have built their barns beside the Susquehanna, but all the
land there's taken. Aaron could have taken a job in Lancaster, too; he could have shaved off his beard, bought a
Chevie and moved to the suburbs, and settled down to
read an English-language Bible in a steepled church. Instead, he signed a homestead-contract for a hundred acres
eighty light-years from home; and set out to plow the land
like his grandpop did. He'll sweat hard for his piece of
Murna, but the Amish always pay well for their land."

"And what do we, the government, I mean, get from the
deal?" the Exec wanted to know. "This wagon of ours
doesn't run on hay, like Aaron's does."

"Cultures skid backwards when they're transplanted,"
the Captain said. "Murnan culture was lifted from Kano,
a modern city by the standards of the time; but, without
tools and with a population too small to support tech-
nology, the West African apostates from Islam who landed
here four hundred years ago slid back to the ways of their
grandparents. We want them to get up to date again. We
want Murna to become a market. That's Aaron's job. Our
Amishman has got to start this planet back toward the
machine age."

"Seems an odd job to give a fellow who won't drive a
car or read by electric light," the Engineer observed.

"Not so odd," the Captain said. "The Amish pretty much
invented American agriculture, you know. They've developed the finest low-energy farming there is. Clover-
growing, crop-rotation, using animal manures, those are
their inventions. Aaron, by his example, will teach the
natives here Pennsylvania farming. Before you can say
Tom Malthus, there'll be steel cities in this wilderness,

filled with citizens eager to open charge accounts for low-gravs and stereo sets."

"You expect our bearded friend to reap quite a harvest, Captain," the Engineer said. "I just hope the natives here let him plant the seed."

"Did you get along with him, Hymie?"

"Sure," the Engineer said. "Aaron even made our smiths, those human sharks bound for Qureysh, act friendly. For all his strange ways, he's a nice guy."

"Nice guy, hell," the Captain said. "He's a genius. That seventeenth-century un-scientist has more feeling for folk-ways in his calloused left hand than you'd find in all the Colonial Survey. How do you suppose the Old Order maintains itself in Pennsylvania, a tiny Deitsch-speaking enclave surrounded by calico suburbs and ten-lane highways? They mind their business and leave the neighbors to theirs. The Amish have never been missionaries—they learned in 1600 that missionaries are resented, and either slaughtered or absorbed."

"Sometimes digestively," the Engineer remarked.

"Since the Thirty Years' War, back when 'Hamlet' was opening in London, these people have been breeding a man who can fit one special niche in society. The failures were killed in the early days, or later went gay and took the trappings of the majority. The successes stayed on the farm, respected and left alone. Aaron has flirted with our century; he and his wife learned some very un-Amish skills at the Homestead School. The skill that makes Aaron worth his fare out here, though, is an Amish skill, and the rarest one of all. He knows the Right Way to Live, and lives it; but he knows, too, that your Truth-of-the-Universe is something different. And right, for you. He's quite a man, our Aaron Stoltzfoos. That's why we dropped him here."

"Better him than me," the Engineer said.

"Precisely," the Captain said. He turned to the Exec. "As soon as we've lifted, ask Colonel Harris to call on me in my cabin, Gene. Our Marines had better fresh-up their swordsmanship and cavalry tactics if they're to help our Inad Tuaregs establish that foundry on Qureysh."

"It sometimes seems you're more Ship's Anthropologist than Captain," the Engineer remarked.

"I'm an anthro-apologist, Hymie, like Mr. Kipling," the Captain said. *"There are nine and sixty ways of construct- ing tribal lays. And—every—single—one—of—them—is— right!"* Bells rang, and the ship surged. "Aaron and Martha, God keep you," the Captain said.

"Whoa!" Aaron shouted. He peered back toward the ship, floating up into grayness, the cavitation of her wake stirring the snow into patterns like fine-veined marble. *"Gott saygen eich,"* he said, a prayer for his departing friends.

His wife shivered. "It's cold enough to freeze the horns off a mooley-cow," she said. She glanced about at the snow- drifted little trees and clutched her black cloak tighter. "I'm feared, Stoltz. There's naught about us now but snow and black heathen."

"It's fear that is the heathen," Aaron said. *"By the word of the Lord were the heavens made; and the host of them by the breath of His mouth."* He kissed her. "I welcome you to our new homeland, wife," he said.

Behind them Wutzchen—"piglet"—grunted. Martha smiled back at the giant porker, perched amongst the cases and bags and household goods like the victim of some bawdy charivari. "I've never heard a pig mutter so," she said.

"If he knew that his business here was to flatter the local lady-pigs with farrow, Wutzchen would hop out and run," Aaron said.

"*Dummel dich,* Stoltz," Martha said. "I've got to make your supper yet, and we don't have so much as a stove lit in our tent."

Stoltzfoos slapped the team back into motion. "What we need for our journey home are a few of the *altie lieder,*" he said, reaching back in the wagon for his scarred guitar. He strummed and hummed, then began singing in his clear baritone: "*In da guut alt Suumer-zeit . . .*

". . . *In da guut alt Suumer-zeit,*" Martha's voice joined him. As they jolted along the path through the pine trees, heading toward Datura-village, near which their homestead stood, they sang the other homey songs to the music of the old guitar. "*Drawk Mich Zrick zu Alt Virginye,*" nostalgic for the black-garbed Plain Folk left at home. Then Aaron's fingers danced a livelier tune on the strings: "*Ich fang 'n neie Fashun aw,*" he crowed, and Martha joined in:

"A new fashion I'll begin," they sang,

"The hay I'll cut in the winter;

"When the sun-heat beats, I'll loaf in the shade

"And feast on cherry-pie.

"I'll get us a white, smearkase cow,

"And a yard full of guinea-hen geese;

"A red-beet tree as high as the moon,

"And a patent-leather fence.

"The chickens I'll keep in the kitchen," they sang; whereupon Martha broke down laughing.

"It's a new world, and for now a cold world; but it's God's world, with home just up ahead," Aaron shouted. He pulled the wagon up next to the arctic tent that was to be their temporary farmhouse, beside the wagon loads of provision he'd brought before. He jumped down and swung Martha to earth. "Light the stove, woman; make your little kitchen bright, while I make our beasts feel welcome."

The Amishwoman pushed aside the entrance flap of the

62 BLIND MAN'S LANTERN

tent. Enclosed was a circle some twelve feet wide. The floor
was bare earth. Once warmed by the pump-up "naphtha"
lantern and the gasoline hotplate, it would become a bog.
Martha went out to the wagon to get a hatchet and set out
for the nearby spinny of pines to trim off some twigs. Old
Order manner forbid decorative floor-coverings as improper worldly show; but a springy carpet of pine-twigs
could be considered as no more than a wooden floor, keeping two Plain Folk from sinking to their knees in mud.

The pots were soon boiling atop the two-burner stove,
steaming the tent's air with onion-tangy *tzvivvele Supp* and
the savory pork-smell of *Schnitz un Knepp,* a cannibal
odor that disturbed not a bit Wutzchen, snoring behind the
cookstove. Chickens, penned beneath the bed, chuckled in
their bedtime caucus. The cow stood cheek-by-jowl with
Yonnie, warming him with platonic graciousness as they
shared the hay Aaron had spread before them. Martha
stirred her soup. "When the bishop married me to you,"
she told Aaron, "he said naught of my having to sleep with
a pig."

"Ah, but I thought you knew that to be the purpose of
Christian marriage, woman," Aaron said, standing close.

"It's Wutz I mean," she said. "Truly, I mind not a bit
living as in one of those automobile-wagons, since it's with
you, and only for a little while."

"I'll hire a crew of our neighbors to help with the barn
tomorrow," Aaron said. "That done, you'll have but one
pig to sleep with."

After grace, they sat on cases of tobacco to eat their meal
from a table of feed sacks covered with oilcloth. "The man
in the ship's little kitchen let me make and freeze pies,
Stoltz," Martha said. "He said we'd have a deepfreeze big
as all outdoors, without electric, so use it. Eat till it's all,
Maan; there's more back."

Yonnie bumped against Aaron's eating-elbow. "No man and his wife have eaten in such a zoo since Noah and his wife left the ark," Aaron said. He cut a slice of Schnitz-pie and palmed it against the bull's big snout to be snuffled up. "He likes your cooking," he said.

"So wash his face," Martha told him.

Outside the tent there was a clatter of horse-iron on frozen ground. "What the die-hinker is that?" Aaron demanded. He stood and picked up the naphtha lantern.

Outside, Aaron saw a tall black stranger, astride a horse as pale as the little Murnan moons that lighted him. *"Rankeshi dade!"* the visitor bellowed.

"May your life be a long one!" Aaron Stoltzfoos repeated in Hausa. Observing that his caller was brandishing a clenched fist, the Amishman observed the same ambiguous courtesy. "If you will enter, O Welcome Stranger, my house will be honored."

"Mother bless thee, Bearded One," the Murnan said. He dismounted, tossing his reins to one of the four retainers who remained on horseback. He entered the tent after Aaron; and stared about him at the animals, letting his dark eyes flick across Martha's unveiled face. At the Amishman's invitation, the visitor sat himself on a tobacco-case, revealing as he crossed his legs elaborately embroidered trousers and boot tops worked with designs that would dazzle a Texan. Martha bustled about hiding the remains of their meal.

The Murnan's outer dress was a woolen *riga*, the neckless gown of his West-African forefathers, with a blanket draped about his shoulders, exactly as those ancestors had worn one in the season of the cold wind called harmattan. Aaron introduced himself as Haruna, the Hausa version of his name; and the guest made himself known as Sarki—Chief—

of the village of Datura. His given name was Kazunzumi.
Wutzchen snuffled in his sleep. The Sarki glanced at the
huge pig and smiled. Aaron relaxed a bit. The Islamic
interdict on swine had been shed by the Murnans when
they'd become apostates, just as Colonial Survey had
guessed.

Stoltzfoos' Hausa, learned at the Homestead School at
Georgetown University, proved adequate to its first challenge in the field, though he discovered, with every experi-
menter in a new language, that his most useful phrase was
magana sanoo-sanoo: "please speak slowly." Aaron let the
Chief commence the desultory conversation that would pre-
cede talk of consequence. Martha, ignored by the men, sat
on the edge of the bed, reading the big German-language
Bible. Aaron and Kazunzumi sang on in the heathen tongue
about weather, beasts, and field-crops.

The Sarki leaned forward to examine Aaron's beard and
shaven upper lip, once; and smiled. The Murnan does not
wear such. He looked at Martha more casually now, seeing
that the husband was not disgraced by his wife's naked
face; and remarked on the whiteness of her skin in the same
tones he'd mentioned Wutzchen's remarkable girth.

Aaron asked when the snows would cease, when the
earth would thaw. The Sarki told him, and said that the
land here was as rich as manure. Gradually the talk worked
round to problems involving carpenters, nails, lumber,
hinges—and money. Aaron was pleased to discover that the
natives thought nothing of digging a cellar and raising a
barn in midwinter, and that workers could be easily hired.

Suddenly Sarki Kazunzumi stood and slapped his palms
together. The tent flap was shoved open. Bowed servants,
who'd shivered outside for over an hour, placed their master's presents on the sack table, on the twig floor, even beside Martha on the bed. There were iron knives, a roast

kid, a basket of peanuts, a sack of roasted coffee beans, a string of dried fruit, and a tiny earthware flask of perfume. There was even a woolen riga for Aaron, black, suggesting that the Survey had said a bit to the natives about Amish custom; and there were bolts of bright-patterned cloth too worldly for aught but quilts and infant-dresses, brightening Martha's eyes.

Aaron stood to accept the guest-gifts with elaborate thanks. Sarki Kazunzumi as elaborately bemeaned his offerings. "Musa the carpenter will appear on tomorrow's tomorrow," he said. "You will, the Mother willing, visit me in Datura tomorrow. We will together purchase lumber worthy of my friend-neighbor's barn-making. May the Mother give you strength to farm, Haruna! May the Mother grant you the light of understanding!"

"*Sannu, sannu!*" Stoltzfoos responded. He stood at the door of his tent, holding his lantern high to watch the Sarki and his servants ride off into the darkness.

"*Er iss en groesie Fisch, nee?*" Martha asked.

"The biggest fish in these parts," Aaron agreed. "Did you understand our talk?"

"The heathen speech is hard for me to learn, Stoltz," Martha admitted, speaking in the dialect they'd both been reared to. "While you had only the alien speech to study, I spent my time learning to grow the buglets and tell the various sorts apart. Besides, *unser guutie Deitschie Schproech, asz unser Erlayser schwetzt, iss guut genunk fa mier.*" (Our honest German tongue, that our Saviour spoke, is good enough for me).

Aaron laughed. "So *altfashuned* a *Maedel* I married," he said. "Woman, you must learn the Hausa, too. We must be friends to these *Schwotzers,* as we were friends with the English-speakers back in the United Schtayts." He pushed

aside the bolt of Murnan cloth to sit beside his wife, and
leafed through the pages of their *Familien-Bibel,* pages
lovingly worn by his father's fingers, and his grandfather's.
"Listen," he commanded:

*"For the Lord thy God bringeth thee into a good land,
a land of brooks of water, of fountains and depths that
spring out of valleys and hills; a land of wheat, and barley,
and vines, and fig trees, and pomegranates; a land of oil
olive, and honey; a land wherein thou shalt eat bread without scarceness, thou shalt not lack any thing in it; a land
whose stones are iron, and out of whose hills thou mayest
dig brass. When thou hast eaten and art full, then thou
shalt bless the Lord thy God for the good land which He
hath given thee."* Aaron closed the big book reverently.
"Awmen," he said.

"Awmen," the woman echoed. "Aaron, with you beside
me, I am not fretful."

"And with the Lord above us, I fear not in a strange land,"
Aaron said. He bent to scrape a handful of earth from beneath Martha's pine-twig carpet. *"Guuter Gruundt,"* he
said. "This will grow tall corn. Tobacco, too; the folk here
relish our leaf. There will be deep grasses for the beasts
when the snow melts. We will prosper here, wife."

The next morning was cold, but the snowfall had ceased
for a spell. The Stoltzfooses had risen well before the dawn;
Martha to feed herself, her husband, and the chickens;
Aaron to ready the horse and wagon for a trip into Datura.
He counted out the hoard of golden cowries he'd been
loaned as grubstake, did some arithmetic, and allowed his
wife to pour him a second cup of coffee for the road. "You
may expect the Sarki's wives to visit while I'm gone," he
remarked.

"I'd be scared half to death!" Martha Stoltzfoos said.
Her hands went to the back of her head, behind the lace

prayer covering. "My hair's all strooby, this place is untidy as an auction yard; besides, how can I talk with those dark and heathen women? Them all decked out in golden bangles and silken clothes, most likely, like the bad lady of Babylon? Aaron Stoltz, I would admire a pretty to ride into town with you."

"Haggling for hired-help is man's *Bissiniss*," he said. "When Kazunzumi's women come, feed them pie and peaches from the can. You'll find a way to talk, or women are not sisters. I'll be back home in time for evening chores."

Bumping along the trail into Datura, Aaron Stoltzfoos studied the land. A world that could allow so much well-drained black soil to go unfarmed was fortunate indeed, he mused. He thought of his father's farm, which would be his elder brother's, squeezed between railroad tracks and a three-lane highway, pressed from the west by an Armstrong Cork plant, the very cornstalks humming in harmony with the electric lines strung across the fields. This land was what the old folks had sought in America so long ago: a wilderness ripe for the plow.

The wagon rumbled along the hoof-packed frozen clay. Aaron analyzed the contours of the hills for watershed and signs of erosion. He studied the patterns of the barren winter fields, fall-plowed and showing here and there the stubble of a crop he didn't recognize. When the clouds scudded for a moment off the sun, he grinned up, and looked back blinded to the road. Good tilth and friendship were promised here, gifts to balance loneliness. Five years from spring, other Amish folk would come to homestead—what a barn-raising they'd have! For now, though, he and Martha, come from a society so close-knit that each had always known the yield-per-acre of their remotest cousin-german, were in a land as strange as the New York City Aaron, stopping

in for a phone-call to the vet, had once glimpsed on the
screen of a gay-German neighbor's stereo-set.

Datura looked to Aaron like a city from the Bible, giving
it a certain vicarious familiarity. The great wall was a block
of sunbaked mud, fifty feet tall at the battlements, forty
feet thick at its base; with bright, meaningless flags spotted
on either side of the entrance tower. The cowhide-shielded
gate was open. Birds popped out of mud nests glued to the
mud wall and chattered at Aaron. Small boys wearing too
little to be warm appeared at the opening like flies at a
hog-slaughtering to add to the din, buzzing and hopping
about and waving their arms as they called companions to
view the black-bearded stranger.

Aaron whoaed his horse and took a handful of *amenes,*
copper tenth-penny bits, to rattle between his hands.
"Zonang!" he shouted: "Come here! Is there a boy amongst
you brave enough to ride with an off-worlder to the Sarki's
house, pointing him the way?"

One of the boys laughed at Aaron's slow, careful Hausa.
"Let Black-Hat's whiskers point him the way!" the boy
yelled.

"Uwaka! Ubaka!" Damning both parents of the rude
one, another youngster trotted up to Aaron's wagon and
raised a skinny brown fist in greeting. "Sir Off-Worlder, I
who am named Waziri, Musa-the-Carpenter's son, would be
honored to direct you to the house of Sarki Kazunzumi."

"The honor, young man, is mine," Stoltzfoos assured the
lad, raising his own fist gravely. "My name is Haruna, son
of Levi," he said, reaching down to hoist the boy up beside him on the wagon's seat. "Your friends have ill manners." He giddapped the horse.

"Buzzard-heads!" Waziri shouted back at his whilom
companions.

"Peace, Waziri!" Aaron protested. "You'll frighten my

poor horse into conniptions. Do you work for your father, the carpenter?"

"*To*, honorable Haruna," the boy said. "Yes." The empty wagon thumped over the wheel-cut streets like a wooden drum. "By the Mother, sir, I have great knowledge of planing and joining; of all the various sorts of wood, and the curing of them; all the tools my father uses are as familiar to me as my own left hand."

"Carpentry is a skillful trade," Aaron said. "Myself, I am but a farmer."

"By Mother's light! So am I!" Waziri said, dazzled by this coincidence. "I can cultivate a field free of all its noxious weeds and touch never a food-plant. I can steer a plow straight as a snapped chalk-string, grade seed with a sure eye; I can spread manure—"

"I'm sure you can, Waziri," Aaron said. "I need a man of just those rare qualifications to work for me. Know you such a paragon?"

"Mother's name! Myself, your Honor!"

Aaron Stoltzfoos shook the hand of his hired man, an alien convention that much impressed Waziri. The boy was to draw three hundred anenes a day, some thirty-five cents, well above the local minimum-wage conventions; and he would get his bed and meals. Aaron's confidence that the boastful lad would make a farmer was bolstered by Waziri's loud calculations: "Three hundred coppers a day make, in ten days' work, a bronze cowrie; ten big bronzes make a silver cowrie, the price of an acre of land. Haruna, will you teach me your off-world farming? Will you allow me to buy land that neighbors yours?"

"*Sei schtill, Buu*," Aaron said, laughing. "Before you reap your first crop, you must find me the Sarki."

"We are here, Master Haruna."

The Sarki's house was no larger than its neighbors, Moorish-styled and domed-roofed like the others; but it wore on its streetside walls designs cut into the stucco, scrolls and arabesques. Just above the doorway, which opened spang onto the broadway of Datura, a grinning face peered down upon the visitors, its eyes ruby-colored glass.

Waziri pounded the door for Aaron, and stepped aside to let his new employer do the speaking. They were admitted to the house by a thin, old man wearing a pink turban. As they followed this butler down a hallway, Aaron and Waziri heard the shrieks and giggles of feminine consternation that told of women being herded into the zenana. The Amishman glimpsed one of the ladies, perhaps Sarki Kazunzumi's most junior wife, dashing toward the female sanctuary. Her eyes were lozenges of antimony; her hands, dipped in henna, seemed clad in pale kid gloves. Aaron, recalling pointers on Murnan etiquette he'd received at Georgetown, elaborately did not see the lady. He removed his hat as the turbaned butler bowed him to a plush-covered sofa. Waziri was cuffed to a mat beside the door.

"*Rankeshi dade!*" the Sarki said. "May the Mother bring you the light of understanding."

"Light and long life, O Sarki," Stoltzfoos said, standing up.

"Will the guest who honors my roof-cup taste coffee with his fortunate host?" the Sarki asked.

"The lucky guest will be ever the Sarki's servant if your Honor allows him to share his pleasure with his fellow-farmer and employee, Waziri the son of Musa," Aaron said.

"You'd better have hired mice to guard your stored grain, O Haruna; and blowflies to curry your cattle, than to have engaged the son of Musa as a farmer," Kazunzumi growled. "Waziri has little light of understanding. He will try to win from the soil what only honest sweat and Mother's grace can cause to grow. This boy will gray your beard, Haruna."

"Perhaps the sun that warms the soil will light his brains to understanding," Aaron suggested.

"Better that your hand should leave the plowhandle from time to time to warm his lazy fundament," the Sarki said.

"Just so, O Sarki," the Amishman said. "If Waziri does not serve me well, I have an enormous boar who will, if kept long enough from wholesomer food, rid me of a lazy farmhand." Waziri grinned at all the attention he was getting from the two most important men in town, and sat expectantly as the turbaned elder brought in coffee.

Stoltzfoos watched the Sarki, and aped his actions. Water was served with the coffee; this was to rinse the mouth that the beverage could be tasted with fresh taste buds. The coffee was brown as floodwater silt, heavy with sugar, and very hot; and the cups had no handles. "You are the first European I have seen for many years, friend Haruna," the Sarki said. "It is five years gone that the white off-worlders came, and with a black man as their voice purchased with silver the land you now farm."

"They bought well," Aaron said; "the seller sold justly. When the fist of winter loosens, the soil will prove as rich as butter."

"When the first green breaks through, and you may break the soil without offense, you will do well," Kazunzumi said. "You are a man who loves the land."

"My fathers have flourished with the soil for twenty generations," the Amishman said. "I pray another twenty may live to inherit my good fortune."

"Haruna," the Sarki said, "I see that you are a man of the book, that volume of which Mother in her grace turns over a fresh page each spring. Though your skin is as pale as the flesh of my palm, though you have but one wife, though you speak throat-deep and strangely, yet you and I are more alike than different. The Mother has given you light, Haruna, her greatest gift."

"I thank the Sarki for his words," Aaron said. "Sir, my good and only wife—I am a poor man, and bound by another law than that of the fortunate Kazunzumi—adds her thanks to mine for the rich gifts the Chief of Datura presented us, his servants. In simple thanks, I have some poor things to tender our benefactor."

Waziri, perceiving the tenor of Aaron's talk, sprang to his feet and hastened out to the wagon for the bundles he'd seen under the seat. He returned, staggering under a seventy-pound bale of long-leaf tobacco, product of Aaron's father's farm. He went back for a bolt of scarlet silk for the Sarki's paramount wife, and strings of candy for the great man's children. He puffed in with one last brown-wrapped parcel, which he unpacked to display a leather saddle. This confection was embossed with a hundred intricate designs, rich with silver; un-Amish as a Christmas tree. Judging from the Sarki's dazzled thanks, the saddle was just the thing for a Murnan Chief.

As soon as Kazunzumi had delivered his pyrotechnic speech of thanks, and had directed that Aaron's gifts be placed on a velvet-draped dais at the end of the room, a roast kid was brought in. Waziri, half drunk with the elegance of it all, fell to like any other adolescent boy, and was soon grease to the armpits. Aaron, more careful, referred his actions to the Sarki's. The bread must be broken, not cut; and it was eaten with the right hand only, the left lying in the lap as though broken. Belching seemed to be *de rigueur* as a tribute to the cuisine, so Aaron belched his stomach flat.

Business could now be discussed. Aaron, having no pencil, traced with a greasy finger on the tile floor the outlines of the barn and farmhouse he envisaged. The Sarki from time to time demanded of young Waziri such facts as a carpenter's son might be expected to know, and added lumber-prices in his head as Aaron's bank-barn and two-story farmhouse took form in his imagination. Finally he told the Amishman what the two buildings would cost. Better pleased by this figure than he'd expected to be, Aaron initiated the long-drawn ceremony required to discharge himself from Kazunzumi's hospitality.

As the Stoltzfoos wagon jolted out the gate of Datura, bearing the cot and clothes-trunk of Waziri together with the owner of those chattels, the boys who'd jeered before now stared with respect. The black-hatted *Turawa* had been to visit the Sarki; this established him as no safe man to mock. Waziri gave his late playmates no notice beyond sitting rather straighter on the wagon seat than was comfortable.

There was light enough left when they got back to the farm for Aaron and Waziri to pace out the dimensions of the barn and house. The bank-barn would go up first, of course. No Christian owner of beasts could consent to being well-housed while his animals steamed and shivered in a cloth-sided tent. Waziri pounded stakes into the frozen ground to mark the corners of the barn. Aaron pointed out the drainage-line that would have to be ditched, and explained how the removed earth would be packed, with the clay dug for the cellar, into a ramp leading to the barn's second story in the back. Come next fall, the hayladder could be pulled right up that driveway to be unloaded above the stalls. Aaron took the boy to the frozen-solid creek to show him where a wheel could be placed to lift water to a spillway for the upper fields. He introduced his new helper to Wutzchen, and was pleased to hear Waziri speak wistfully of pork chops. Waziri didn't want to meet Martha yet, though. As a proper Murnan boy, he was not eager to be introduced to the boss' barefaced wife, though she bribed him with a fat wedge of applecake.

When Waziri set out with the lantern to tend to the final outdoor chores, Aaron inquired of his wife's day. The Sarki's Paramount Wife, with two servants, had indeed visited, bringing more gifts of food and clothing. Somehow the four of them had managed to breach the Hausa-*Pennsylfawnisch Deitsch* curtain. "What in the world did you talk about?" Aaron asked.

"First, not knowing what to say, I showed the ladies a drop of vinegar under the microscope," Martha said. "They screamed when they saw all the wriggly worms, and I was put to it to keep them from bundling back home. Then we talked about you, Stoltz, and about the farm; and when would I be giving you *Kinner* to help with all the work," she said. Martha fiddled with the cloak she was sewing for her husband. "It was largely their heathen speech we used, so I understood only what they pointed at; but they ate hearty of anything without vinegar in it, and I laughed with them like with friends at a quilting-bee. My, Stoltz! Those *Nayyer* women are lovely, all jeweled like queens, even the servant girls; even though they have no proper understanding of Christian behavior."

"Did they make you feel welcome, then?" Aaron asked.

"*Ach, ja!* They pitied me, I thought," Martha said. "They said you must be poor, to have but one wife to comfort you; but they said that if the crops be good, you can earn a second woman by next winter. *Chuudes Paste!*"

"I hope you told the Sarki's woman we've been married only since haying-time," Aaron said, "and it's a bit previous for you to be giving me little farmhands."

"I did that," Martha said. "I told them, too, that by the

time the oak leaves are the size of squirrel's ears—if this place has oaks, indeed, or squirrels—we'd have a youngling squalling in our house, loud as any of the Sarki's."

Waziri, crouched near the tent to pick up such talk as might pass inside concerning himself, was at first dismayed by Aaron's whoops of joy. Then Martha joined her husband in happy laughter. Since her tiny-garments line had been delivered in Low Dutch, the young Murnan chose to believe that the enthusiastic sounds he heard within the tent reflected joy at his employment.

It was cold the week the barn was raised, and the mattocks had heavy work gouging out frozen earth to be heaped into the bank leading up the back. The Murnan laborers seemed to think midwinter as appropriate as any other time for building; they said the Mother slept, and would not be disturbed. Martha served coffee and buttermilk-pop at breaktime, and presided over noontime feasts, served in several sittings, in the tent. Before the workers left in the evening, Aaron would give each a drink out back, scharifer cider, feeling that they'd steamed hard enough to earn a sip of something volatile. There are matters, he mused, in which common sense can blink at a bishop; as in secretly trimming one's beard a bit, for example, to keep it out of one's soup; or plucking a guitar to raise the spirits.

When the fortnight's cold work was done, the Stoltzfoos Farm was like nothing seen before on Murna. The bankbarn was forty feet high. On its lee side, Aaron had nailed thin, horizontal strips of wood about a foot apart, hoping to encourage the mud-daubing birds he'd seen on the wall at Datura to plaster their nests onto his barn, and shop for insects in his fields. Lacking concrete, he'd constructed a roofless stone hut abutting the barn to serve as his manure shed. The farmhouse itself was a bit gay, having an inside

toilet to cheat the Murnan winters and a sunporch for
Martha's bacteriological equipment. As the nearest Amish
Volle Diener—Congregational Bishop—was eighty light-
years off, and as the circumstances were unusual, Aaron
felt that he and Martha were safe from the shunning—
Meidung—that was the Old Order's manner of punishing
Amischers guilty of "going gay" by breaking the church
rules against worldly show.

A third outbuilding puzzled the Murnan carpenters even
more than the two-storied wooden house and the enormous
barn. This shed had hinged sidings that could be propped
out to let breezes sweep through the building. Aaron explained to Musa the function of this tobacco shed, where
he would hang his lathes of long-leafed tobacco to cure
from August through November. The tobacco seedlings
were already sprouting in Mason jars on the sunporch win-
dow-sills. The bank-barn's basement was also dedicated to
tobacco. Here, in midwinter, Aaron and Martha and Waziri
would strip, size, and grade the dry leaves for sale in
Datura. Tobacco had always been a prime cash-crop for
Levi, Aaron's father. After testing the bitter native leaf,
Aaron knew that his Pennsylvania Type 41 would sell better here than anything else he could grow.

Martha Stoltzfoos was as busy in her new farmhouse as
Aaron and Waziri were in the barn. Her kitchen stove
burned all day. Nothing ever seen in Lancaster County, this
stove was built of fireclay and brick; but the food it heated
was honest Deitsch. There were pickled eggs and red beets,
ginger tomatoes canned back home, spiced peaches, pickled
pears, mustard pickles and chowchow, pickled red cabbage,
Schnitz un Knepp, shoo-fly pie, vanilla pie, rhubarb sauce,
Cheddar cheeses the size of Waziri's head, haystacks of
sauerkraut, slices off the great slab of home-preserved

chipped beef, milk by the gallon, stewed chicken, popcorn
soup, rashers of bacon, rivers of coffee. In the evenings, protecting her fingers from the sin of idleness, Martha quilted
and cross-stitched by lamplight. Already her parlor wall
boasted a framed motto that reduced to half a dozen German words, the Amish philosophy of life: "What One Likes
Doing is No Work."

For all the chill of the late-winter winds, Aaron kept himself and his young helper in a sweat. Martha's cooking and
the heavy work were slabbing muscle onto Waziri's lean,
brown frame. Aaron's farming methods, so much different
to Murnan routines, puzzled and intrigued the boy. Aaron
was equally bemused by the local taboos. Why, for example,
did all the politer Murnans eat with the right hand only?
Why did the women veil themselves in his presence? And
what was this Mother-goddess worship that seemed to require no more of its adherents than the inclusion of their
deity's name in every curse, formal and profane? "Think
what you please, but not too loud," Aaron cautioned himself, and carefully commenced to copy those Murnan
speech-forms, gestures, and attitudes that did not conflict
with his own deep convictions.

But the soil was his employment, not socializing. Aaron
wormed his swine, inspected his horse-powered plow and
harrow, gazed at the sun, palpated the soil, and prayed for
an early spring to a God who understood German. Each
day, to keep mold from strangling the moist morsels, he
shook the jars of tobacco seed, whose hair-fine sprouts were
just splitting the hulls.

The rations packaged in Pennsylvania were shrinking.
The Stoltzfoos stake of silver and gold cowries was wasting
away. Each night, bruised with fatigue, Aaron brought his
little household into the parlor while he read from the Book
that had bound his folk to the soil. Waziri bowed, honor-

ing his master's God in his master's manner, but understood nothing of the hard High German: *"For the Lord God will help me: therefore shall I not be confounded: therefore have I set my face like a flint, and I know I shall not be ashamed. Awmen."*

"Awmen," said Martha.

"Awmen," said Waziri, fisting his hand in respect to his friend's bearded God.

The Murnan neighbors, to whom late winter was the slackest season in the farm-year, visited often to observe and comment on the off-worlder's work. Aaron Stoltzfoos privately regarded the endless conversations as too much of a good thing; but he realized that his answering the Murnans' questions helped work off the obligation he owed the government for the eighty light-years' transportation it had given him, the opportunity he'd been given to earn this hundred acres with five years' work, and the interest-free loans that had put up his barn and farmhouse.

With Waziri hovering near, Aaron's proud lieutenant, the neighbors would stuff their pipes with native tobacco, a leaf that would have gagged one of Sir Walter Raleigh's Indian friends, while the Amishman lit a stogie in self-defense. Why, the neighbor farmers demanded, did Aaron propose to dust his bean-seeds with a powder that looked like soot? Martha's microscope, a wonder, introduced the Murnans to bacteria; and Aaron tediously translated his knowledge of the nitrogen-fixing symbiotes into Hausa. But there were other questions. What was the purpose of the brush stacked on top of the smooth-raked beds where Aaron proposed to plant his tobacco-seedlings? He explained that fire, second best to steaming, would kill the weed-seeds in the soil, and give the tobacco uncrowded beds to prosper in.

Those needles with which he punctured the flanks of his

swine and cattle: what devils did they exorcise? Back to the
microscope for an explanation of the disease-process, a so-
phistication the Murnans had lost in the years since they'd
left Kano. What were the bits of blue and pink paper Aaron
pressed into mudballs picked up in the various precincts of
his property? Why did those slips oftentime change color,
from blue to pink, or pink-to-blue? What was in those sacks
of stuff—no dung of animals, but a sort of flour—that he intended to work into his soil? Aaron answered each question
as best he could, Waziri supplying—and often inventing—
Hausa words for concepts like phosphorous, ascarid worms,
and litmus.

Aaron had as much to learn from his brown-skinned
neighbors as he had to teach them. He was persuaded to lay
in a supply of seed-yams, guaranteeing a crop that would
bring bronze cowries next fall in Datura, the price of next
year's oil and cloth and tools. The peanut, a legume Aaron
had no experience of beyond purchasing an occasional
tooth-ful at the grocery-store, won half a dozen acres from
Korean lespedeza, the crop he'd at first selected as his soil-
improver there. He got acquainted with a plant no Amishman before him had ever sown, a crabgrass called fonio, a
staple cereal and source of beer-malt on Murna, imported
with the first Nigerian colonists.

Aaron refused to plant any lalle, the henna-shrub from
which the Murnans made the dye to stain their women's
hands, feeling that it would be improper for him to contribute to such a vanity. Bulrush millet, another native crop,
was ill suited to Aaron's well-drained fields. He planned to
grow corn, though, the stuff his people called *Welschkarn*
—alien corn. Though American enough, maize had been a
foreigner to the first Amish farmers, and still carried history
in its name. This crop was chiefly for Wutzchen, whose

bloodlines, Aaron was confident, would lead to a crop of pork of a quality these heretics from Islam had never tasted before.

Work wasn't everything. One Sunday, after he and Martha had sung together from the *Ausbund,* and Aaron had read from the *Schrift* and the *Martyr's Mirror,* there was time to play.

Sarki Kazunzumi and several other gentlemen who enjoyed City Hall or Chamber of Commerce standing in Datura had come to visit the Stoltzfooses after lunch; as had Musa the carpenter and his older son, Dauda, Waziri's brother. Also on the premises were about a dozen of the local farmers and craftsmen, inspecting the curious architecture the off-worlder had introduced to their planet. Aaron, observing that the two classes of his guests were maintaining a polite fiction, each that the other was not present, had an idea. He'd seen Murnans in town at the midwinter festival, their status-consciousness forgotten in mutual quaffs of fonio-beer or barley-brandy, betting together at horse-races and wheels-of-fortune. "My friends," the Amishman addressed the Murnans gathered in his barn, inspecting Wutzchen, "let's play a game of ball."

Kazunzumi looked interested. As the local Chief of State, the Sarki's approval guaranteed the enthusiasm of all the lesser ranks.

Aaron explained the game he had in mind. It wasn't baseball, an "English" sport foreign to Amishmen, who can get through their teens without having heard of either Comiskey Park or the World Series. Their game, *Mosch Balle,* fits a barnyard better.

In lieu of the regulation softball used in the game of Corner Ball, Martha had stitched together a sort of large beanbag. The playing-field Aaron set up with the help of his visitors was a square some twelve yards on a side, fence-rails being propped up to mark its boundaries and fresh straw forked onto it six inches deep as footing.

Aaron's eight-man team was chosen from the working-stiffs. The opposing eight were the Brass. To start the game, four of the proletarians stood at the corners of the square; and two men of Kazunzumi's team waited warily within.

Aaron commenced to explain the game. To say that the object of *Mosch Balle* is for a member of the outer, offensive, team to strike an inner, defensive man with the ball is inadequate; such an explanation is as lacking as to explain baseball as the pitcher's effort to throw a ball so well that it's hittable, and so very well that it yet goes unhit. Both games have their finer points.

"Now," Aaron told his guests on the field, "we four on the corners will toss the ball back and forth amongst ourselves, shouting *Hah, Oh, Tay,* with each pitch. Whoever has the ball on *Tay* has to fling it at one of the two men inside the square. If he misses, he's Out; and one of the other men on our team takes his place. If he hits his target-man, the target's Out, and will be replaced by another man from the Sarki's team. The team with the last man left on the straw wins the first half. *Des iss der Weeg wie mir's diehne.* O.K.?"

"*Afuwo!*" the Sarki yelled, a woman's call, grinning, crouched to spring aside. "Hah!" Aaron shouted, and tossed the ball to Waziri's older brother, Dauda. "Oh!" Dauda yelled, and threw the ball to the shoemaker. "Tay!" the cobbler exulted, and slammed the ball at the lower-ranking of the two men within the square, the village banker. The shoemaker missed, and was retired.

The Daturans were soon stripped down to trousers and boots, their black torsos steaming in the cold air. Aaron removed his shirt—but not his hat—and so far forgot his

Hausa in the excitement that he not only rooted for his teammates in *Pennsylfawnisch Deitsch,* but even punctuated several clumsy plays with raw *Fadomm's.*

Aaron's skill won the first half for his team. Blooded, the Chamber of Commerce Eight fought through to win the second half. A tie. The play-off saw the Working-Man's League pummeled to a standstill by the C-of-C, who took the laurels with a final slam that knocked Waziri into the straw, protesting that it was an accident.

Sweating, laughing, social status for the moment forgotten, the teams and their mobs of fans surged into the farmhouse to demand of Martha wedges of raisin pie and big cups of strong coffee. As the guests put their rigas and their white caps back on, and assumed therewith their game-discarded rank of class, they assured Aaron that the afternoon at the ball game had been a large success.

The next day was crisp and cold. With nothing more to be done till the soil thawed, Aaron took Waziri down to the creek to investigate his project of irrigating the hilltop acres. The flow of water was so feeble that the little stream was ice to its channel. "Do you have hereabouts a digger-of-water-holes?" Aaron asked the boy. Waziri nodded, and supplied the Hausa phrase for this skill. "Good. *Wonn's Gottes wille iss,* I will find a spot for them to dig, smelling out the water as can my cousin Blue Ball Benjamin Blank," Aaron said. "Go get from the barn the pliers, the hand-tool that pinches."

Waziri trotted off and brought back the pliers. "What are you up to, Haruna-boss?" he asked. Aaron was holding the bulldog pliers out before him, one handle in each hand, parallel to the ground.

"I am smelling for the well-place," the Amishman said, pacing deliberately across the field. The boy scampered along beside him. "We will need at least one well to be safe from August drought. Cousin Benjamin found the wet depths in this fashion; perhaps it will work for me." Aaron walked, arms outstretched, for half an hour before his face grew taut. He slowed his walking and began to work toward the center of a spiral. Waziri could see the sweat springing up on the young farmer's brow and fingers, despite the cold breeze that blew. The bulldog pliers trembled as though responding to the throbbing of an engine. Suddenly, as though about to be jerked from Aaron's hands, the pliers tugged downward so forceably that he had to lift his elbows and flex his wrists to hold onto them. "Put a little pile of stones here, Waziri," he said. "We'll have the diggers visit as soon as the ground thaws."

Waziri shook his head. "Haruna, they will not touch soft earth until the first grass sprouts," he said.

"Time enough," Aaron said. He looked up to satisfy himself that his prospective well-site was high enough to avoid drainage from his pig-yard, then left the Murnan boy to pile up a cairn for the diggers. It would be good to have a windmill within earshot of the house, he mused; its squeaking would ease Martha with a homey sound. Alone for a few minutes, Aaron retired to the workshop in the cellar of the barn. He planed and sanded boards of a native lumber very like to tulipwood. Into the headboard of the cradle he was making, he keyhole-sawed the same sort of broad Dutch heart that had marked his own cradle, and the cradles of all his family back to the days in the Rhineland, before they'd been driven to America.

Martha Stoltzfoos was speaking Hausa better than she'd spoken English since grade-school days, and she kept busy in the little bacteriological laboratory on her sunporch, keeping fresh the skills she'd learned at Georgetown and might some day need in earnest; but she still grew homesick

as her child-coming day drew nearer. It was wrong, she told
Aaron, for an Amishwoman to have heathen midwives at
her lying-in. For all their kindness, the Murnan women
could never be as reassuring as the prayer-covered, black-
aproned matrons who'd have attended Martha back home.
"Ach, Stoltz," she told her husband, "if only a few other of
unser sart Leit could have come here with us."

"Don't worry, Love," Aaron said. "I've eased calves and
colts enough into the world; man-children can't come so
different."

"You talk like a man," Martha accused him. "I wish my
Mem was just down the road a piece, ready to come a-run-
ning when my time came," she said. She put one hand on
her apron. "*Chuudes Paste!* The little rascal is wild as a colt,
indeed. Feel him, Stoltz!"

Aaron dutifully placed his hand to sense the child's
quickening. "He'll be of help on the farm, so strong as he
is," he remarked. Then, tugging his hat down tight, Aaron
went outdoors, bashful before this mystery.

The little creek had thawed, and the light of the sun on
a man's face almost gave back the heat the air extorted.
Waziri had gone to town today for some sort of Murnan
spring-festival, eager to celebrate his hard-earned wealth on
his first day off in months. The place seemed deserted,
Aaron felt, without the boy; without the visitors he'd played
ball and talked crops with, striding up in their scarlet-
trimmed rigas to gossip with their friend Haruna.

Between the roadway and the house, Aaron knelt to rake
up with his fingers a handful of the new-thawed soil. He
squeezed it. The clod in his hand broke apart of its own
weight: it was not too wet to work. Festival-day though it
was to his *Schwotzer* neighbors, he was eager to spear this
virgin soil with his plow blade.

Aaron strode back to the barn. He hitched Rosina—the

dappled mare, named "Raisin" for her spots—to the plow
and slapped her into motion. Sleek with her winter's idleness, Rosina was at first unenthusiastic about the plow; but
the spring sun and honest exercise warmed her quickly.
Within half an hour she was earning her keep. Though
Aaron was plowing shallow, the compact soil broke hard.
Rosina leaned into the traces, leaving hoofprints three
inches deep. No gasoline tractor, Aaron mused, could ever
pull itself through soil so rich and damp. *Geilsgrefte*, horse-
power, was best exerted by a horse, he thought.

The brown earth-smells were good. Aaron kicked apart
the larger clods, fat with a planet-life of weather and rich
decay. This land would take a good deal of disking to get it
into shape. His neighbors, who'd done their heavy plowing
just after last fall's first frost, were already well ahead of
him. He stabled Rosina at sundown, and went in to sneak a
well-earned glass of hard cider past Martha's teetotaling eye.

Musa the carpenter brought his son home well after dark.
Waziri had had adventures, the old man said; dancing,
gambling on the Fool's Wheel, sampling fonio-beer, cele-
brating his own young life's springtime with the earth's.
Both the old man and the boy were barefoot, Aaron noticed; but said nothing: perhaps shoelessness was part of
their spring-festival.

Waziri, a bit *geschwepst* with the beer, tottered off to bed.
"Thanks to you, friend Haruna, that boy became a man today," the carpenter said. He accepted a glass of Aaron's
cider. "Today Waziri's wallet jingled with bronze and copper earned by his own sweat, a manful sound to a lad of
fifteen summers. I ask pardon for having returned your la-
borer in so damaged a condition, brother Haruna; but you
may be consoled with the thought that the Mother's festival
comes but once in the twelve-month."

"No harm was done, brother Musa," Aaron said, offering his visitor tobacco. "In my own youth, I sometimes danced with beer-light feet to the music of worldly guitars; and yet I reached a man's estate."

Offered a refill for his pipe, Musa raised a hand in polite refusal. "Tomorrow's sun will not wait on our conversation, and much must be done, in the manner of racers waiting the signal, before the first blade breaks the soil," he said. "Good night, brother Haruna; and may Mother grant you light!"

"Mother keep you, brother Musa," Aaron murmured the heathen phrase without embarrassment. "I'll guide your feet to your wagon, if I may."

Aaron, carrying the naphtha lantern, led the way across the strip of new-plowed soil. Set by frost into plastic mounds and ridges, the earth bent beneath his shoes and the carpenter's bare feet. Aaron swung Musa's picket-iron, the little anchor to which his horse was tethered, into the wagon, noticing that it had been curiously padded with layers of quilted cloth. "May you journey home in good health, brother Musa," he said.

"*Uwaka!*" Musa shouted, staring at the plow-cuts.

Aaron Stoltzfoos dropped the lantern to his side, amazed that the dignified old man could be guilty of such an obscenity. Perhaps he'd misheard. "Haruna, you have damned yourself!" Musa bellowed. "Cursed be this farm! Cursed be thy farming! May thy seedlings rot, may thy corn sprout worms for tassles, may your cattle stink and make early bones!"

"Brother Musa!" Aaron said.

"I am no sib to you, O Bearded One," Musa said. "Nor will I help you carry the curse you have brought upon yourself by today's ill-doing." He darted back to the farmhouse, where he ordered half-wakened Waziri to pad barefoot after

him to the wagon, rubbing his eyes. "Come, son," Musa said.
"We must flee these ill-omened fields." Without another
word to his host, the carpenter hoisted his boy into the
wagon, mounted, and set off into the night. The hoofs of
his horse padded softly against the dirt road, unshod.

Martha met the bewildered Aaron at the door, wakened
by Musa's shouting. *"Wass gibt,* Stoltz?" she asked. "What
for was all the carry-on?"

Aaron tugged at his beard. "I don't know, woman," he
admitted. "Musa the carpenter took one look at the plowing
I did today, then cursed me as though he'd caught me spit-
ting in his well. He got Waziri up from bed and took him
home." He took his wife's hand. "I'm sorry he woke you up,
Liebchen."

"It was not so much the angry carpenter who waked me
as the little jack rabbit you're father to," Martha said. "As
you say, a *Buu* who can kick so hard, and barefoot, too,
will be a strong one once he's born."

Aaron was staring out the window onto the dark road.
"Farwas hot Musa sell gehuh?" he asked himself. "What for
did Musa do such a thing? He knows that our ways are different to his. If I did aught wrong, Musa must know it was
done not for want to harm. I will go to the village tomorrow;
Musa must forgive me and explain."

"He will, Stoltz," Martha said. *"Kuum, schloef.* You'll be
getting up early."

"How can I sleep, not knowing how I have hurt my
friend?" Aaron asked.

"You must," Martha urged him. "Let your cares rest for
the night, Aaron."

In the morning, Stoltzfoos prepared for his trip into
Datura by donning his Sunday-best. He clipped a black
patent-leather bow tie, a wedding gift, onto his white shirt;
and fastened up his best broadfall trousers with his dress

suspenders. Over this, Aaron put his *Mutzi,* the tailed frock coat that fastened with hooks-and-eyes. When he'd exchanged his broad-brimmed black felt working-hat for another just the same, but unsweated, Aaron was dressed as he'd be on his way to a House-Amish Sunday meeting back home. "I expect no trouble here, Martha," he said, tucking a box of stogies under his arm as a little guest-gift for the old carpenter.

"Hurry home, Stoltz; I feel wonderful busy about the middle," Martha said. There was a noise out on the road. "Listen!" she said. "Go look the window out, now; someone is coming the yard in!"

Aaron hastened to lift the green roller-blind over the parlor window. "Ach; it is the *groesie Fisch,* Sarki Kazunzumi, with half the folk from town," he said. "Stay here, woman. I will go out and talk with them."

The Sarki sat astride his white pony, staring as Aaron approached him. Behind their chief, on lesser beasts, sat Kazunzumi's retainers, each with a bundle in his arms. "Welcome, O Sarki!" Aaron said, raising his fist.

Kazunzumi did not return the Amishman's salute. "I return your gifts, Lightless One," he announced. "They are tainted with your blasphemy." He nodded, and his servants dismounted to stack at the side of the road Aaron's guest-gifts of months before. The bale of tobacco was set down, the bolt of scarlet silk, the chains of candy, the silver-filigreed saddle. "Now that I owe you naught, Bearded One, we have no further business with one another." He reined his horse around. "I go in sadness, Haruna," he said.

"What did I do, Kazunzumi?" Aaron asked. "What am I to make of your displeasure?"

"You have failed us, who was my friend," the Sarki said. "You will leave this place, taking your woman and your beasts and your sharp-shod horses."

"Sir, where am I to go?"

"Whence came you, Haruna?" the Sarki asked. "Return to your own black-garbed folk, and injure the Mother no longer with your lack of understanding."

"Sarki Kazunzumi, I know not how I erred," Stoltzfoos said. "As for returning to my own country, that I cannot. The off-world vessel that brought us here is star-far away; and it will not return until we are all five summers older. My Martha is besides with child, and cannot safely travel. My land is ripe for seeding. How can I go now?"

"There is wilderness to the south, where no son of the Mother lives," the Sarki said. "Go there. I care not for heathen who are out of my sight."

"Sir, show us mercy," Aaron said.

Kazunzumi danced his shoeless horse around to face Aaron. "Haruna, who was my friend, whom I thought to stand with me in Mother's light, I would be merciful; but I cannot be weak. It is not me whom you must beseech, but the Mother who feeds us all. Make amends to Her, then Sarki Kazunzumi will give his ear to your pleas. Without amends, Haruna, you must go from here within the week." Kazunzumi waved his arm and galloped off toward Datura. His servants followed quickly. On the roadside lay the gifts, dusted from the dirt raised by the horses.

The Amishman turned toward the house. Martha's face was at the parlor window, quizzical under her prayer-covering, impatient to hear what had happened. Aaron plodded back to the house with the evil news, stumbling over a clod of earth in the new-turned furrows near the road. Martha met him at the door. *"Waas will er?"* she demanded.

"He says we must leave our farm."

"Why for?" she asked.

"Somehow, I have offended their *fadommt* Mum-god,"

Aaron said. "The Sarki has granted us a week to make ready to go into the wilderness." He sat on a coffee-colored kitchen chair, his head bowed and his big hands limp between his knees.

"Stoltz, where can we go?" Martha asked. "We have no *Freindschaft,* no kin, in all this place."

Aaron tightened his hands into fists. "We will not go!" he vowed. "I will find a way for us to stay." He broke open the box of cigars that had been meant as a gift for Musa and clamped one of the black stogies between his teeth. "What is their *heidisch* secret?" he demanded. "What does the Mother want of me?"

"Aaron Stoltz," Martha said vigorously, "I'll have no man of mine offering dignity to a heathen god. The *Schrift* orders us to cut down the groves of the alien gods, to smash their false images; not to bow before them. Will you make a golden calf here, as did your namesake Aaron of Egypt, for whose sin the Children of Israel were plagued?"

"Woman, I'll not have you preach to me like a servant of the Book," Aaron said. "It is not for you to cite Scripture." He stared through the window. "What does the Mother want of me?"

"As you shout, do not forget that I am a mother, too," Martha said. She dabbed a finger at her eye.

"Fagep mir, Liebling," Aaron said. He walked behind the chair where his wife sat. Tenderly, he kneaded the muscles at the back of her neck. "I am trying to get inside Musa's head, and Kazunzumi's; I am trying to see their world through their eyes. It is not an easy thing to do, Martha. Though I lived for a spell among the 'English,' my head is still House-Amish; a fat, Dutch cheese."

"It is a good head," Martha said, relaxing under his massage, "and if there be cheese-heads hereabouts, it's these blackfolk that wear them, and not my man."

"If I knew what the die-hinker our neighbors mean by their Mother-talk, it might be I could see myself through Murnan eyes, as I can hear a bit with Hausa ears," Aaron said. *"Iss sell nix so,* Martha?"

"We should have stood at home, and thought with our own good heads," she said.

"Let me think," Aaron said. "If I were to strike you, wife," he mused, "it could do you great hurt, and harm our unborn child, *Nee?"*

"Aaron!" Martha scooted out from under her husband's kneading hands.

"Druuvel dich net!" he said. "I am only thinking. These blackfolk now, these neighbors who were before last night our friends, speak of Light as our bishop at home speaks of Grace. To have it is to have all, to be one with the congregation. If I can find this Light, we and the Sarki and his people can again be friends." Aaron sat down. "I must learn what I have done wrong," he said.

"Other than drink a glass of cider now and then, and make worldly music with a guitar, you've done no wrong," Martha said stubbornly. "You're a good man."

"In the Old Order, I am a good man, so long as no *Diener* makes trouble over a bit of singing or cider," Aaron said. "As a guest on Murna, I have done some deed that has hurt this Mother-god, whom our neighbors hold dear."

"Heathenish superstition!"

"Martha, love, I am older than you, and a man," Aaron said. "Give me room to think! If the goddess-Mother is heathen as Baal, it matters not; these folk who worship her hold our future in their hands. Besides, we owe them the courtesy not to dance in their churches nor to laugh at their prayers; even the 'English' have more grace than that."

Aaron pondered. "Something in the springtime is the
Murnan Mother's gift, her greatest gift. What?"

"Blaspheme not," Martha said. "Remember Him who
*causeth the grass to grow for the cattle, and herb for the
service of man: that he may bring forth food out of the
earth.*"

"Wife, is the True God less, if these people call Him
Mother?" Aaron demanded.

"We are too far from home," the woman sighed. "Such
heavy talk is wearisome; it is for bishops to discourse so,
not ordinary folk like us."

"If I can't find the light," Aaron said, "this farm we live
on, and hoped to leave to our children, isn't worth the water in a dish of soup." He slapped his hands together and
stood to pace. "Martha, hear me out," he said. "If a woman
be with child, and a man takes her with lust and against her
will, is not that man accursed?"

"Aaron!" she said. *"Haagott,* such wicked talk you make!"

"Seen with Murnan eyes, have I not done just such a
cursed thing?" Aaron demanded. "The Mother-god of this
world is *mit Kinndt,* fat with the bounty of springtime. So
tender is the swollen belly of the earth that the people here,
simple folk with no more subtle God, strip the iron from
the hoofs of their horses not to bruise her. They bare their
feet in her honor, treat her with the tenderness I treat my
beloved Martha. And to this Goddess, swollen earth, I took
the plow! Martha, we are fortunate indeed that our neighbors are gentle people, or I would be hanged now, or stoned
to death like the wicked in the old days. *Ich hot iere Got-
terin awgepockt:* I raped their Goddess!"

Martha burst into tears. When Aaron stepped forward to
comfort her, she struck his chest with her balled fists.
"Stoltz, I wed you despite your beer-drinking from cans at

the Singing, though you play a worldly guitar and sing the English songs, though people told me you drove your gay Uncle Amos' black-bumpered Ford before you membered to the district; still, house-Amish pure Old Order though my people are, I married you, from love and youngness and girlish ignorance. But I do not care, even in this wilderness you've brought us to in that big English ship, to hear such vileness spoke out boldly. Leave me alone."

"I'll not."

"You'd best," she said. "I'm sore offended in the lad I'm wifed to."

"Love, *Ich bin sorry,*" Aaron said. "The Book, though, says just what our neighbors told me: Ye shall know the truth, and the truth shall set you free. I have found the truth, the truth of our dark-skinned friends. I did not want to wound the ears of *da Oppel fuun mein Awk,* apple-of-mine-eye sweet Martha; but I must speak out the truth."

"It is not good enough," Martha sobbed, "that you accept this brown-skinned, jewel-bedizzened woman-god; but you must make love to her; and I, wed to you by the Book, nine months gone with *Kinndt,* am to make no fuss."

"I loved the Mother-god with the plow, and accidentally," Aaron bellowed. *"Haagott!* woman; have you no funny?"

"I will birth our child in my lap from laughing," Martha said, weeping. "Aaron, do what you will. I can hardly walk home to my Mem to bear a son in my girlhood bedroom. We are like *Awduum uuu Ayf,* like you said; but the serpent in this Eden pleases me not."

"When I spoke of colts, and the borning of them," Aaron said, "I forgot me that mares are more sensible than human women. Martha, *liebe* Martha, you wed a man when you married me. All your vapors are naught against my having seen the light. If to stay here, on this land already watered with my hard sweat, I had to slaughter cattle in sacrifice to the Mother, I'd pick up the knife gladly, and feel it no blasphemy against our God."

"Aaron Stoltz," Martha said, "I forbid you to lend honor to this god!"

Aaron sat. He unlaced his shoes and tugged them off. "Woman," he asked softly, "you forbid me? Martha, for all the love I bear you, there is one rule of our folk that's as holy as worship; and that's that the man is master in his house." He pulled off his black stockings and stood, barefoot, with calluses won on the black earth of his father's farm; dressed otherwise meetly as a deacon. "I will walk to Datura on my naked feet to show our friends I know my wrongdoing, that I have hurt the belly of the pregnant earth. I will tell Sarki Kazunzumi that I have seen his light; that my horses will be unshod as I am, that the Mother will not feel my plow again until the grasses spring, when her time will be accomplished."

Martha crossed her hands about her middle. "Ach, Stoltz," she said. "Our *Buu iss reddi far geh,* I think. Today will be his birthday. Don't let your tenderness to the earth keep you from walking swiftly to Datura; and when you return, come in a wagon with the Sarki's ladies, who understand midwifery. I think they will find work here."

"I will hurry, Mother," Aaron promised.

JUNIOR ACHIEVEMENT

by William Lee

"What would you think," I asked Marjorie over supper, "if I should undertake to lead a junior achievement group this summer?"

She pondered it while she went to the kitchen to bring in the dessert. It was dried apricot pie, and very tasty, I might add.

"Why Donald," she said, "it could be quite interesting, if I understand what a junior achievement group is. What gave you the idea?"

"It wasn't my idea, really," I admitted. "Mr. McCormack called me to the office today, and told me that some of the children in the lower grades wanted to start one. They need adult guidance of course, and one of the group suggested my name."

I should explain, perhaps, that I teach a course in general science in our Ridgeville Junior High School, and another in general physics in the Senior High School. It's a privilege which I'm sure many educators must envy, teaching in Ridgeville, for our new school is a fine one, and our academic standards are high. On the other hand, the fathers of most of my students work for the Commission and a constant awareness of the Commission and its work pervades the town. It is an uneasy privilege then, at least

sometimes, to teach my old fashioned brand of science to
these children of a new age.

"That's very nice," said Marjorie. "What does a junior
achievement group do?"

"It has the purpose," I told her, "of teaching the members something about commerce and industry. They manufacture simple compositions like polishing waxes and sell
them from door-to-door. Some groups have built up tidy
little bank accounts which are available for later educa-
tional expenses."

"Gracious, you wouldn't have to sell from door to door,
would you?"

"Of course not. I'd just tell the kids how to do it."

Marjorie put back her head and laughed, and I was
forced to join her, for we both recognize that my understanding and "feel" for commercial matters—if I may use
that expression—is almost nonexistent.

"Oh, all right," I said, "laugh at my commercial aspira-
tions. But don't worry about it, really. Mr. McCormack
said we could get Mr. Wells from Commercial Department to help out if he was needed. There is one problem,
though. Mr. McCormack is going to put up fifty dollars to
buy any raw materials wanted and he rather suggested that
I might advance another fifty. The question is, could we
do it?"

Marjorie did mental arithmetic. "Yes," she said, "yes, if
it's something you'd like to do."

We've had to watch such things rather closely for the
last ten—no, eleven years. Back in the old Ridgeville, fifty
odd miles to the south, we had our home almost paid for,
when the accident occurred. It was in the path of the
heaviest fall out, and we couldn't have kept on living there
even if the town had stayed. When Ridgeville moved to its

present site, so, of course, did we, which meant starting mortgage payments all over again.

Thus it was that on a Wednesday morning about three weeks later, I was sitting at one end of a plank picnic table with five boys and girls lined up along the sides. This was to be our headquarters and factory for the summer—a roomy unused barn belonging to the parents of one of the group members, Tommy Miller.

"O.K.," I said, "let's relax. You don't need to treat me as a teacher, you know. I stopped being a school teacher when the final grades went in last Friday. I'm on vacation now. My job here is only to advise, and I'm going to do that as little as possible. You're going to decide what to do, and if it's safe and legal and possible to do with the starting capital we have, I'll go along with it and help in any way I can. This is your meeting."

Mr. McCormack had told me, and in some detail, about the youngsters I'd be dealing with. The three who were sitting to my left were the ones who had proposed the group in the first place.

Doris Enright was a grave young lady of ten years, who might, I thought, be quite a beauty in a few more years, but was at the moment rather angular—all shoulders and elbows. Peter Cope, Jr. and Hilary Matlack were skinny kids, too. The three were of an age and were all tall for ten-year-olds.

I had the impression during that first meeting that they looked rather alike, but this wasn't so. Their features were quite different. Perhaps from association, for they were close friends, they had just come to have a certain similarity of restrained gesture and of modulated voice. And they were all tanned by sun and wind to a degree that made their eyes seem light and their teeth startlingly white.

The two on my right were cast in a different mold. Mary McCready was a big husky redhead of twelve, with a face full of freckles and an infectious laugh, and Tommy Miller, a few months younger, was just an average extroverted well adjusted youngster, noisy and restless, tee shirted and butch barbered.

The group exchanged looks to see who would lead off, and Peter Cope seemed to be elected.

"Well, Mr. Henderson, a junior achievement group is a bunch of kids who get together to manufacture and sell things, and maybe make some money."

"Is that what you want to do," I asked, "make money?"

"Why not?" Tommy asked. "There's something wrong with making money?"

"Well sure, I suppose we want to," said Hilary. "We'll need some money to do the things we want to do later."

"And what sort of things would you like to make and sell?" I asked.

The usual products, of course, with these junior achievement efforts, are chemical specialties that can be made safely and that people will buy and use without misgivings—solvent to free up rusty bolts, cleaner to remove road tar, mechanics hand soap—that sort of thing. Mr. McCormack had told me, though, that I might find these youngsters a bit more ambitious. "The Miller boy and Mary McCready," he had said, "have exceptionally high IQ's—around one forty or one fifty. The other three are hard to classify. They have some of the attributes of exceptional pupils, but much of the time they seem to have little interest in their studies. The junior achievement idea has sparked their imaginations. Maybe it'll be just what they need."

Mary said, "Why don't we make a freckle remover? I'd be our first customer."

"The thing to do," Tommy offered, "is to figure out what people in Ridgeville want to buy, then sell it to them."

"I'd like to make something by powder metallurgy techniques," said Pete. He fixed me with a challenging eye. "You should be able to make ball bearings by molding, then densify them by electroplating."

"And all we'd need is a hydraulic press," I told him, "which, on a guess, might cost ten thousand dollars. Let's think of something easier."

Pete mulled it over and nodded reluctantly. "Then maybe something in the electronics field. A hi-fi sub assembly of some kind."

"How about a new detergent," Hilary put in.

"Like the liquid dishwashing detergents?" I asked.

He was scornful. "No, they're formulations—you know, mixtures. That's cookbook chemistry. I mean a brand new synthetic detergent. I've got an idea for one that ought to be good even in the hard water we've got around here."

"Well now," I said, "organic synthesis sounds like another operation calling for capital investment. If we should keep the achievement group going for several summers, it might be possible later on to carry out a safe synthesis of some sort. You're Dr. Matlack's son, aren't you? Been dipping into your father's library?"

"Some," said Hilary, "and I've got a home laboratory."

"How about you, Doris," I prompted. "Do you have a special field of interest?"

"No." She shook her head in mock despondency. "I'm not very technical. Just sort of miscellaneous. But if the group wanted to raise some mice, I'd be willing to turn over a project I've had going at home."

"You could sell mice?" Tommy demanded incredulously.

"Mice," I echoed, then sat back and thought about it. "Are they a pure strain? One of the recognized laboratory strains? Healthy mice of the right strain," I explained to Tommy, "might be sold to laboratories. I have an idea the Commission buys a supply every month."

"No," said Doris, "these aren't laboratory mice. They're fancy ones. I got the first four pairs from a pet shop in Denver, but they're red—sort of chipmunk color, you know. I've carried them through seventeen generations of careful selection."

"Well now," I admitted, "the market for red mice might be rather limited. Why don't you consider making an aftershave lotion? Denatured alcohol, glycerine, water, a little color and perfume. You could buy some bottles and have some labels printed. You'd be in business before you knew it."

There was a pause, then Tommy inquired, "How do you sell it?"

"Door to door."

He made a face. "Never build up any volume. Unless it did something extra. You say we'd put color in it. How about enough color to leave your face looking tanned. Men won't use cosmetics and junk, but if they didn't have to admit it, they might like the shave lotion."

Hilary had been deep in thought. He said suddenly, "Gosh, I think I know how to make a—what do you want to call it—a before-shave lotion."

"What would that be?" I asked.

"You'd use it before you shaved."

"I suppose there might be people who'd prefer to use it beforehand," I conceded.

"There will be people," he said darkly, and subsided.

Mrs. Miller came out to the barn after a while, bringing a bucket of soft drinks and ice, a couple of loaves of bread and ingredients for a variety of sandwiches. The parents had agreed to underwrite lunches at the barn and Betty

Miller philosophically assumed the role of commissary officer. She paused only to say hello and to ask how we were progressing with our organization meeting.

I'd forgotten all about organization, and that, according to all the articles I had perused, is most important to such groups. It's standard practice for every member of the group to be a company officer. Of course a young boy who doesn't know any better, may wind up a sales manager.

Over the sandwiches, then, I suggested nominating company officers, but they seemed not to be interested. Peter Cope waved it off by remarking that they'd each do what came naturally. On the other hand, they pondered at some length about a name for the organization, without reaching any conclusions, so we returned to the problem of what to make.

It was Mary, finally, who advanced the thought of kites. At first there was little enthusiasm, then Peter said, "You know, we could work up something new. Has anybody ever seen a kite made like a wind sock?"

Nobody had. Pete drew figures in the air with his hands. "How about the hole at the small end?"

"I'll make one tonight," said Doris, "and think about the small end. It'll work out all right."

I wished that the youngsters weren't starting out by inventing a new article to manufacture, and risking an almost certain disappointment, but to hold my guidance to the minimum, I said nothing, knowing that later I could help them redesign it along standard lines.

At supper I reviewed the day's happenings with Marjorie and tried to recall all of the ideas which had been propounded. Most of them were impractical, of course, for a group of children to attempt, but several of them appeared quite attractive.

Tommy, for example, wanted to put tooth powder into tablets that one would chew before brushing the teeth. He thought there should be two colors in the same bottle—orange for morning and blue for night, the blue ones designed to leave the mouth alkaline at bed time.

Pete wanted to make a combination nail and wood screw. You'd drive it in with a hammer up to the threaded part, then send it home with a few turns of a screwdriver.

Hilary, reluctantly forsaking his ideas on detergents, suggested we make black plastic discs, like poker chips but thinner and as cheap as possible, to scatter on a snowy sidewalk where they would pick up extra heat from the sun and melt the snow more rapidly. Afterward one would sweep up and collect the discs.

Doris added to this that if you could make the discs light enough to float, they might be colored white and spread on the surface of a reservoir to reduce evaporation.

These latter ideas had made unknowing use of some basic physics, and I'm afraid I relapsed for a few minutes into the role of teacher and told them a little bit about the laws of radiation and absorption of heat.

"My," said Marjorie, "they're really smart boys and girls. Tommy Miller does sound like a born salesman. Somehow I don't think you're going to have to call in Mr. Wells."

I do feel just a little embarrassed about the kite, even now. The fact that it flew surprised me. That it flew so confoundedly well was humiliating. Four of them were at the barn when I arrived next morning; or rather on the rise of ground just beyond it, and the kite hung motionless and almost out of sight in the pale sky. I stood and watched for a moment, then they saw me.

"Hello, Mr. Henderson," Mary said, and proffered the cord which was wound on a fishing reel. I played the kite up and down for a few minutes, then reeled it in. It was, almost exactly, a wind sock, but the hole at the small end was shaped—by wire—into the general form of a kidney bean. It was beautifully made, and had a sort of professional look about it.

"It flies too well," Mary told Doris. "A kite ought to get caught in a tree sometimes."

"You're right," Doris agreed. "Let's see it." She gave the wire at the small end the slightest of twists. "There, it ought to swoop."

Sure enough, in the moderate breeze of that morning, the kite swooped and yawed to Mary's entire satisfaction. As we trailed back to the barn I asked Doris, "How did you know that flattening the lower edge of the hole would create instability?" She looked doubtful.

"Why it would have to, wouldn't it? It changed the pattern of air pressures." She glanced at me quickly. "Of course, I tried a lot of different shapes while I was making it."

"Naturally," I said, and let it go at that. "Where's Tommy?"

"He stopped off at the bank," Pete Cope told me, "to borrow some money. We'll want to buy materials to make some of these kites."

"But I said yesterday that Mr. McCormack and I were going to advance some cash to get started."

"Oh sure, but don't you think it would be better to borrow from a bank? More businesslike?"

"Doubtless," I said, "but banks generally want some security." I would have gone on and explained matters further, except that Tommy walked in and handed me a pocket check book.

"I got two hundred and fifty," he volunteered—not without a hint of complacency in his voice. "It didn't take long,

but they sure made it out a big deal. Half the guys in the
bank had to be called in to listen to the proposition. The
account's in your name, Mr. Henderson and you'll have to
make out the checks. And they want you to stop in at the
bank and give them a specimen signature. Oh yes, and
cosign the note."

My heart sank. I'd never had any dealings with banks
except in the matter of mortgages, and bank people make
me most uneasy. To say nothing of finding myself responsible for a two hundred and fifty dollar note—over two
weeks salary. I made a mental vow to sign very few checks.

"So then I stopped by at Apex Stationers," Tommy went
on, "and ordered some paper and envelopes. We hadn't
picked a name yesterday, but I figured what's to lose, and
picked one. Ridge Industries, how's that?" Everybody
nodded.

"Just three lines on the letterhead," he explained. "Ridge
Industries—Ridgeville—Montana."

I got my voice back and said, "Engraved, I trust."

"Well sure," he replied. "You can't afford to look
chintzy."

My appetite was not at its best that evening, and Marjorie recognized that something was concerning me, but
she asked no questions, and I only told her about the success of the kite, and the youngsters embarking on a shop-
ping trip for paper, glue and wood splints. There was no
use in both of us worrying.

On Friday we all got down to work, and presently had
a regular production line under way; stapling the wood
splints, then wetting them with a resin solution and shaping them over a mandrel to stiffen, cutting the plastic film
around a pattern, assembling and hanging the finished
kites from an overhead beam until the cement had set. Pete

Cope had located a big roll of red plastic film from somewhere, and it made a wonderful looking kite. Happily, I didn't know what the film cost until the first kites were sold.

By Wednesday of the following week we had almost three hundred kites finished and packed into flat cardboard boxes, and frankly I didn't care if I never saw another. Tommy, who by mutual consent, was our authority on sales, didn't want to sell any until we had, as he put it, enough to meet the demand, but this quantity seemed to satisfy him. He said he would sell them the next week and Mary McCready, with a fine burst of confidence, asked him in all seriousness to be sure to hold out a dozen.

Three other things occurred that day, two of which I knew about immediately. Mary brought a portable typewriter from home and spent part of the afternoon banging away at what seemed to me, since I use two fingers only, a very creditable speed.

And Hilary brought in a bottle of his new detergent. It was a syrupy yellow liquid with a nice collar of suds. He'd been busy in his home laboratory after all, it seemed.

"What is it?" I asked. "You never told us."

Hilary grinned. "Lauryl benzyl phosphonic acid, dipotassium salt, in 20% solution."

"Goodness," I protested, "it's been twenty-five years since my last course in chemistry. Perhaps if I saw the formula—."

He gave me a singularly adult smile and jotted down a scrawl of symbols and lines. It meant little to me.

"Is it good?"

For answer he seized the ice bucket, now empty of its soda bottles, trickled in a few drops from the bottle and swished the contents. Foam mounted to the rim and spilled over. "And that's our best grade of Ridgeville water," he pointed out. "Hardest in the country."

The third event of Wednesday came to my ears on
Thursday morning.

I was a little late arriving at the barn, and was taken a
bit aback to find the roadway leading to it rather full of
parked automobiles, and the barn itself rather full of people, including two policemen. Our Ridgeville police are
quite young men, but in uniform they still look ominous
and I was relieved to see that they were laughing and evidently enjoying themselves.

"Well now," I demanded, in my best classroom voice.
"What is all this?"

"Are you Henderson?" the larger policeman asked.

"I am indeed," I said, and a flash bulb went off. A young
lady grasped my arm.

"Oh please, Mr. Henderson, come outside where it's
quieter and tell me all about it."

"Perhaps," I countered, "somebody should tell me."

"You mean you don't know, honestly? Oh it's fabulous. Best story I've had for ages. It'll make the city papers." She led me around the corner of the barn to a spot
of comparative quiet.

"You didn't know that one of your junior whatsisnames
poured detergent in the Memorial Fountain basin last
night?"

I shook my head numbly.

"It was priceless. Just before rush hour. Suds built up in
the basin and overflowed, and down the library steps and
covered the whole street. And the funniest part was they
kept right on coming. You couldn't imagine so much suds
coming from that little pool of water. There was a three-
block traffic jam and Harry got us some marvelous pictures
—men rolling up their trousers to wade across the street.
And this morning," she chortled, "somebody phoned in an
anonymous tip to the police—of course it was the same boy

that did it—Tommy—Miller?—and so here we are. And we just saw a demonstration of that fabulous kite and saw all those simply captivating mice."

"Mice?"

"Yes, of course. Who would ever have thought you could breed mice with those cute furry tails?"

Well after a while things quieted down. They had to. The police left after sobering up long enough to give me a serious warning against letting such a thing happen again. Mr. Miller, who had come home to see what all the excitement was, went back to work and Mrs. Miller went back to the house and the reporter and photographer drifted off to file their story or whatever it is they do. Tommy was jubilant.

"Did you hear what she said? It'll make the city papers. I wish we had a thousand kites. Ten thousand. Oh boy, selling is fun. Hilary, when can you make some more of that stuff? And Doris, how many mice do you have?"

Those mice! I have always kept my enthusiasm for rodents within bounds, but I must admit they were charming little beasts, with tails as bushy as miniature squirrels.

"How many generations?" I asked Doris.

"Seventeen. No, eighteen, now. Want to see the genetic charts?"

I won't try to explain it as she did to me, but it was quite evident that the new mice were breeding true. Presently we asked Betty Miller to come back down to the barn for a conference. She listened and asked questions. As last she said, "Well all right, if you promise me they can't get out of their cages. But heaven knows what you'll do when fall comes. They won't live in an unheated barn and you can't bring them into the house."

"We'll be out of the mouse business by then," Doris predicted. "Every pet shop in the country will have them and they'll be down to nothing apiece."

Doris was right, of course, in spite of our efforts to protect the market. Anyhow that ushered in our cage building phase, and for the next week—with a few interruptions—we built cages, hundreds of them, a good many for breeding, but mostly for shipping.

It was rather regrettable that, after the *Courier* gave us most of the third page, including photographs, we rarely had a day without a few visitors. Many of them wanted to buy mice or kites, but Tommy refused to sell any mice at retail and we soon had to disappoint those who wanted kites. The Supermarket took all we had—except a dozen—and at a dollar fifty each. Tommy's ideas of pricing rather frightened me, but he set the value of the mice at ten dollars a pair and got it without any arguments.

Our beautiful stationery arrived, and we had some invoice forms printed up in a hurry—not engraved, for a wonder.

It was on Tuesday—following the Thursday—that a lanky young man disentangled himself from his car and strolled into the barn. I looked up from the floor where I was tacking squares of screening onto wooden frames.

"Hi," he said. "You're Donald Henderson, right? My name is McCord—Jeff McCord—and I work in the Patent Section at the Commission's downtown office. My boss sent me over here, but if he hadn't, I think I'd have come anyway. What are you doing to get patent protection on Ridge Industries' new developments?"

I got my back unkinked and dusted off my knees. "Well now," I said, "I've been wondering whether something shouldn't be done, but I know very little about such matters—."

"Exactly," he broke in, "we guessed that might be the

case, and there are three patent men in our office who'd
like to chip in and contribute some time. Partly for the
kicks and partly because we think you may have some
things worth protecting. How about it? You worry about
the filing and final fees. That's sixty bucks per brainstorm.
We'll worry about everything else."

"What's to lose," Tommy interjected.

And so we acquired a patent attorney, several of them,
in fact.

The day that our application on the kite design went to
Washington, Mary wrote a dozen toy manufacturers scattered from New York to Los Angeles, sent a kite to each
one and offered to license the design. Result, one licensee
with a thousand dollar advance against next season's
royalties.

It was a rainy morning about three weeks later that I
arrived at the barn. Jeff McCord was there, and the whole
team except Tommy. Jeff lowered his feet from the picnic
table and said "Hi."

"Hi yourself," I told him. "You look pleased."

"I am," he replied, "in a cautious legal sense, of course.
Hilary and I were just going over the situation on his phos-
phonate detergent. I've spent the last three nights studying
the patent literature and a few standard texts touching on
phosphonates. There are a zillion patents on synthetic detergents and a good round fifty on phosphonates, but it
looks"—he held up a long admonitory hand—"it just looks
as though we had a clear spot. If we do get protection,
you've got a real salable property."

"That's fine, Mr. McCord," Hilary said, "but it's not
very important."

"No?" Jeff tilted an inquiring eyebrow at me, and I

handed him a small bottle. He opened and sniffed at it gingerly. "What gives?"

"Before-shave lotion," Hilary told him. "You've shaved this morning, but try some anyway."

Jeff looked momentarily dubious, then puddled some in his palm and moistened his jaw line. "Smells good," he noted, "and feels nice and cool. Now what?"

"Wipe your face." Jeff located a handkerchief and wiped, looked at the cloth, wiped again, and stared.

"What is it?"

"A whisker stiffener. It makes each hair brittle enough to break off right at the surface of your skin."

"So I perceive. What is it?"

"Oh just a mixture of stuff. Cookbook chemistry. Cysteine thiolactone and a fat soluble magnesium compound."

"I see. Just a mixture of stuff. And do your whiskers grow back the next day?"

"Right on schedule," I said.

McCord unfolded his length and stood staring out into the rain. Presently he said, "Henderson, Hilary and I are heading for my office. We can work there better than here, and if we're going to break the hearts of the razor industry, there's no better time to start than now."

When they had driven off I turned and said, "Let's talk a while. We can always clean mouse cages later. Where's Tommy?"

"Oh he stopped at the bank to get a loan."

"What on earth for? We have over six thousand in the account."

"Well," Peter said, looking a little embarrassed, "we were planning to buy a hydraulic press. You see, Doris put some embroidery on that scheme of mine for making ball bearings." He grabbed a sheet of paper. "Look, we make a roller bearing, this shape only it's a permanent magnet. Then you see—." And he was off.

"What did they do today, dear?" Marge asked as she refilled my coffee cup.

"Thanks," I said. "Let's see, it was a big day. We picked out a hydraulic press, Doris read us the first chapter of the book she's starting, and we found a place over a garage on Fourth Street that we can rent for winter quarters. Oh yes, and Jeff is starting action to get the company incorporated."

"Winter quarters," Marge repeated. "You mean you're going to try to keep the group going after school starts?"

"Why not? The kids can sail through their courses without thinking about them, and actually they won't put in more than a few hours a week during the school year."

"Even so, it's child labor, isn't it?"

"Child labor nothing. They're the employers. Jeff McCord and I will be the only employees—just at first, anyway."

Marge choked on something. "Did you say you'd be an employee?"

"Sure," I told her. "They've offered me a small share of the company, and I'd be crazy to turn it down. After all, what's to lose?"

NOVICE

by James H. Schmitz

There was, Telzey Amberdon thought, someone besides
TT and herself in the garden. Not, of course, Aunt Halet,
who was in the house waiting for an early visitor to arrive,
and not one of the servants. Someone or something else
must be concealed among the thickets of magnificently
flowering native Jontarou shrubs about Telzey.

She could think of no other way to account for Tick-
Tock's spooked behavior—nor, to be honest about it, for
the manner her own nerves were acting up without visible
cause this morning.

Telzey plucked a blade of grass, slipped the end between her lips and chewed it gently, her face puzzled and
concerned. She wasn't ordinarily afflicted with nervousness. Fifteen years old, genius level, brown as a berry and
not at all bad looking in her sunbriefs, she was the young-
est member of one of Orado's most prominent families and
a second-year law student at one of the most exclusive
schools in the Federation of the Hub. Her physical, mental,
and emotional health, she'd always been informed, were
excellent. Aunt Halet's frequent cracks about the inherent
instability of the genius level could be ignored; Halet's
own stability seemed questionable at best.

But none of that made the present odd situation any
less disagreeable . . .

The trouble might have begun, Telzey decided, during the night, within an hour after they arrived from the spaceport at the guest house Halet had rented in Port Nichay for their vacation on Jontarou. Telzey had retired at once to her second-story bedroom with Tick-Tock; but she barely got to sleep before something awakened her again. Turning over, she discovered TT reared up before the window, her forepaws on the sill, big cat-head outlined against the star-hazed night sky, staring fixedly down into the garden.

Telzey, only curious at that point, climbed out of bed and joined TT at the window. There was nothing in particular to be seen, and if the scents and minor night-sounds which came from the garden weren't exactly what they were used to, Jontarou was after all an unfamiliar planet. What else would one expect here?

But Tick-Tock's muscular back felt tense and rigid when Telzey laid her arm across it, and except for an absent-minded dig with her forehead against Telzey's shoulder, TT refused to let her attention be distracted from whatever had absorbed it. Now and then, a low, ominous rumble came from her furry throat, a half-angry, half-questioning sound. Telzey began to feel a little uncomfortable. She managed finally to coax Tick-Tock away from the window, but neither of them slept well the rest of the night. At breakfast, Aunt Halet made one of her typical nasty-sweet remarks.

"You look so fatigued, dear—as if you were under some severe mental strain . . . which, of course, you might be," Halet added musingly. With her gold-blond hair piled high on her head and her peaches and cream complexion, Halet looked fresh as a daisy herself . . . a malicious daisy. "Now wasn't I right in insisting to Jessamine that you needed a vacation away from that terribly intellectual school?" She smiled gently.

"Absolutely," Telzey agreed, restraining the impulse to fling a spoonful of egg yolk at her father's younger sister. Aunt Halet often inspired such impulses, but Telzey had promised her mother to avoid actual battles on the Jontarou trip, if possible. After breakfast, she went out into the back garden with Tick-Tock, who immediately walked into a thicket, camouflaged herself and vanished from sight. It seemed to add up to something. But what?

Telzey strolled about the garden a while, maintaining a pretense of nonchalant interest in Jontarou's flowers and colorful bug life. She experienced the most curious little chills of alarm from time to time, but discovered no signs of a lurking intruder, or of TT either. Then, for half an hour or more, she'd just sat cross-legged in the grass, waiting quietly for Tick-Tock to show up of her own accord. And the big lunkhead hadn't obliged.

Telzey scratched a tanned kneecap, scowling at Port Nichay's park trees beyond the garden wall. It seemed idiotic to feel scared when she couldn't even tell whether there was anything to be scared about! And, aside from that, another unreasonable feeling kept growing stronger by the minute now. This was to the effect that she should be doing some unstated but specific thing . . .

In fact, that Tick-Tock *wanted* her to do some specific thing!

Completely idiotic!

Abruptly, Telzey closed her eyes, thought sharply, "Tick-Tock?" and waited—suddenly very angry at herself for having given in to her fancies to this extent—for whatever might happen.

She had never really established that she was able to tell, by a kind of symbolic mind-picture method, like a short waking dream, approximately what TT was thinking and feeling. Five years before, when she'd discovered Tick-Tock—an odd-looking and odder-behaved stray kitten then —in the woods near the Amberdons' summer home on Orado, Telzey had thought so. But it might never have been more than a colorful play of her imagination; and after she got into law school and grew increasingly absorbed in her studies, she almost forgot the matter again.

Today, perhaps because she was disturbed about Tick-Tock's behavior, the customary response was extraordinarily prompt. The warm glow of sunlight shining through her closed eyelids faded out quickly and was replaced by some inner darkness. In the darkness there appeared then an image of Tick-Tock sitting a little way off beside an open door in an old stone wall, green eyes fixed on Telzey. Telzey got the impression that TT was inviting her to go through the door, and, for some reason, the thought frightened her.

Again, there was an immediate reaction. The scene with Tick-Tock and the door vanished; and Telzey felt she was standing in a pitch-black room, knowing that if she moved even one step forwards, something that was waiting there silently would reach out and grab her.

Naturally, she recoiled . . . and at once found herself sitting, eyes still closed and the sunlight bathing her lids, in the grass of the guest house garden.

She opened her eyes, looked around. Her heart was thumping rapidly. The experience couldn't have lasted more than four or five seconds, but it had been extremely vivid, a whole, compact little nightmare. None of her earlier experiments at getting into mental communication with TT had been like that.

It served her right, Telzey thought, for trying such a childish stunt at the moment! What she should have done at once was to make a methodical search for the foolish beast—TT was bound to be *somewhere* nearby—locate her behind her camouflage, and hang on to her then until this nonsense in the garden was explained! Talented as Tick-Tock was at blotting herself out, it usually was possible to spot her if one directed one's attention to shadow patterns. Telzey began a surreptitious study of the flowering bushes about her.

Three minutes later, off to her right, where the ground was banked beneath a six-foot step in the garden's terraces, Tick-Tock's outline suddenly caught her eye. Flat on her belly, head lifted above her paws, quite motionless, TT seemed like a transparent wraith stretched out along the terrace, barely discernible even when stared at directly. It was a convincing illusion; but what seemed to be rocks, plant leaves, and sun-splotched earth seen through the wraith-outline was simply the camouflage pattern TT had printed for the moment on her hide. She could have changed it completely in an instant to conform to a different background.

Telzey pointed an accusing finger.

"See you!" she announced, feeling a surge of relief which seemed as unaccountable as the rest of it.

The wraith twitched one ear in acknowledgment, the head outlines shifting as the camouflaged face turned towards Telzey. Then the inwardly uncamouflaged, very substantial looking mouth opened slowly, showing Tick-Tock's red tongue and curved white tusks. The mouth stretched in a wide yawn, snapped shut with a click of meshing teeth, became indistinguishable again. Next, a pair of camouflaged lids drew back from TT's round, brilliant-green eyes. The eyes stared across the lawn at Telzey.

Telzey said irritably, "Quit clowning around, TT!"

The eyes blinked, and Tick-Tock's natural bronze-brown

color suddenly flowed over her head, down her neck and across her body into legs and tail. Against the side of the terrace, as if materializing into solidity at that moment, appeared two hundred pounds of supple, rangy, long-tailed cat . . . or catlike creature. TT's actual origin had never been established. The best guesses were that what Telzey had found playing around in the woods five years ago was either a biostructural experiment which had got away from a private laboratory on Orado, or some spaceman's lost pet, brought to the capital planet from one of the remote colonies beyond the Hub. On top of TT's head was a large, fluffy pompom of white fur, which might have looked ridiculous on another animal, but didn't on her. Even as a fat kitten, hanging head down from the side of a wall by the broad sucker pads in her paws, TT had possessed enormous dignity.

Telzey studied her, the feeling of relief fading again. Tick-Tock, ordinarily the most restful and composed of companions, definitely was still tensed up about something. That big, lazy yawn a moment ago, the attitude of stretched-out relaxation . . . all pure sham!

"What *is* eating you?" she asked in exasperation.

The green eyes stared at her, solemn, watchful, seeming for that fleeting instant quite alien. And why, Telzey thought, should the old question of what Tick-Tock really was pass through her mind just now? After her rather alarming rate of growth began to taper off last year, nobody had cared any more.

For a moment, Telzey had the uncanny certainty of having had the answer to this situation almost in her grasp. An answer which appeared to involve the world of Jontarou, Tick-Tock, and of all unlikely factors—Aunt Halet.

She shook her head. TT's impassive green eyes blinked.

Jontarou? The planet lay outside Telzey's sphere of personal interests, but she'd read up on it on the way here from
Orado. Among all the worlds of the Hub, Jontarou was *the*
paradise for zoologists and sportsmen, a gigantic animal
preserve, its continents and seas swarming with magnificent game. Under Federation law, it was being retained
deliberately in the primitive state in which it had been
discovered. Port Nichay, the only city, actually the only inhabited point on Jontarou, was beautiful and quiet, a pattern of vast but elegantly slender towers, each separated
from the others by four or five miles of rolling parkland
and interconnected only by the threads of transparent sky-
ways. Near the horizon, just visible from the garden, rose
the tallest towers of all, the green and gold spires of the
Shikaris' Club, a center of Federation affairs and of social
activity. From the aircar which brought them across Port
Nichay the evening before, Telzey had seen occasional
strings of guest houses, similar to the one Halet had rented,
nestling along the park slopes.

Nothing very sinister about Port Nichay or green Jontarou, surely!

Halet? That blond, slinky, would-be Machiavelli? What
could—?

Telzey's eyes narrowed reflectively. There'd been a
minor occurrence—at least, it had seemed minor—just before the spaceliner docked last night. A young woman from
one of the newscasting services had asked for an interview
with the daughter of Federation Councilwoman Jessamine
Amberdon. This happened occasionally; and Telzey had
no objections until the newshen's gossipy persistence in inquiring about the "unusual pet" she was bringing to Port
Nichay with her began to be annoying. TT might be somewhat unusual, but that was not a matter of general interest;
and Telzey said so. Then Halet moved smoothly into the

act and held forth on Tick-Tock's appearance, habits, and mysterious antecedents, in considerable detail.

Telzey had assumed that Halet was simply going out of her way to be irritating, as usual. Looking back on the incident, however, it occurred to her that the chatter between her aunt and the newscast woman had sounded oddly stilted—almost like something the two might have rehearsed.

Rehearsed for what purpose? Tick-Tock . . . Jontarou.

Telzey chewed gently on her lower lip. A vacation on Jontarou for the two of them and TT had been Halet's idea, and Halet had enthused about it so much that Telzey's mother at last talked her into accepting. Halet, Jessamine explained privately to Telzey, had felt they were intruders in the Amberdon family, had bitterly resented Jessamine's political honors and, more recently, Telzey's own emerging promise of brilliance. This invitation was Halet's way of indicating a change of heart. Wouldn't Telzey oblige?

So Telzey had obliged, though she took very little stock in Halet's change of heart. She wasn't, in fact, putting it past her aunt to have some involved dirty trick up her sleeve with this trip to Jontarou. Halet's mind worked like that.

So far there had been no actual indications of purposeful mischief. But logic did seem to require a connection between the various puzzling events here . . . A newscaster's rather forced looking interest in Tick-Tock—Halet could easily have paid for that interview. Then TT's disturbed behavior during their first night in Port Nichay, and Telzey's own formless anxieties and fancies in connection with the guest house garden.

The last remained hard to explain. But Tick-Tock . . . and Halet . . . might know something about Jontarou that she didn't know.

Her mind returned to the results of the half-serious attempt she'd made to find out whether there was something Tick-Tock "wanted her to do." An open door? A darkness where somebody waited to grab her if she took even one step forwards? It couldn't have had any significance. Or could it?

So you'd like to try magic, Telzey scoffed at herself. Baby games . . . How far would you have got at law school if you'd asked TT to help with your problems?

Then why had she been thinking about it again?

She shivered, because an eerie stillness seemed to settle on the garden. From the side of the terrace, TT's green eyes watched her.

Telzey had a feeling of sinking down slowly into a sunlit dream, into something very remote from law school problems.

"Should I go through the door?" she whispered.

The bronze cat-shape raised its head slowly. TT began to purr.

Tick-Tock's name had been derived in kittenhood from the manner in which she purred—a measured, oscillating sound, shifting from high to low, as comfortable and often as continuous as the unobtrusive pulse of an old clock. It was the first time, Telzey realized now, that she'd heard the sound since their arrival on Jontarou. It went on for a dozen seconds or so, then stopped. Tick-Tock continued to look at her.

It appeared to have been an expression of definite assent . . .

The dreamlike sensation increased, hazing over Telzey's thoughts. If there was nothing to this mind-communication thing, what harm could symbols do? This time, she wouldn't let them alarm her. And if they did mean something . . .

She closed her eyes.

The sunglow outside faded instantly. Telzey caught a fleeting picture of the door in the wall, and knew in the same moment that she'd already passed through it.

She was not in the dark room then, but poised at the edge of a brightness which seemed featureless and without limit, spread out around her with a feeling-tone like "sea" or "sky." But it was an unquiet place. There was a sense of unseen things on all sides watching her and waiting.

Was this another form of the dark room—a trap set up in her mind? Telzey's attention did a quick shift. She was seated in the grass again; the sunlight beyond her closed eyelids seemed to shine in quietly through rose-tinted curtains. Cautiously, she let her awareness return to the bright area; and *it* was still there. She had a moment of excited elation. She was controlling this! And why not, she asked herself. These things were happening in *her* mind, after all!

She would find out what they seemed to mean; but she would be in no rush to . . .

An impression as if, behind her, Tick-Tock had thought, "Now I can help again!"

Then a feeling of being swept swiftly, irresistibly forwards, thrust out and down. The brightness exploded in thundering colors around her. In fright, she made the effort to snap her eyes open, to be back in the garden; but now she couldn't make it work. The colors continued to roar about her, like a confusion of excited, laughing, triumphant voices. Telzey felt caught in the middle of it all, suspended in invisible spider webs. Tick-Tock seemed to be somewhere nearby, looking on. Faithless, treacherous TT!

Telzey's mind made another wrenching effort, and there was a change. She hadn't got back into the garden, but the noisy, swirling colors were gone and she had the feeling of reading a rapidly moving microtape now, though she didn't actually see the tape.

The tape, she realized, was another symbol for what was happening, a symbol easier for her to understand. There were voices, or what might be voices, around her; on the invisible tape she seemed to be reading what they said.

A number of speakers, apparently involved in a fast, hot argument about what to do with her. Impressions flashed past . . .

Why waste time with her? It was clear that kitten-talk was all she was capable of! . . . Not necessarily; that was a normal first step. Give her a little time! . . . But what—exasperatedly—could *such* a small-bite *possibly* know that would be of significant value?

There was a slow, blurred, awkward-seeming interruption. Its content was not comprehensible to Telzey at all, but in some unmistakable manner it was defined as Tick-Tock's thought.

A pause as the circle of speakers stopped to consider whatever TT had thrown into the debate.

Then another impression . . . one that sent a shock of fear through Telzey as it rose heavily into her awareness. Its sheer intensity momentarily displaced the tape-reading symbolism. A savage voice seemed to rumble:

"Toss the tender small-bite to *me*"—malevolent crimson eyes fixed on Telzey from somewhere not far away—"and let's be done here!"

Startled, stammering protest from Tick-Tock, accompanied by gusts of laughter from the circle. Great sense of humor these characters had, Telzey thought bitterly. That crimson-eyed thing wasn't joking at all!

More laughter as the circle caught her thought. Then a kind of majority opinion found sudden expression:

"Small-bite *is* learning! No harm to wait—We'll find out quickly—Let's . . ."

The tape ended; the voices faded; the colors went blank. In whatever jumbled-up form she'd been getting the impressions at that point—Telzey couldn't have begun to describe it—the whole thing suddenly stopped.

She found herself sitting in the grass, shaky, scared, eyes open. Tick-Tock stood beside the terrace, looking at her. An air of hazy unreality still hung about the garden.

She might have flipped! She didn't think so; but it certainly seemed possible! Otherwise . . . Telzey made an attempt to sort over what had happened.

Something *had* been in the garden! Something had been inside her mind. Something that was at home on Jontarou.

There'd been a feeling of perhaps fifty or sixty of these . . . well, beings. Alarming beings! Reckless, wild, hard . . . and that red-eyed nightmare! Telzey shuddered.

They'd contacted Tick-Tock first, during the night. TT understood them better than she could. Why? Telzey found no immediate answer.

Then Tick-Tock had tricked her into letting her mind be invaded by these beings. There must have been a very definite reason for that.

She looked over at Tick-Tock. TT looked back. Nothing stirred in Telzey's thoughts. Between *them* there was still no direct communication.

Then how had the beings been able to get through to her?

Telzey wrinkled her nose. Assuming this was real, it seemed clear that the game of symbols she'd made up between herself and TT had provided the opening. Her whole experience just now had been in the form of symbols, translating whatever occurred into something she could consciously grasp.

"Kitten-talk" was how the beings referred to the use of

symbols; they seemed contemptuous of it. Never mind, Telzey told herself; they'd agreed she was learning.

The air over the grass appeared to flicker. Again she had the impression of reading words off a quickly moving, not quite visible tape.

"You're being taught and you're learning," was what she seemed to read. "The question was whether you were capable of partial understanding as your friend insisted. Since you were, everything else that can be done will be accomplished very quickly."

A pause, then with a touch of approval, "You're a well-informed mind, small-bite! Odd and with incomprehensibilities, but well-formed—"

One of the beings, and a fairly friendly one—at least not unfriendly. Telzey framed a tentative mental question. "Who are you?"

"You'll know very soon." The flickering ended; she realized she and the question had been dismissed for the moment. She looked over at Tick-Tock again.

"Can't *you* talk to me now, TT?" she asked silently.

A feeling of hesitation.

"Kitten-talk!" was the impression that formed itself with difficulty then. It was awkward, searching; but it came unquestionably from TT. "Still learning, too, Telzey!" TT seemed half anxious, half angry. "We—"

A sharp buzz-note reached Telzey's ears, wiping out the groping thought-impression. She jumped a little, glanced down. Her wrist-talker was signaling. For a moment, she seemed poised uncertainly between a world where unseen, dangerous-sounding beings referred to one as small-bite and where TT was learning to talk, and the familiar other world where wrist-communicators buzzed periodically in a matter-of-fact manner. Settling back into the more familiar world, she switched on the talker.

"Yes?" she said. Her voice sounded husky.

"Telzey, dear," Halet murmured honey-sweet from the talker, "would you come back into the house, please? The living room—We have a visitor who very much wants to meet you."

Telzey hesitated, eyes narrowing. Halet's visitor wanted to meet *her?*

"Why?" she asked.

"He has something *very* interesting to tell you, dear." The edge of triumphant malice showed for an instant, vanished in murmuring sweetness again. "So please hurry!"

"All right." Telzey stood up. "I'm coming."

"Fine, dear!" The talker went dead.

Telzey switched off the instrument, noticed that Tick-Tock had chosen to disappear meanwhile.

Flipped? She wondered, starting up towards the house. It was clear Aunt Halet had prepared some unpleasant surprise to spring on her, which was hardly more than normal behavior for Halet. The other business? She couldn't be certain of anything there. Leaving out TT's strange actions —which might have a number of causes, after all—that entire string of events could have been created inside her head. There was no contradictory evidence so far.

But it could do no harm to take what *seemed* to have happened at face value. Some pretty grim event might be shaping up, in a very real way, around here . . .

"You reason logically!" The impression now was of a voice speaking to her, a voice that made no audible sound. It was the same being who'd addressed her a minute or two ago.

The two worlds between which Telzey had felt suspended seemed to glide slowly together and become one.

"I go to Law school," she explained to the being, almost absently.

Amused agreement. "So we heard."

"What do you want of me?" Telzey inquired.

"You'll know soon enough."

"Why not tell me now?" Telzey urged. It seemed about to dismiss her again.

Quick impatience flared at her. "Kitten-pictures! Kitten-thoughts! Kitten-talk! Too slow, too slow! YOUR pictures —too much YOU! Wait till the . . ."

Circuits close . . . channels open . . . Obstructions clear? What *had* it said? There'd been only the blurred image of a finicky, delicate, but perfectly normal technical operation of some kind.

". . . Minutes now!" the voice concluded. A pause, then another thought tossed carelessly at her. "This is more important to you, small-bite, than to *us!*" The voice impression ended as sharply as if a communicator had snapped off.

Not *too* friendly! Telzey walked on towards the house, a new fear growing inside her . . . a fear like the awareness of a storm gathered nearby, still quiet—deadly quiet, but ready to break.

"Kitten-pictures!" a voice seemed to jeer distantly, a whispering in the park trees beyond the garden wall.

Halet's cheeks were lightly pinked; her blue eyes sparkled. She looked downright stunning, which meant to anyone who knew her that the worst side of Halet's nature was champing at the bit again. On uninformed males it had a dazzling effect, however; and Telzey wasn't surprised to find their visitor wearing a tranced expression when she came into the living room. He was a tall, outdoorsy man with a tanned, bony face, a neatly trained black mustache, and a scar down one cheek which would have seemed dashing if it hadn't been for the stupefied look. Beside his chair stood a large, clumsy instrument which might have been some kind of telecamera.

Halet performed introductions. Their visitor was Dr. Droon, a zoologist. He had been tuned in on Telzey's newscast interview on the liner the night before, and wondered whether Telzey would care to discuss Tick-Tock with him.

"Frankly, no," Telzey said.

Dr. Droon came awake and gave Telzey a surprised look. Halet smiled easily.

"My niece doesn't intend to be discourteous, doctor," she explained.

"Of course not," the zoologist agreed doubtfully.

"It's just," Halet went on, "that Telzey is a little, oh, sensitive where Tick-Tock is concerned. In her own way, she's attached to the animal. Aren't you, dear?"

"Yes," Telzey said blandly.

"Well, we hope this isn't going to disturb you too much, dear." Halet glanced significantly at Dr. Droon. "Dr. Droon, you must understand, is simply doing . . . well, there is something very important he must tell you now."

Telzey transferred her gaze back to the zoologist. Dr. Droon cleared his throat. "I, ah, understand, Miss Amberdon, that you're unaware of what kind of creature your, ah, Tick-Tock is?"

Telzey started to speak, then checked herself, frowning. She had been about to state that she knew exactly what kind of creature TT was . . . but she didn't, of course!

Or did she? She . . .

She scowled absent-mindedly at Dr. Droon, biting her lip.

"Telzey!" Halet prompted gently.

"Huh?" Telzey said. "Oh . . . please go on, doctor!"

Dr. Droon steepled his fingers. "Well," he said, "she . . .

your pet . . . is, ah, a young crest cat. Nearly full grown
now, apparently, and—"

"Why, yes!" Telzey cried.

The zoologist looked at her. "You knew that—"

"Well, not really," Telzey admitted. "Or sort of." She
laughed, her cheeks flushed. "This is the most . . . go
ahead please! Sorry I interrupted." She stared at the wall
beyond Dr. Droon with a rapt expression.

The zoologist and Halet exchanged glances. Then Dr.
Droon resumed cautiously. The crest cats, he said, were a
species native to Jontarou. Their existence had been known
for only eight years. The species appeared to have had a
somewhat limited range—the Baluit mountains on the opposite side of the huge continent on which Port Nichay had
been built . . .

Telzey barely heard him. A very curious thing was happening. For every sentence Dr. Droon uttered, a dozen
other sentences appeared in her awareness. More accu-
rately, it was as if an instantaneous smooth flow of information relevant to whatever he said arose continuously from
what might have been almost her own memory, but wasn't.
Within a minute or two, she knew more about the crest
cats of Jontarou than Dr. Droon could have told her in
hours . . . much more than he'd ever known.

She realized suddenly that he'd stopped talking, that he
had asked her a question. "Miss Amberdon?" he repeated
now, with a note of uncertainty.

"Yar-rrr-REE!" Telzey told him softly. "I'll drink your
blood!"

"Eh?"

Telzey blinked, focused on Dr. Droon, wrenching her
mind away from a splendid view of the misty-blue peaks
of the Baluit range.

"Sorry," she said briskly. "Just a joke!" She smiled. "Now what were you saying?"

The zoologist looked at her in a rather odd manner for a moment. "I was inquiring," he said then, "whether you were familiar with the sporting rules established by the various hunting associations of the Hub in connection with the taking of game trophies?"

Telzey shook her head. "No, I never heard of them."

The rules, Dr. Droon explained, laid down the type of equipment . . . weapons, spotting and tracking instruments, number of assistants, and so forth . . . a sportsman could legitimately use in the pursuit of any specific type of game. "Before the end of the first year after their discovery," he went on, "the Baluit crest cats had been placed in the ultra-equipment class."

"What's ultra-equipment?" Telzey asked.

"Well," Dr. Droon said thoughtfully, "it doesn't quite involve the use of full battle armor . . . not quite! And, of course, even with that classification the sporting principle of mutual accessibility must be observed."

"Mutual . . . oh, I see!" Telzey paused as another wave of silent information rose into her awareness; went on, "So the game has to be able to get at the sportsman too, eh?"

"That's correct. Except in the pursuit of various classes of flying animals, a shikari would not, for example, be permitted the use of an aircar other than as a means of simple transportation. Under these conditions, it was soon established that crest cats were being obtained by sportsmen who went after them at a rather consistent one-to-one ratio."

Telzey's eyes widened. She'd gathered something similar from her other information source but hadn't quite believed it. "One hunter killed for each cat bagged?" she said. "That's pretty rough sport, isn't it?"

"Extremely rough sport!" Dr. Droon agreed dryly. "In fact, when the statistics were published, the sporting interest in winning a Baluit cat trophy appears to have suffered a sudden and sharp decline. On the other hand, a more scientific interest in these remarkable animals was coincidingly created, and many permits for their acquisition by the agents of museums, universities, public and private collections were issued. Sporting rules, of course, do not apply to that activity."

Telzey nodded absently. "I see! *They* used aircars, didn't they? A sort of heavy knockout gun—"

"Aircars, long-range detectors and stunguns are standard equipment in such work," Dr. Droon acknowledged. "Gas and poison are employed, of course, as circumstances dictate. The collectors were relatively successful for a while.

"And then a curious thing happened. Less than two years after their existence became known, the crest cats of the Baluit range were extinct! The inroads made on their numbers by man cannot begin to account for this, so it must be assumed that a sudden plague wiped them out. At any rate, not another living member of the species has been seen on Jontarou until you landed here with your pet last night."

Telzey sat silent for some seconds. Not because of what he had said, but because the other knowledge was still flowing into her mind. On one very important point *that* was at variance with what the zoologist had stated; and from there a coldly logical pattern was building up. Telzey didn't grasp the pattern in complete detail yet, but what she saw of it stirred her with a half incredulous dread.

She asked, shaping the words carefully but with only a small part of her attention on what she was really saying, "Just what does all that have to do with Tick-Tock, Dr. Droon?"

Dr. Droon glanced at Halet, and returned his gaze to Telzey. Looking very uncomfortable but quite determined, he told her, "Miss Amberdon, there is a Federation law which states that when a species is threatened with extinction, any available survivors must be transferred to the Life Banks of the University League, to insure their indefinite preservation. Under the circumstances, this law applies to, ah, Tick-Tock!"

So that had been Halet's trick. She'd found out about the crest cats, might have put in as much as a few months arranging to make the discovery of TT's origin on Jontarou seem a regrettable mischance—something no one could have foreseen or prevented. In the Life Banks, from what Telzey had heard of them, TT would cease to exist as an individual awareness while scientists tinkered around with the possibilities of reconstructing her species.

Telzey studied her aunt's carefully sympathizing face for an instant, asked Dr. Droon, "What about the other crest cats you said were collected before they became extinct here? Wouldn't they be enough for what the Life Banks need?"

He shook his head. "Two immature male specimens are known to exist, and they are at present in the Life Banks. The others that were taken alive at the time have been destroyed . . . often under nearly disastrous circumstances. They are enormously cunning, enormously savage creatures, Miss Amberdon! The additional fact that they can conceal themselves to the point of being virtually indetectable except by the use of instruments makes them one of the most dangerous animals known. Since the young female which you raised as a pet has remained docile . . . so far . . . you may not really be able to appreciate that."

"Perhaps I can," Telzey said. She nodded at the

heavy-looking instrument standing beside his chair. "And that's—?"

"It's a life detector combined with a stungun, Miss Amberdon. I have no intention of harming your pet, but we can't take chances with an animal of that type. The gun's charge will knock it unconscious for several minutes—just long enough to let me secure it with paralysis belts."

"You're a collector for the Life Banks, Dr. Droon?"

"That's correct."

"Dr. Droon," Halet remarked, "has obtained a permit from the Planetary Moderator, authorizing him to claim Tick-Tock for the University League and remove her from the planet, dear. So you see there is simply nothing we can do about the matter! Your mother wouldn't like us to attempt to obstruct the law, would she?" Halet paused. "The permit should have your signature, Telzey, but I can sign in your stead if necessary."

That was Halet's way of saying it would do no good to appeal to Jontarou's Planetary Moderator. She'd taken the precaution of getting his assent to the matter first.

"So now if you'll just call Tick-Tock, dear . . ." Halet went on.

Telzey barely heard the last words. She felt herself stiffening slowly, while the living room almost faded from her sight. Perhaps, in that instant, some additional new circuit had closed in her mind, or some additional new channel had opened, for TT's purpose in tricking her into contact with the reckless, mocking beings outside was suddenly and numbingly clear.

And what it meant immediately was that she'd have to get out of the house without being spotted at it, and go some place where she could be undisturbed for half an hour.

She realized that Halet and the zoologist were both staring at her.

"Are you ill, dear?"

"No." Telzey stood up. It would be worse than useless to try to tell these two anything! Her face must be pretty white at the moment—she could feel it—but they assumed, of course, that the shock of losing TT had just now sunk in on her.

"I'll have to check on that law you mentioned before I sign anything," she told Dr. Droon.

"Why, yes . . ." He started to get out of his chair. "I'm sure that can be arranged, Miss Amberdon!"

"Don't bother to call the Moderator's office," Telzey said. "I brought my law library along. I'll look it up myself." She turned to leave the room.

"My niece," Halet explained to Dr. Droon who was beginning to look puzzled, "attends law school. She's always so absorbed in her studies . . . Telzey?"

"Yes, Halet?" Telzey paused at the door.

"I'm very glad you've decided to be sensible about this, dear. But don't take too long, will you? We don't want to waste Dr. Droon's time."

"It shouldn't take more than five or ten minutes," Telzey told her agreeably. She closed the door behind her, and went directly to her bedroom on the second floor. One of her two valises was still unpacked. She locked the door behind her, opened the unpacked valise, took out a pocket edition law library and sat down at the table with it.

She clicked on the library's view-screen, tapped the clearing and index buttons. Behind the screen, one of the multiple rows of pinhead tapes shifted slightly as the index was flicked into reading position. Half a minute later, she was glancing over the legal section on which Dr. Droon

had based his claim. The library confirmed what he had
said.

Very neat of Halet, Telzey thought, very nasty . . . and
pretty idiotic! Even a second-year law student could think
immediately of two or three ways in which a case like that
could have been dragged out in the Federation's courts for
a couple of decades before the question of handing Tick-
Tock over to the Life Banks became too acute.

Well, Halet simply wasn't really intelligent. And the plot
to shanghai TT was hardly even a side issue now.

Telzey snapped the tiny library shut, fastened it to the
belt of her sunsuit and went over to the open window. A
two-foot ledge passed beneath the window, leading to the
roof of a patio on the right. Fifty yards beyond the patio,
the garden ended in a natural-stone wall. Behind it lay
one of the big wooded park areas which formed most of the
ground level of Port Nichay.

Tick-Tock wasn't in sight. A sound of voices came from
ground-floor windows on the left. Halet had brought her
maid and chauffeur along; and a chef had showed up in
time to make breakfast this morning, as part of the city's
guest house service. Telzey took the empty valise to the
window, set it on end against the left side of the frame, and
let the window slide down until its lower edge rested on the
valise. She went back to the house guard-screen panel beside the door, put her finger against the lock button, and
pushed.

The sound of voices from the lower floor was cut off as
outer doors and windows slid silently shut all about the
house. Telzey glanced back at the window. The valise had
creaked a little as the guard field drove the frame down
on it, but it was supporting the thrust. She returned to the
window, wriggled feet foremost through the opening,
twisted around and got a footing on the ledge.

A minute later, she was scrambling quietly down a vine-covered patio trellis to the ground. Even after they discovered she was gone, the guard screen would keep everybody in the house for some little while. They'd either have to disengage the screen's main mechanisms and start poking around in them, or force open the door to her bedroom and get the lock unset. Either approach would involve confusion, upset tempers, and generally delay any organized pursuit.

Telzey edged around the patio and started towards the wall, keeping close to the side of the house so she couldn't be seen from the windows. The shrubbery made minor rustling noises as she threaded her way through it . . . and then there was a different stirring which might have been no more than a slow, steady current of air moving among the bushes behind her. She shivered involuntarily but didn't look back.

She came to the wall, stood still, measuring its height, jumped and got an arm across it, swung up a knee and squirmed up and over. She came down on her feet with a small thump in the grass on the other side, glanced back once at the guest house, crossed a path and went on among the park trees.

Within a few hundred yards, it became apparent that she had an escort. She didn't look around for them, but spread out to right and left like a skirmish line, keeping abreast with her, occasional shadows slid silently through patches of open, sunlit ground, disappeared again under the trees. Otherwise, there was hardly anyone in sight. Port Nichay's human residents appeared to make almost no personal use of the vast parkland spread out beneath their tower apartments; and its traffic moved over the airways, visible from the ground only as rainbow-hued ribbons which bisected the sky between the upper tower levels. An occasional private aircar went by overhead.

Wisps of thought which were not her own thoughts flicked through Telzey's mind from moment to moment as the silent line of shadows moved deeper into the park with her. She realized she was being sized up, judged, evaluated again. No more information was coming through; they had given her as much information as she needed. In the main perhaps, they were simply curious now. This was the first human mind they'd been able to make heads or tails of, and that hadn't seemed deaf and silent to their form of communication. They were taking time out to study it. They'd been assured she would have something of genuine importance to tell them; and there was some derision about that. But they were willing to wait a little, and find out. They were curious and they liked games. At the moment, Telzey and what she might try to do to change their plans was the game on which their attention was fixed.

Twelve minutes passed before the talker on Telzey's wrist began to buzz. It continued to signal off and on for another few minutes, then stopped. Back in the guest house they couldn't be sure yet whether she wasn't simply locked inside her room and refusing to answer them. But Telzey quickened her pace.

The park's trees gradually became more massive, reached higher above her, stood spaced more widely apart. She passed through the morning shadow of the residential tower nearest the guest house, and emerged from it presently on the shore of a small lake. On the other side of the lake, a number of dappled grazing animals like long-necked, tall horses lifted their heads to watch her. For some seconds they seemed only mildly interested, but then a breeze moved across the lake, crinkling the surface of the water; and as it touched the opposite shore, abrupt panic exploded among the grazers. They wheeled, went flashing away in effortless twenty-foot strides, and were gone among the trees.

Telzey felt a crawling along her spine. It was the first objective indication she'd had of the nature of the company she had brought to the lake, and while it hardly came as a surprise, for a moment her urge was to follow the example of the grazers.

"Tick-Tock?" she whispered, suddenly a little short of breath.

A single up-and-down purring note replied from the bushes on her right. TT was still around, for whatever good that might do. Not too much, Telzey thought, if it came to serious trouble. But the knowledge was somewhat reassuring . . . and this, meanwhile, appeared to be as far as she needed to get from the guest house. They'd be looking for her by aircar presently, but there was nothing to tell them in which direction to turn first.

She climbed the bank of the lake to a point where she was screened both by thick, green shrubbery and the top of a single immense tree from the sky, sat down on some dry, mossy growth, took the law library from her belt, opened it and placed it in her lap. Vague stirrings indicated that her escort was also settling down in an irregular circle about her; and apprehension shivered on Telzey's skin again. It wasn't that their attitude was hostile; they were simply overawing. And no one could predict what they might do next. Without looking up, she asked a question in her mind.

"Ready?"

Sense of multiple acknowledgment, variously tinged— sardonic; interestedly amused; attentive; doubtful. Impatience quivered through it too, only tentatively held in restraint, and Telzey's forehead was suddenly wet. Some of them seemed on the verge of expressing disapproval with what was being done here—

Her fingers quickly flicked in the index tape, and the stir of feeling about her subsided, their attention captured again for the moment. Her thoughts became to some degree detached, ready to dissect another problem in the familiar ways and present the answers to it. Not a very involved problem essentially, but this time it wasn't a school exercise. Her company waited, withdrawn, silent, aloof once more, while the index blurred, checked, blurred and checked. Within a minute and a half, she had noted a dozen reference symbols. She tapped in another of the pinhead tapes, glanced over a few paragraphs, licked salty sweat from her lip, and said in her thoughts, emphasizing the meaning of each detail of the sentence so that there would be no misunderstanding, "This is the Federation law that applies to the situation which existed originally on this planet. . . ."

There were no interruptions, no commenting thoughts, no intrusions of any kind, as she went step by step through the section, turned to another one, and another. In perhaps twelve minutes she came to the end of the last one, and stopped. Instantly, argument exploded about her.

Telzey was not involved in the argument; in fact, she could grasp only scraps of it. Either they were excluding her deliberately, or the exchange was too swift, practiced and varied to allow her to keep up. But their vehemence was not encouraging. And was it reasonable to assume that the Federation's laws would have any meaning for minds like these? Telzey snapped the library shut with fingers that had begun to tremble, and placed it on the ground. Then she stiffened. In the sensations washing about her, a special excitement rose suddenly, a surge of almost gleeful wildness that choked away her breath. Awareness followed of a pair of malignant crimson eyes fastened on her, moving steadily closer. A kind of nightmare paralysis seized Telzey—they'd turned her over to that red-eyed horror! She sat still, feeling mouse-sized.

Something came out with a crash from a thicket behind her. Her muscles went tight. But it was TT who rubbed a hard head against her shoulder, took another three stiff-legged steps forward and stopped between Telzey and the bushes on their right, back rigid, neck fur erect, tail twisting.

Expectant silence closed in about them. The circle was waiting. In the greenery on the right something made a slow, heavy stir.

TT's lips peeled back from her teeth. Her head swung towards the motion, ears flattening, transformed to a split, snarling demon-mask. A long shriek ripped from her lungs, raw with fury, blood lust and challenge.

The sound died away. For some seconds the tension about them held; then came a sense of gradual relaxation mingled with a partly amused approval. Telzey was shaking violently. It had been, she was telling herself, a deliberate test . . . not of herself, of course, but of TT. And Tick-Tock had passed with honors. That *her* nerves had been half ruined in the process would seem a matter of no consequence to this rugged crew . . .

She realized next that someone here was addressing her personally.

It took a few moments to steady her jittering thoughts enough to gain a more definite impression than that. This speaker, she discovered then, was a member of the circle of whom she hadn't been aware before. The thought-impressions came hard and cold as iron—a personage who was very evidently in the habit of making major decisions

and seeing them carried out. The circle, its moment of
sport over, was listening with more than a suggestion of
deference. Tick-Tock, far from conciliated, green eyes still
blazing, nevertheless was settling down to listen, too.

Telzey began to understand.

Her suggestions, Iron Thoughts informed her, might appear without value to a number of foolish minds here, but
he intended to see they were given a fair trial. Did he perhaps hear, he inquired next of the circle, throwing in a
casual but horridly vivid impression of snapping spines and
slashed shaggy throats spouting blood, any objection to
that?

Dead stillness all around. There was, definitely, no objection! Tick-Tock began to grin like a pleased kitten.

That point having been settled in an orderly manner
now, Iron Thoughts went on coldly to Telzey, what
specifically did she propose they should do?

Halet's long, pearl-gray sportscar showed up above the
park trees twenty minutes later. Telzey, face turned down
towards the open law library in her lap, watched the car
from the corner of her eyes. She was in plain view, sitting
beside the lake, apparently absorbed in legal research.
Tick-Tock, camouflaged among the bushes thirty feet higher
up the bank, had spotted the car an instant before she did
and announced the fact with a three-second break in her
purring. Neither of them made any other move.

The car was approaching the lake but still a good distance off. Its canopy was down, and Telzey could just make
out the heads of three people inside. Delquos, Halet's
chauffeur, would be flying the vehicle, while Halet and Dr.
Droon looked around for her from the sides. Three hundred yards away, the aircar began a turn to the right. Del-

quos didn't like his employer much; at a guess, he had just spotted Telzey and was trying to warn her off.

Telzey closed the library and put it down, picked up a handful of pebbles and began flicking them idly, one at a time, into the water. The aircar vanished to her left.

Three minutes later, she watched its shadow glide across the surface of the lake towards her. Her heart began to thump almost audibly, but she didn't look up. Tick-Tock's purring continued, on its regular, unhurried note. The car came to a stop almost directly overhead. After a couple of seconds, there was a clicking noise. The purring ended abruptly.

Telzey climbed to her feet as Delquos brought the car down to the bank of the lake. The chauffeur grinned ruefully at her. A side door had been opened, and Halet and Dr. Droon stood behind it. Halet watched Telzey with a small smile while the naturalist put the heavy life-detector-and-stungun device carefully down on the floorboards.

"If you're looking for Tick-Tock," Telzey said, "she isn't here."

Halet just shook her head sorrowfully.

"There's no use lying to us, dear! Dr. Droon just stunned her."

They found TT collapsed on her side among the shrubs, wearing her natural color. Her eyes were shut; her chest rose and fell in a slow breathing motion. Dr. Droon, looking rather apologetic, pointed out to Telzey that her pet was in no pain, that the stungun had simply put her comfortably to sleep. He also explained the use of the two sets of webbed paralysis belts which he fastened about TT's legs. The effect of the stun charge would wear off in a few minutes, and contact with the inner surfaces of the energized belts would then keep TT anesthetized and unable to move until the belts were removed. She would, he repeated, be suffering no pain throughout the process.

Telzey didn't comment. She watched Delquos raise TT's limp body above the level of the bushes with a gravity hoist belonging to Dr. Droon, and maneuver her back to the car, the others following. Delquos climbed into the car first, opened the big trunk compartment in the rear. TT was slid inside and the trunk compartment locked.

"Where are you taking her?" Telzey asked sullenly as Delquos lifted the car into the air.

"To the spaceport, dear," Halet said. "Dr. Droon and I both felt it would be better to spare your feelings by not prolonging the matter unnecessarily."

Telzey wrinkled her nose disdainfully, and walked up the aircar to stand behind Delquos' seat. She leaned against the back of the seat for an instant. Her legs felt shaky.

The chauffeur gave her a sober wink from the side.

"That's a dirty trick she's played on you, Miss Telzey!" he murmured. "I tried to warn you."

"I know." Telzey took a deep breath. "Look, Delquos, in just a minute something's going to happen! It'll look dangerous, but it won't be. Don't let it get you nervous . . . right?"

"Huh?" Delquos appeared startled, but kept his voice low. "Just *what's* going to happen?"

"No time to tell you. Remember what I said."

Telzey moved back a few steps from the driver's seat, turned around, said unsteadily, "Halet . . . Dr. Droon—"

Halet had been speaking quietly to Dr. Droon; they both looked up.

"If you don't move, and don't do anything stupid," Telzey said rapidly, "you won't get hurt. If you do . . . well,

I don't know! You see, there's another crest cat in the car . . ." In her mind she added, "Now!"

It was impossible to tell in just what section of the car Iron Thoughts had been lurking. The carpeting near the rear passenger seats seemed to blur for an instant. Then he was there, camouflage dropped, sitting on the floorboards five feet from the naturalist and Halet.

Halet's mouth opened wide; she tried to scream but fainted instead. Dr. Droon's right hand started out quickly towards the big stungun device beside his seat. Then he checked himself and sat still, ashen-faced.

Telzey didn't blame him for changing his mind. She felt he must be a remarkably brave man to have moved at all. Iron Thoughts, twice as broad across the back as Tick-Tock, twice as massively muscled, looked like a devil-beast even to her. His dark-green marbled hide was criss-crossed with old scar patterns; half his tossing crimson crest appeared to have been ripped away. He reached out now in a fluid, silent motion, hooked a paw under the stungun and flicked upwards. The big instrument rose in an incredibly swift, steep arc eighty feet into the air, various parts flying away from it, before it started curving down towards the treetops below the car. Iron Thoughts lazily swung his head around and looked at Telzey with yellow fire-eyes.

"Miss Telzey! Miss Telzey!" Delquos was muttering behind her. "You're *sure* it won't . . ."

Telzey swallowed. At the moment, she felt barely mouse-sized again. "Just relax!" she told Delquos in a shaky voice. "He's really quite t-t-t-tame."

Iron Thoughts produced a harsh but not unamiable chuckle in her mind.

The pearl-gray sportscar, covered now by its stream-lining canopy, drifted down presently to a parking plat-

form outside the suite of offices of Jontarou's Planetary
Moderator, on the fourteenth floor of the Shikaris' Club
Tower. An attendant waved it on into a vacant slot.

Inside the car, Delquos set the brakes, switched off the
engine, asked, "Now what?"

"I think," Telzey said reflectively, "we'd better lock you
in the trunk compartment with my aunt and Dr. Droon
while I talk to the Moderator."

The chauffeur shrugged. He'd regained most of his
aplomb during the unhurried trip across the parklands.
Iron Thoughts had done nothing but sit in the center of
the car, eyes half shut, looking like instant death enjoying
a dignified nap and occasionally emitting a ripsawing noise
which might have been either his style of purring or a snore.
And Tick-Tock, when Delquos peeled the paralysis belts
off her legs at Telzey's direction, had greeted him with her
usual reserved affability. What the chauffeur was suffering
from at the moment was intense curiosity, which Telzey
had done nothing to relieve.

"Just as you say, Miss Telzey," he agreed. "I hate to miss
whatever you're going to be doing here, but if you *don't*
lock me up now, Miss Halet will figure I was helping you
and fire me as soon as you let her out."

Telzey nodded, then cocked her head in the direction of
the rear compartment. Faint sounds coming through the
door indicated that Halet had regained consciousness and
was having hysterics.

"You might tell her," Telzey suggested, "that there'll be
a grown-up crest cat sitting outside the compartment door."
This wasn't true, but neither Delquos nor Halet could know
it. "If there's too much racket before I get back, it's likely
to irritate him . . ."

A minute later, she set both car doors on lock and went

outside, wishing she were less informally clothed. Sunbriefs and sandals tended to make her look juvenile.

The parking attendant appeared startled when she approached him with Tick-Tock striding alongside.

"They'll never let you into the offices with that thing, miss," he informed her. "Why, it doesn't even have a collar!"

"Don't worry about it," Telzey told him aloofly.

She dropped a two-credit piece she'd taken from Halet's purse into his hand, and continued on towards the building entrance. The attendant squinted after her, trying unsuccessfully to dispel an odd impression that the big catlike animal with the girl was throwing a double shadow.

The Moderator's chief receptionist also had some doubts about TT, and possibly about the sunbriefs, though she seemed impressed when Telzey's identification tag informed her she was speaking to the daughter of Federation Councilwoman Jessamine Amberdon.

"You feel you can discuss this . . . emergency . . . only with the Moderator himself, Miss Amberdon?" she repeated.

"Exactly," Telzey said firmly. A buzzer sounded as she spoke. The receptionist excused herself and picked up an earphone. She listened a moment, said blandly, "Yes . . . Of course . . . Yes, I understand," replaced the earphone and stood up, smiling at Telzey.

"Would you come with me, Miss Amberdon?" she said. "I think the Moderator will see you immediately . . ."

Telzey followed her, chewing thoughtfully at her lip. This was easier than she'd expected—in fact, too easy! Halet's work? Probably. A few comments to the effect of "A highly imaginative child . . . overexcitable," while Halet was arranging to have the Moderator's office authorize Tick-Tock's transfer to the Life Banks, along with the implication that Jessamine Amberdon would appreciate a discreet handling of any disturbance Telzey might create as a result. It was the sort of notion that would appeal to Halet—

They passed through a series of elegantly equipped offices and hallways, Telzey grasping TT's neck-fur in lieu of a leash, their appearance creating a tactfully restrained wave of surprise among secretaries and clerks. And if somebody here and there was troubled by a fleeting, uncanny impression that not one large beast but two seemed to be trailing the Moderator's visitor down the aisles, no mention was made of what could have been only a momentary visual distortion. Finally, a pair of sliding doors opened ahead, and the receptionist ushered Telzey into a large, cool balcony garden on the shaded side of the great building. A tall, gray-haired man stood up from the desk at which he was working, and bowed to Telzey. The receptionist withdrew again.

"My pleasure, Miss Amberdon," Jontarou's Planetary Moderator said, "Be seated, please." He studied Tick-Tock with more than casual interest while Telzey was settling herself into a chair, added, "And what may I and my office do for you?"

Telzey hesitated. She'd observed his type on Orado in her mother's circle of acquaintances—a senior diplomat, a man not easy to impress. It was a safe bet that he'd had her brought out to his balcony office only to keep her occupied while Halet was quietly informed where the Amberdon problem child was and requested to come over and take charge.

What she had to tell him now would have sounded rather wild even if presented by a presumably responsible adult. She could provide proof, but until the Moderator was already nearly sold on her story, that would be a very unsafe thing to do. Old Iron Thoughts was backing her up, but if it didn't look as if her plans were likely to succeed, he would be willing to ride herd on his devil's pack just so long . . .

Better start the ball rolling without any preliminaries, Telzey decided. The Moderator's picture of her must be that of a spoiled, neurotic brat in a stew about the threatened loss of a pet animal. He expected her to start arguing with him immediately about Tick-Tock.

She said, "Do you have a personal interest in keeping the Baluit crest cats from becoming extinct?"

Surprise flickered in his eyes for an instant. Then he smiled.

"I admit I do, Miss Amberdon," he said pleasantly. "I should like to see the species re-established. I count myself almost uniquely fortunate in having had the opportunity to bag two of the magnificent brutes before disease wiped them out on the planet."

The last seemed a less than fortunate statement just now. Telzey felt a sharp tingle of alarm, then sensed that in the minds which were drawing the meaning of the Moderator's speech from her mind there had been only a brief stir of interest.

She cleared her throat, said, "The point is that they weren't wiped out by disease."

He considered her quizzically, seemed to wonder what she was trying to lead up to. Telzey gathered her courage, plunged on, "Would you like to hear what did happen?"

"I should be much interested, Miss Amberdon," the Moderator said without change of expression. "But first, if you'll excuse me a moment . . ."

There had been some signal from his desk which Telzey hadn't noticed, because he picked up a small communicator now, said, "Yes?" After a few seconds, he resumed, "That's rather curious, isn't it? . . . Yes, I'd try that . . . No, that

shouldn't be necessary . . . Yes, please do. Thank you."
He replaced the communicator, his face very sober; then,
his eyes flicking for an instant to TT, he drew one of the
upper desk drawers open a few inches, and turned back to
Telzey.

"Now, Miss Amberdon," he said affably, "you were about
to say? About these crest cats . . ."

Telzey swallowed. She hadn't heard the other side of
the conversation, but she could guess what it had been
about. His office had called the guest house, had been told
by Halet's maid that Halet, the chauffeur and Dr. Droon
were out looking for Miss Telzey and her pet. The Moderator's office had then checked on the sportscar's communication number and attempted to call it. And, of
course, there had been no response.

To the Moderator, considering what Halet would have
told him, it must add up to the grim possibility that the
young lunatic he was talking to had let her three-quarters-
grown crest cat slaughter her aunt and the two men when
they caught up with her! The office would be notifying the
police now to conduct an immediate search for the missing
aircar.

When it would occur to them to look for it on the Moderator's parking terrace was something Telzey couldn't
know. But if Halet and Dr. Droon were released before
the Moderator accepted her own version of what had occurred, and the two reported the presence of wild crest
cats in Port Nichay, there would be almost no possibility
of keeping the situation under control. Somebody was
bound to make some idiotic move, and the fat would be
in the fire . . .

Two things might be in her favor. The Moderator seemed
to have the sort of steady nerve one would expect in a man

who had bagged two Baluit crest cats. The partly opened desk drawer beside him must have a gun in it; apparently he considered that a sufficient precaution against an attack by TT. He wasn't likely to react in a panicky manner. And the mere fact that he suspected Telzey of homicidal tendencies would make him give the closest attention to what she said. Whether he believed her then was another matter, of course.

Slightly encouraged, Telzey began to talk. It did sound like a thoroughly wild story, but the Moderator listened with an appearance of intent interest. When she had told him as much as she felt he could be expected to swallow for a start, he said musingly, "So they weren't wiped out— they went into hiding! Do I understand you to say they did it to avoid being hunted?"

Telzey chewed her lip frowningly before replying. "There's something about that part I don't quite get," she admitted. "Of course I don't quite get either why you'd want to go hunting . . . twice . . . for something that's just as likely to bag you instead!"

"Well, those are, ah, merely the statistical odds," the Moderator explained. "If one has enough confidence, you see—"

"I don't really. But the crest cats seem to have felt the same way—at first. They were getting around one hunter for every cat that got shot. Humans were the most exciting game they'd ever run into.

"But then that ended, and the humans started knocking them out with stunguns from aircars where they couldn't be got at, and hauling them off while they were helpless. After it had gone on for a while, they decided to keep out of sight.

"But they're still around . . . thousands and thousands of them! Another thing nobody's known about them is that

they weren't only in the Baluit mountains. There were crest
cats scattered all through the big forests along the other
side of the continent."

"Very interesting," the Moderator commented. "Very interesting, indeed!" He glanced towards the communicator,
then returned his gaze to Telzey, drumming his fingers
lightly on the desk top.

She could tell nothing at all from his expression now,
but she guessed he was thinking hard. There was supposed
to be no native intelligent life in the legal sense on Jontarou, and she had been careful to say nothing so far to
make the Baluit cats look like more than rather exceptionally intelligent animals. The next—rather large—question should be how she'd come by such information.

If the Moderator asked her that, Telzey thought, she
could feel she'd made a beginning at getting him to buy
the whole story.

"Well," he said abruptly, "if the crest cats are not extinct or threatened with extinction, the Life Banks obviously have no claim on your pet." He smiled confidingly
at her. "And that's the reason you're here, isn't it?"

"Well, no," Telzey began, dismayed. "I—"

"Oh, it's quite all right, Miss Amberdon! I'll simply
rescind the permit which was issued for the purpose. You
need feel no further concern about that." He paused. "Now,
just one question . . . do you happen to know where your
aunt is at present?"

Telzey had a dead, sinking feeling. So he hadn't believed
a word she said. He'd been stalling her along until the
aircar could be found.

She took a deep breath. "You'd better listen to the rest
of it."

"Why, is there more?" the Moderator asked politely.

"Yes. The important part! The kind of creatures they are, they wouldn't go into hiding indefinitely just because someone was after them."

Was there a flicker of something beyond watchfulness in his expression. "What would they do, Miss Amberdon?" he asked quietly.

"If they couldn't get at the men in the aircars and couldn't communicate with them"—the flicker again!—"they'd start looking for the place the men came from, wouldn't they? It might take them some years to work their way across the continent and locate us here in Port Nichay. But supposing they did it finally and a few thousand of them are sitting around in the parks down there right now? They could come up the side of these towers as easily as they go up the side of a mountain. And supposing they'd decided that the only way to handle the problem was to clean out the human beings in Port Nichay?"

The Moderator stared at her in silence a few seconds. "You're saying," he observed then, "that they're rational beings—above the Critical I. Q. level."

"Well," Telzey said, "legally they're rational. I checked on that. About as rational as we are, I suppose."

"Would you mind telling me now how you happen to know this?"

"They told me," Telzey said.

He was silent again, studying her face. "You mentioned, Miss Amberdon, that they have been unable to communicate with other human beings. This suggests then that you are a xenotelepath . . ."

"I am?" Telzey hadn't heard the term before. "If it means that I can tell what the cats are thinking, and they can tell what I'm thinking, I guess that's the word for it." She considered him, decided she had him almost on the ropes, went on quickly.

"I looked up the laws, and told them they could conclude a treaty with the Federation which would establish them as an Affiliated Species . . . and that would settle everything the way they would want it settled, without trouble. Some of them believed me. They decided to wait until I could talk to you. If it works out, fine! If it doesn't"—she felt her voice falter for an instant—"they're going to cut loose fast!"

The Moderator seemed undisturbed. "What am I supposed to do?"

"I told them you'd contact the Council of the Federation on Orado."

"Contact the Council?" he repeated coolly. "With no more proof for this story than your word Miss Amberdon?"

Telzey felt a quick, angry stirring begin about her, felt her face whiten.

"All right," she said. "I'll give you proof! I'll have to now. But that'll be it. Once they've tipped their hand all the way, you'll have about thirty seconds left to make the right move. I hope you remember that!"

He cleared his throat. "I—"

"NOW!" Telzey said.

Along the walls of the balcony garden, beside the ornamental flower stands, against the edges of the rock pool, the crest cats appeared. Perhaps thirty of them. None quite as physically impressive as Iron Thoughts who stood closest to the Moderator; but none very far from it. Motionless as rocks, frightening as gargoyles, they waited, eyes glowing with hellish excitement.

"This is *their* council, you see," Telzey heard herself saying.

The Moderator's face had also paled. But he was, after all, an old shikari and a senior diplomat. He took an unhurried look around the circle, said quietly, "Accept my

profound apologies for doubting you, Miss Amberdon!"
and reached for the desk communicator.

Iron Thoughts swung his demon head in Telzey's direction. For an instant, she picked up the mental impression
of a fierce yellow eye closing in an approving wink.

". . . An open transmitter line to Orado," the Moderator was saying into the communicator. "The Council. And
snap it up! Some very important visitors are waiting . . ."

The offices of Jontarou's Planetary Moderator became
an extremely busy and interesting area then. Quite two
hours passed before it occurred to anyone to ask Telzey
again whether she knew where her aunt was at present.

Telzey smote her forehead.

"Forgot all about that!" she admitted, fishing the sportscar's keys out of the pocket of her sunbriefs. "They're out
on the parking platform . . ."

The preliminary treaty arrangements between the Federation of the Hub and the new Affiliated Species of the
Planet of Jontarou were formally ratified two weeks later,
the ceremony taking place on Jontarou, in the Champagne
Hall of the Shikaris' Club.

Telzey was able to follow the event only by news viewer
in her ship-cabin, she and Halet being on the return trip
to Orado by then. She wasn't too interested in the treaty's
details—they conformed almost exactly to what she had
read out to Iron Thoughts and his co-chiefs and companions in the park. It was the smooth bridging of the wide
language gap between the contracting parties by a row of
interpreting machines and a handful of human xenotele-
paths which held her attention.

As she switched off the viewer, Halet came wandering
in from the adjoining cabin.

"I was watching it, too!" Halet observed. She smiled. "I was hoping to see dear Tick-Tock."

Telzey looked over at her. "Well, TT would hardly be likely to show up in Port Nichay," she said. "She's having too good a time now finding out what life in the Baluit range is like."

"I suppose so," Halet agreed doubtfully, sitting down on a hassock. "But I'm glad she promised to get in touch with us again in a few years. I'll miss her."

Telzey regarded her aunt with a reflective frown. Halet meant it quite sincerely, of course; she had undergone a profound change of heart during the past two weeks. But Telzey wasn't without some doubts about the actual value of a change of heart brought on by telepathic means. The learning process the crest cats had started in her mind appeared to have continued automatically several days longer than her rugged teachers had really intended; and Telzey had reason to believe that by the end of that time she'd developed associated latent abilities of which the crest cats had never heard. She'd barely begun to get it all sorted out yet, but . . . as an example . . . she'd found it remarkably easy to turn Halet's more obnoxious attitudes virtually upside down. It had taken her a couple of days to get the hang of her aunt's personal symbolism, but after that there had been no problem.

She was reasonably certain she'd broken no laws so far, though the sections in the law library covering the use and abuse of psionic abilities were veiled in such intricate and downright obscuring phrasing—deliberately, Telzey suspected—that it was really difficult to say what they did mean. But even aside from that, there were a number of arguments in favor of exercising great caution.

Jessamine, for one thing, was bound to start worrying about her sister-in-law's health if Halet turned up on Orado in her present state of mind, even though it would make for a far more agreeable atmosphere in the Amberdon household.

"Halet," Telzey inquired mentally, "do you remember what an all-out stinker you used to be?"

"Of course, dear," Halet said aloud. "I can hardly wait to tell dear Jessamine how much I regret the many times I . . ."

"Well," Telzey went on, still verbalizing it silently, "I think you'd really enjoy life more if you were, let's say, about halfway between your old nasty self and the sort of sickening-good kind you are now."

"Why, Telzey!" Halet cried out with dopey amiability. "What a delightful idea!"

"Let's try it," Telzey said.

There was silence in the cabin for some twenty minutes then while she went painstakingly about remolding a number of Halet's character traits for the second time. She still felt some misgiving about it; but if it became necessary, she probably could always restore the old Halet *in toto*.

These, she told herself, definitely were powers one should treat with respect! Better rattle through law school first; then, with that out of the way, she could start hunting around to see who in the Federation was qualified to instruct a genius-level novice in the proper handling of psionics . . .

ETHICAL QUOTIENT

by John T. Phillifent

Gordon Spencer sat up on his bunk with a stifled sigh. For more than an hour, now, he had been trying to settle down to sleep. A glowing dial on the bulkhead warned him that one sixth of the rest period was gone. The ship around him was quiet, silent but for the hardly-heard mumble of power. But his brain seethed with nagging, unanswerable questions. The cabin, the very bunk itself, posed one set. This was luxury, far beyond anything he had ever wanted, or been able to afford—but it was more than that.

At his first despairing sigh, and wriggle to sit up, it had shifted its contours to assist him. Had he wanted to go far- ther, to swing his legs over the side and get out, it would have tilted, obligingly, for him. In the same moment, the cabin lights would have glowed into discreet illumination, and the deep pile rug on the floor would have warmed to greet his feet. If he had then stood up, the bunk, if he had wanted it to, would have folded itself neatly away. Spencer knew all this, because he had tried it out.

And this luxury—almost dreamlike, to Spencer's way of thinking—had been provided for him without request, and without argument. His discreet inquiries had told him that this cabin had been booked, for the trip from Hanlar to Chaldun, by some merchant-tycoon or other. In Galactalk it translated out as a "High Born," or Prince, of the Ferl, who ruled this sector of the Galactic Federation. Yet this eminent person had immediately surrendered his booking, had changed his own schedule, to oblige Spencer, whom he had never seen. And this was only the pale fringe of the incredible.

He, Gordon Spencer, an obscure and non-aspiring science-historian, thirty-five, unmarried, unambitious, unpretentious, was sitting here in a luxury cabin, in a luxury warp-ship of the Ferl, arrowing its way deep into the heart of the Ferl sector, many hundreds of light-years from his home—all without cost to himself, or any Solarian institution or association—and he was being treated as an honored guest. It was fantastic. He said as much, aloud, into the dimness of the quiet cabin.

"This is fantastic. It is also ridiculous. All this, just because I was lucky enough to guess the right answers to a quiz game?"

At this, his innate honesty put up a gentle but firm correction. It hadn't been quite *that* simple. Nevertheless, that silly quiz had started it all. He leaned back against the obliging bunk-bed, crossing one knee over the other, and groped for a cigarette. Then he remembered that he'd put them away in a drawer, in the table which had, since, withdrawn into the wall. He got to his feet, padded across, and the table slid out to meet him, opening its drawer and offering a light, all ready. Back on the bunk again, he grinned, wryly, into the gloom. This cabin was well-nigh human.

He'd heard of psionics, on an academic level. Fringes of rumor had come his way, along with the occasional paper on the theory of it. He knew, also academically, that what was a half-scorned rumor to Solarians was an everyday commonplace throughout the whole of the galaxy wherever humanoid life-forms were found. In Galactalk, it was "personal-energy-control." But to meet it in practice, to be im-

mersed in it like this, was a different order of things, was
slightly unnerving. His fingers went, self-consciously, to the
almost invisible bulge under the skin of his right temple,
where a micro-miniaturized device was concealed, and he
recalled his conversation with Captain Wakely, at the
jump-off outpost on Ganymede.

"Beyond this point, Spencer, you're in Galactic territory"
Wakely had said, crisply. "Who you are, where you're
bound, why—those things don't concern me—have been
taken care of by other people. All I need to know is that
you're cleared, that the Galactics are giving you the veep
treatment—which is very nice for you, but none of my affair.
But you are still an Earthman, and that is very much my
affair." The immediate effect, Spencer had learned, was that
he would have to endure a delicate operation on a tooth, a
bit of minor surgery to the side of his head, and absorb some
crucial advice. Wakely had supplied the last item.

"Think of it this way," he had suggested. "Out there, you'll
be on your own, among people who look a lot like us. But
they can, they do, and they have been in the habit of doing,
for centuries, things which look like magic to us. They don't
shake hands when they meet, as we do. You know why we
do? It's a hold-over from the past, when you needed to be
able to weigh up the strength of the possible opposition, and
hold him still, at the same time. And we still do it. But they
shake minds. They reach out and 'feel' each other. Also,
they open doors, switch things on and off, run power-units
fast or slow, and manipulate objects—that kind of thing."

Spencer had been sensible enough not to interrupt, although Wakely was not telling him anything he didn't already know. The captain had gone on.

"Now, you have to be protected against that, for a start.
This gadget will take care of it for you. The tooth has a

three-position switch. Off . . . one . . . two. Off, and you're normal, defenseless, like any other human."

"They could read my mind, do you mean?"

"No. That's one bogey nobody has to fear, after all. Putting it very simply, reading is reading no matter how you do it. And Greek is greek, if you don't understand it. But they can, and would, catch your emotions, feelings, reactions—that level of thought. And influence them. Also a certain degree of physical control is possible. They could hinder your movements, slow you down. So, you move to position one and you are blanked off, totally, so far as they are concerned. Nothing for them to touch."

"I see!" Spencer had been interested, now. This was something definite. "At position one, I would be just 'not there' to them, on a psionic level?" Wakely's eye had gone bleak, suddenly.

"Right!" he had confirmed. "You catch on quick, mister. Now, do you mind telling me how come you're so quick with the 'psionics'? I don't recall mentioning the word!"

"The history and philosophy of science is my field," Spencer had explained, hastily. "I've heard of this kind of thing. Nothing as advanced as this, of course. But I've heard of it. What puzzles me is—if you have this thing developed to this degree, why isn't it more common? Why all the hush-hush?" It had been a naïve question, nicely calculated to reassure Wakely, and set him off on an explanation, most of which Spencer had guessed, anyway.

"Position two gives you an imitation of the kind of thing the Galactics can do—object-control—pick-up and transmission of emotions. It's not the same as theirs, so far as we can tell. Think of it as being on the order of trying to pick up AM broadcasts on an FM set and you have an idea. But this gadget, mister, is about as hard to get as a permit to enter Fort Knox with a bag. You have to be the right sort of person, just to get to know of its existence. You're getting it just because you're going out of the system. When you come back, you won't get any farther than this, *with* it. Every man on this outpost wears a shut-off model, but there are very few who ever get to wear the Mark II that you have." His expression had gone even more bleak.

"Just try to imagine what it would be like if a thing like this was let loose to every Tom and Dick. You'd have shambles, in a hurry. And I'm not just thinking of the criminal element, either. That thing spells 'power', the power to control and enslave. It could knock a man right off balance. Even a good, honest man."

Spencer nodded to himself, in the dark. Wakely hadn't said as much, but had inferred that such power needed its own ethic. And ethics had been a fadword, for a while, when the Solar worlds had learned that it was highly valued throughout the rest of the galaxy. For a while, it had caught on, become a "gimmick." Hence the ridiculous quiz that had started everything. But, where the fad had run its course and died out, speeded by the realization that you can't, in the nature of things, win big money prizes for being "ethical," the effects of that first quiz had gone on snow-balling, for Spencer.

He muttered, "Who'd have dreamed it would come to anything like this." He had been on position two ever since he'd reached the solitude of this cabin, in an attempt to gain familiarity with the power. He got to his feet again, "wanted" the bunk to flatten itself out and slide into its recess. He "wished" the cabin lights into brightness, and dim again, adjusted the air temperature, even wished the door open, all without moving a muscle. Cold logic told him that there wasn't a lot of power involved, not in the sense of moving mountains. This wasn't that kind of power. It wasn't free ergs from thin air. It just enabled a man to employ his personal quota of energy, to apply the tug of a hand or the pressure of a finger—at a distance—just by "wanting" it. The same cold logic told him that this was only a degree more weird than the actual fact of a "want" making his fingers splay out, or knot into a fist.

But, cold logic or not, it was a weird sensation. As Wakely had said, this kind of thing could knock a man off balance. It was tempting, and frightening, at the same time. He shivered, and "wished" the door shut again. This kind of thing shook one's ideas about privacy. It was no longer just a matter of keeping other people out. You needed to be able to keep yourself in. When your thoughts, pictures, emotions and urges were impotent within your own skull, you could let them run. But when their effect was extended outside your own skin, that was a new kind of responsibility. You needed control. And it was difficult. Spencer frowned as he began to realize just how difficult.

Sinkingly, he thought, "If I can't take charge of my thinking, here and now, in this privacy, what chance do I have in company?" He moved his tongue, to set the switch to the "blank" position, where it had been, safely, from the time he had left Wakely on Ganymede, until reaching this cabin. "Psionics is not for me," he decided, "not on any level." But, before he could shift the switch, he felt a sudden sharp-edged touch of menace. It was so vivid that he whirled, ducked—and the cabin lights flared . . . all in one swift reaction.

But he was quite alone. Relaxing, he frowned again, trying to sort his impressions. Somebody yearned to commit mayhem on somebody else, that much was sure. And not too far away, either. But it couldn't be anything to do with him, surely? He must have eavesdropped into someone else's problems. The question, now, was—what did he do about it, if anything? Did one interfere in someone else's quarrel? That "feel" came again, stronger, and he revised the word "quarrel." By the impact of it, nothing less than bloody murder was being planned.

But, he reasoned, standing quite still, whoever that was intended for must surely be able to detect it? Unless, of course, he was asleep, or doped, or handicapped in some other way. Fascinated in spite of himself, Spencer "wished" to home in on that ferocious thought, to know more of it, shutting his eyes to aid concentration. He cringed a little as the thrust of hate became a mental shout. But it wasn't hate, at all. It was the blind unthinking "feel" of somebody under orders, and rationalizing them, who was saying to himself: "He is to be killed. It is for the best." Not an honest fire of rage, but the dim reaction of a stupid servant. Or—it could be there were two of them. It felt like it. Gaining facility, Spencer began to gather a picture of the victim. It clarified, suddenly, and he was watching, as if through a distorting lens, the spaceport at Hanlar, the warpship gangway, the thin stream of passengers going aboard. One figure highlighted—one oddly incongruous, hatted and sober-suited figure, among the colorful flamboyant rest. One lone Earthman.

"Me?" he gasped, as the mind-picture wavered, shifted through a closeup of his own unremarkable features, to a dim-lit view of a corridor, and the door of a cabin. This cabin. "They're after me!" he breathed, not wanting to believe it, utterly baffled as to why, but unable to argue with what he had "seen." All at once, he felt vulnerable, and foolish, standing there in just the nether half of his plain and unbeautiful pajamas. Scream for help? He didn't know how, and dismissed the thought. With it went all his puzzlement and unbelief. Personal danger drove all else into second place, sharpened his attention to immediate matters.

How many? Two. What, exactly, did they have in mind? He got the convincing impression that each was carrying something which equated with "knife."

He glanced round, urgently, seeking something to swing, to wield, to hit with—but there was nothing. This was one class of luxury the cabin did not have. In desperation, he "wanted" the top quilt of his bunk, and it wrapped itself, obediently, around his left forearm. Something, but not much. He wished the cabin into darkness, and felt a stab of dismay. It would be the acme of insanity to confuse himself with his amateurish psi-powers at a time like this. He couldn't hope to compete, on that level. Flipping the tooth-switch to a safe "blank," he slid to the wall, flattening himself alongside the door, and tried to iron out the tension of waiting by controlling his breathing. He might be outclassed on a psionic level, but, in a staid and uneventful life, he had made something of a fetish of physical fitness, often to the amusement and gentle ribbing of his colleagues so the thugs were not going to have things *all* their own way.

The moments seemed to crawl, and he found time to wonder what this was all about. More importantly, "who" had given the order. Who wanted him killed, and why? Then the door sighed, and a thin thread of light showed from the corridor. He readied to chop down on the arm moving that door, and remembered, just in time, that there need not be one, that the person moving that door might be all of a foot away from it. The door slid wide, a dark bulk showed, came through, moving none too quietly. He caught the glint of a bright blade, and a second shadow. There was a sheen of light on yellow skin. These men were about his own size, and kilted to the knee. That meant they were servant-class. And they were heavy-footed and careless. Overconfident. As the second man came clear of the doorway, Spencer reached out, tapped him on the shoulder.

The intruder jerked, swung round, to meet a right-handed smash that had traveled all the way from the wall, with all the hit that Spencer could pack into it. Shaking his arm, filled with an unholy joy at the sweetness of that punch, he stepped back to the wall again, plus a knife. The handle felt odd, in his hand, but the odds were considerably more even, now. He saw the leading thug pause, spin round, and almost stumble over the prone figure of his companion. Then the lights blazed, the door hissed shut, and Spencer was face-to-face with deliberate murder.

The yellow man betrayed only a slight oddness about his shaven skull and the set of his eyes to mark him as other than Terran. Physically, he matched Spencer's six-foot height, with possibly a slight advantage in reach and weight. And he had psi-power. Spencer hunched himself, anxiously alert for anything, trying to read that dull face. It was a mask that told him very little. The man stood heavily, flat-footed, as if unready and surprised. Then he lifted his knife hand. Spencer swayed. Suddenly, with no muscular cue, the nine-inch blade darted, like an arrow of light, and Spencer snatched up his quilted arm to fend it off. The blade sliced into the quilt, burned his arm, and half-an-inch of it bit into his forehead.

Blinded with the pain, Spencer grabbed for the weapon, got it. Then both knives, in his hands, jerked to be free. Only just in time, he slapped his hands together and squeezed, getting them apart with a squirming knife firmly gripped in each. For a moment, it was muscles against mind-power, and muscles were winning, but it was only a shred of consolation.

"This is crazy," he thought, desperately. "I'm no knife-artist. I have to eliminate these, somehow." Pressing his back to the paneled bulkhead, he clutched the two writhing weapons, and stabbed back and down, so that they were jammed into the hard wood. Then he went forward again, caught a flicker of surprise on that yellow face. "Slow on the uptake," he thought, with rising hope. Then the quilt on his arm went crazy and whipped itself up, over his face and head, smothering and blinding him. Snatching frantically at it, he caught a brief glimpse of his opponent coming forward, and barked in agony to a vicious kick in the belly. He went down in a knotted heap, whooping for breath, and was just able to ward off the next kick, to roll with it. The quilt began to wrap itself around his neck. Desperately, he flicked his tooth-switch to control, ordered the quilt to lie down and stay down. Up on one knee, he ducked away from a mighty but unskilled swipe from the enemy, and managed to stagger to his feet. Backing up, he pushed away the first feeling of despair. How could a man put up a decent fight, when the odd items in the environment couldn't be counted on to stay put?

The yellow man came forward, heavily, launched another kick, telegraphing the movement all the way. Spencer swayed, lashed out a chopping right, and his opponent staggered, off-balance. Stepping in, Spencer slammed him upright with a left, smashed across a right, and swayed back. The yellow man reeled, glassy-eyed. "That shakes up your psionics I'll bet," Spencer thought, grimly. The thug reeled back, dazed but game, putting up his arms in a clumsy guard. Spencer brushed one arm aside, easily, hit him once . . . twice . . . with the ache in his belly to add fuel to the punches . . . and it was all over. He stood, flexed his stinging knuckles, and then stepped heavily over the two bodies, called out his bunk, sat on it, and panted, rubbing his middle. On a sudden afterthought, he moved his tooth-switch to "blank." And wondered what he ought to do, now?

"Excuse, please, if I intrude," came a voice, soft and melodious, in careful Galactalk. "I felt pain, distress, and trouble. Do you need help?"

He looked up, hurriedly. A girl—or a young woman, he couldn't be sure which—stood in his doorway. Her golden hair gleamed in disarray around an elfin face where dark-blue eyes watched him in wide curiosity. The rest of her was hidden in a cloud of mist that was all shades of restless green fire.

"I'm sorry—" He got up, awkwardly and embarrassed, feeling for the right word-sounds. Galactalk was poorly equipped for delicate nuances. "There has been trouble. These men came to attack me. They had weapons. I do not know why, nor what is the approved next action." Her eyes had been active during his halting explanation, but were now back on him, and with a sudden understanding.

"Of course—" she breathed, in a subtly different tone. "I am sorry, I was still half asleep. You are the Solarian Great One, the Ethical Absolute. I should have known. My cabin adjoins yours. Please command me. The distress and hurt could not have come from you, because all know that Solarians are . . . deficient." She gave the word an inflection of delicate distaste, hurried on, "It must have been from these, when you struck them down. But you *are* injured." Suddenly he was aware of the sticky trickle of blood down the side of his face, and from his arm.

"It is trivial," he mumbled, also becoming aware of his half-nakedness, his pajamas, his bare feet. "These are more important, surely?" and he nodded to the two bodies. She became brisk.

"I will see to everything."

Within seconds his cabin was invaded by competent and helpful people. A gray-skinned, placid-faced, medical attendant dealt with his cuts, sealing them with quick-drying spray. The duty officer, grim-faced, stood by while crewmen seized the two bodies and removed them. And their knives. Spencer had a moment of intrigued wonder, as he pictured the task of securing a man who has psionic ability. The brig, or its equivalent, would have to be something really special, he thought. Possibly with a locking system designed to operate only on a private code of thought-patterns—or to a certain brain-pattern, even. The officer himself lingered only long enough to be sure that Spencer was comfortable.

"All will be dealt with, immediately after the rest period," he said. "They will be put to the question. You need trouble yourself no further. I hope you will sleep well, now . . ." and he finished on a word which sent Spencer groping through his Galactalk vocabulary vainly. The intergalactic language was a minor interest, on Earth. Spencer had acquired what little he knew out of a necessity to be able to read the few scientific papers which filtered in from outside. When this trip had become a possibility he had made efforts to brush up on it. But that word had him stopped. He turned to where the girl sat on the bunk, discreetly distant but attentive.

"I am grateful," he said. "May I know your name, to thank you properly? Mine is Gordon Spencer. Of Earth, as you seem to know already."

"And *what* are you?" she asked, curiously. "What is your function?" This was another stopper, as Galactalk had no precise synonym either for "history" or "science." The nearest he could get to history was "that which has happened." Science, all science, in Galactalk, was subsumed in a word which meant "cosmology." There was a deal of philosophical truth in that, Spencer thought, but it didn't help in translation.

"I teach," he said, "or, better, I make programs for a machine to be used by those who wish to know just how the

Universe came to be the way it is, and how much we know about the process." Her eyes rounded.

"This is a work truly befitting a Great One!"

"I'm no great one," he denied, hurriedly. "On Earth I am of little importance. Such activities are of minor value and there are many hundreds of thousands equal, or superior, to me."

"I do not understand this," she shook her head, "although I know you speak true, being Ethical Absolute. Still"—she made a tiny gesture of amusement—"there are things I do not yet understand."

"Myself, also," he said, feelingly. "But you have not told me who you are."

"I am Delyra Taynee. As yet, I have no function. This was my father's cabin, and he should have traveled in your place. I have been thinking that this accounts for your disturbance. The attack was meant for my father, not for you." Spencer bit back his denial of this. He knew different, but he couldn't say so without disclosing just how he knew, and he wasn't ready for that, yet. Besides, he had just caught on to a clue to something else.

"Your father," he murmured, "is a personage, as I understand it. Excuse my awkward words, but he would be called 'noble,' I think? High-born? Then you, also. You are a Princess?" She nodded, gravely. "Then I know, now, what the duty-officer meant. He called you 'Highness'. I am honored, and very sorry that I have caused you such disturbance." She eyed him with a delicate frown, then shook her head.

"Again, I do not understand. The officer was speaking to you. I am of rank, it is true, but through the blood and by material possessions only. You are Ethical Absolute. You are the Great One, the Highness. The honor is mine." She frowned even more deeply at his involuntary gape. "You did not know this? Yours must be a strange world, indeed. See now, in all the galaxy of people such as we, there are great numbers, beyond counting. Of these there are Ethical Absolutes, like you, only one in every million of millions. This is a truth that all children are taught. Think . . . all on this ship . . . in Hanlar, whence we came . . . in Chaldun, where we are bound . . . all who have seen you . . . they will count it a great thing, to speak of to less-fortunate friends. Now do you understand?"

"I hear your words," Spencer mumbled, "but they do not make sense to me. Look, after the rest period there will be some time before we arrive. You are the first person I have met"—he managed to catch the correct personal-formal inflection—"so I would ask you to join me for—" but now he had lost the word altogether, so substituted, hastily—"for the first meal. Will you? There is so much to explain."

"It will be a great honor."

"No, not as an honor," he objected. "As a gesture, to me-as-a-person?"

"That, also!" she smiled. "I will come for you."

Leaning back on the bunk, after she had gone, he wished, belatedly, that he had asked the medico for something to quell the headache he could feel beginning to swell behind his eyes. But perhaps these people could dismiss a thing like that with a thought? He moved his switch, tried it, and wished he hadn't. The dial on the wall indicated a third of the rest period gone. He needed sleep. It occurred to him that a well-appointed cabin ought to have something to take care of such things, so he "ached" his head—so successfully that it made his scalp tighten—and a panel slid back. He hadn't seen this one before, but the shelf full of bottles was unmistakable, even at a distance. Drinks. Wrong signal, he mused, unhappily. He didn't want a hangover. Just the opposite.

All the same, he went across to it, stooped painfully, and peered at a cluster of smaller bottles, each labeled. Fortunately, chemical formulae followed the same logical system, here, as on Earth. Only the symbols were different. He translated, laboriously, through a headache that was excruciatingly genuine, now. Eventually he found one bottle, translating twice to make quite sure—$C_2H_5O.C_6H_4.NH.CO.CH_3$—aceto-p-phenetidine—phenacetin. That would do him very well.

Back on the bunk again, he tried to relax. What had been bewilderment before was now explained, but the explanation was worse than the puzzle. He had her word, and her obvious sincerity, that he was a Great One, an Ethical Absolute. She believed it. By the evidence, so did a whole lot of other people. Ethical Absolute. One in a million of millions. The words rolled in his mind. He tried to view them objectively. Whether they were true or not was beside the point. What mattered was that "they" accepted this, and gave him honor as a consequence. He tried to feel great, and worthy, and the attempt was a miserable failure. He still knew himself as ordinary and unspectacular.

Then there was that delicate hint of hers, that he was a freak. Well, deficient, anyway, like all Solarians. He seized on that, followed it back in his mind, curiously—ten years back, to First Contact. Captain . . . later major . . . John Field, and his hand-picked international crew of six, making the very first interstellar jump, with the first, primitive but workable, star-drive. Then their return, and the stunning news. There were people out there, by the myriad. Civilizations, races, systems, cultures—so many as to stagger the biggest imagination, and all peacefully and freely interlinked in a loose framework of trade and commerce. A galaxy-wide Federation, many hundreds of centuries old.

Were they interested in us? Mildly. Not very much.

What were their aims, their objectives, their motivations? None, save a mild interest, friendly neutrality, and a willingness—nothing more—to trade and exchange, on a material basis.

But what about their cultures, their technologies, the great scientific secrets, the social advances, the treasures they might have—must have—what about them? What did we do now—tremble? Or exult? Or what?

Spencer could recall, almost word for word, the public answer John Field had made to that question.

"They class us as a lesser culture. With respect, but primitive. Not important. Their values differ in many ways from ours, which is not surprising. But we were given to understand that we would not be interfered with. They respect our right to do just whatever we please, within our own system. Beyond that, though, we would have to *ask* to be admitted, on a low level, as a member of this sector of the Federation. Under the managership and control of the particular Overlord of this sector. Known as the Ferl. So far as we could make out, the Ferl control, directly, some fifty-odd planetary systems, all bigger than ours, and are administratively responsible for some five hundred more. Also, as far as we could discover, this Overlordship is benevolent.

"But, if we wanted any part of it, we would have to ask. And qualify. And agree to their management—on their terms. I consulted with my colleagues, but it was obvious, to me, at least, that my duty was to tell them that, we of the Solarian planets, if we *had* to make the choice between submitting to alien domination, no matter how, or what the material gain—between that and the freedom to go our own

way, in our own way—then we would choose freedom. That
was the answer I gave. I did add that we were not an authoritative body, and that if the folks back home didn't en-
dorse that, there would be another ship making the trip, to
talk business. But I had no doubt, in my own mind!"

Brave words, Spencer mused, sleepily. And John Field
had judged rightly. His choice had been endorsed by every
responsible Solarian body that could get a hearing. There
had been a few heretical voices, a scientist or two, a few
sociologists, a handful of adventurous spirits, to mutter a
protest. But the great mass had been unanimous. It wasn't
the first time Man had had to rescale his yardstick of values.
Once, Earth had been the center of the Universe. Then it
had been demoted to just one of a system of planets, with
Sol as the center. In its turn, Sol had shrunk to just a minor
star among many millions, a speck in a galaxy. And the
galaxy itself had become just one average specimen among
many million. And none of these changes in perspective
had affected, in any way, the everyday problems of living.
People ate, slept, fought, and tried to plan for the morrow,
just as they had always done. Thus it was no effort at all to
relegate the stupendous Galactic Federation of alien hu-
manoids into the same limbo of incomprehensible academic
things. The stars didn't look any different, did they?

A small outpost grew up, on Ganymede, built with Ferl
co-operation. There was a very small trickle of two-way
communication and information—nothing shattering. And
that was all. But Spencer was groping for something else.
Something important—

He woke to the sound of a gently insistent gong-with-
bells—a sound so pleasant that he lay a while to listen, and
was thus wide awake when he sat up. And he had it. His
subconscious had rounded up the missing item while he

slept. The lucky charms! Field and all his crew had worn good-luck mascots of a special kind, had even wanted to call their ship the "Lucky Charm" instead of the official "Stellar One." Only a handful of people knew why.

Spencer rolled out of his bunk, yawned, "wanted" a shower and shave, and went, almost unthinkingly, to the stall which opened out for him. He was steamed, oiled, sprayed, massaged and depilated, delicately and in comfort, the while his mind dredged up old half-forgotten references. Psi-phenomena, for instance. They had been studied, in a left-handed fashion, as far back as the middle nineteen hundreds, but all attempts to hammer out a workable theory had failed. On an analogy with sight, it had been the same kind of failure that would come from studying only the physical mechanism involved. There had to be a consideration of the personal factor involved. And this was difficult. Some progress had been made, a few minor factors established beyond doubt. One was that mental power, personality, character and dominant emotions were all interlinked. Another was that the influence of the "person" undoubtedly extended beyond the barriers of his skin. Or, in more effective terms, a man operating a machine could, and did, have an effect on it, over and above the control movements he made with his hands, or feet.

This distinctly uncomfortable truth became crucial during the construction and trials of the first star-drive. Time and again, things went wrong, components failed, blew out, reversed function, or just went insanely unstable, against all reason. The point was reached when the whole experimental team, in their out-of-harm's-way Lunar Base, were good and ready to quit. In sheer desperation, the authorities heeded the words of a dedicated group of psi-believers. They couldn't do worse than fail. They might, just, succeed. So the "magic" men had swarmed into Star-base, armed with a jury-rigged theory compounded of equal parts auto-suggestion, witchcraft, voodoo, symbolism and pure guess-work, plus a passion for trial-and-error on a lunatic scale. They had begun by hexing every section, and then every component of every section. And the thin red line on the progress-flow charts had begun to take its first upward bend.

Now the magicians changed their tactics, and went for the key-personnel involved. Try a talisman, a mascot, a luck-piece—anything—just to see. And, more by feel than anything else, they evolved a luck-charm that worked. Not until long after was it discovered that the luck-charm effectively interposed a barrier between a man's worries, fears, nervousness—and the delicate and sensitive machinery he was working on. And the same barrier was a shield against the psionic Galactics those same men met, later. So it was that all Solarians were "known" to be deficient.

Spencer grinned to himself as he finished dressing, but the grin faded as he looked ahead to the prospect of entertaining a princess in a public dining-place. That was going to be an ordeal. Belatedly, he blanked himself off, and then wondered if it would occur to her to wonder how he had managed to "operate" this cabin. This, he thought, grimly, was what happened once you started a falsehood. You had to go along with it, getting more and more involved. He didn't like doing it, but the secret was not his alone to throw away. Being ethical had its drawbacks, he mused, and managed to regain a wry smile. The cabin door slid open so smoothly, without warning, that she caught the grin still on his face.

"Why do you smile?" she asked.

"With my people," he countered, swiftly, "it is the custom to knock, to announce, before entering." She put a hand to her mouth in quick contrition.

"I am sorry. I did not know that. We secure a door with

a 'do-not-enter' thought, if we desire privacy. A clear door is a welcome. I should have known it would be otherwise—"

"That's all right. My fault. I'll learn as I go. Now . . . breakfast?" He had recalled the correct word now, and gestured for her to go ahead.

"If it is your wish," she hesitated, "but . . . perhaps you would prefer to eat here? There will be many eyes, watching, out there. Here, is private."

"I'd like that," he admitted, "but I thought . . . perhaps—" He tried for a rendering of "convention," and floundered. She smiled, understandingly.

"It is the same, with us. But you are Ethical Absolute. So, it is all right, you see?" And she proceeded to take charge, without further comment. Spencer sat, watching, and thinking. It was all right, in her sense. He was Ethical Absolute— at least, he was known to be such. And that, in her culture, was good enough for her. He had to admit that it simplified things. That is, if you could accept as infallible the results of a quiz.

He let the ideas slip, and gave attention to the meal provided by soft-footed stewards. He cleaned his palate with an iced liquid that was acid-fruit; used ornate tongs to eat meat-chunks that were tender, juicy, and delicious; chewed a mouthful of blue berries that stung his tongue, and smoothed away the sting with a green cream that was as bland as a caress. And, surprisingly, he had had enough. Watching her, he had managed to avoid gross mistakes, but if she was deliberately cueing him, it didn't show. He could have used a cup of coffee, or something similar, but here his language failed completely. She knew of no equivalent. To her, it seemed, stimulants were in a medical category, to be taken only as needed. Giving it up, he got out his cigarettes,

offered her one. She refused, delicately, but inviting him
to go ahead.

"A fine meal," he said. "I'm obliged to you. But I wish I
knew what this is all about." She looked her puzzlement
and he elaborated. "What am I supposed to be doing, here,
and why? It is costing somebody a lot to get me to Chaldun.
For what? And why me?"

"To decide, of course!" She said it as if it meant something. "You are to be one of a Great Five—five Ethical Absolutes—meeting to decide some great issue."

"But *what* issue? And how can I have an opinion on a
Galactic matter? I've never been off Earth before. What
would I know about it?"

"You will know the question, when it is put. And you
will have a valid opinion, because it will be an ethical matter, and you—"

"All right," he interrupted. "Don't say it again. I wish it
meant as much to me as it obviously does to you. All I did
was to guess the right . . . the obvious . . . answers to a
lot of obvious questions. That makes me a great somebody?" He aimed for a tone of chagrin, amusement and
disbelief.

"You will see!" She was gently positive. "It so happens
that I know what will happen to you. Our port of arrival on
Chaldun is Pellau, a great city. My father's estate is on the
outskirts. That is where the Great Five is to meet. We
offered our hospitality, and it was accepted. It is a great
honor." He got up, restlessly.

"I'll grant you the honor part," he said. "That's your
values. But why me? I'm no great statesman, or politician—"
He left it there, because her face told him he wasn't getting
across, at all. Changing the subject, he asked, "What's happening about the two assassins? Will I have to report to
somebody?"

"I will inquire." She got up, went to yet another panel, which opened out to meet her, and spent a few moments in communication with someone. Then she was back, smiling. "Captain Elbet will attend you, at once." Spencer shook his head and stifled a sigh. Like it or not, these people were determined to treat him as an eminence.

Captain Elbet was short and thick-set, gray-skinned and with jut ears, his face rugged, his hair an astonishingly bright red. But his uniform gleamed and his manner was placatory.

"We put them to the question," he said, in careful Galactalk, "but, Highness, they chose to die, rather than speak, which is the way of such." He used the term which meant "self-death," and Spencer hid a twinge of distaste. Suicide, here, had a different value.

"What are the prospects of tracing them back, discovering who gave them the orders for what they did?"

"All is being done. They were a crew, taken aboard at Hanlar because of an accidental shortage. Word has been sent to the Lord Taynee, there. He will, doubtless, press the matter."

"You're satisfied that it was meant for him, then?"

"But what else?" Elbet was shocked, his mouth pushing out in a gesture of distaste. "Not even subclasses such as they would offer violence to a Great One, knowingly. It was an error. I am greatly thankful that little hurt has come to you. Had you been seriously harmed, I should have been ruined, disgraced. For such a thing to happen, on my ship . . . it would have been very bad."

Spencer frowned. Could he have been wrong, after all? There was only that mental picture to go by. The other theory certainly made more sense. Perhaps Lord Taynee would turn up the evidence to decide it, one way or the other.

"All right," he shrugged. "No reflection on you, sir. I'm none the worse, so we'll say no more about it." The captain showed his relief, his gratitude, and something else. He hesitated, awkwardly. Delyra Taynee broke in.

"Captain Elbet is curious, Highness . . . and I, also . . . as to how you managed to overpower and strike down the two men. Both were armed, were strong. You were defenseless, and lacking personal-energy-control!" She said it very tactfully. Spencer eyed her, and the captain, and something began to be very clear to him, all at once. The word "compensation" came to him, and he earmarked it for future deliberation. He couldn't explain it, here. He had no way of explaining, at all.

"I took away their knives," he said, simply. "Then I struck them, thus . . ." and he made motions with his fists. "That was all." It meant nothing to them. Elbet withdrew, pleading the urgencies of approaching landing-time. Delyra made no secret of her bewilderment.

"You are a strange man. So many contradictions. Ethical Absolute, yet humble thinking. Deficient, yet powerful. Are all Earth people like you?"

"That's too big a question to go into, right now," he grinned. "If you don't mind, I'd like you to help me with a little experiment, though . . ." and it wasn't until after he had said it that he realized the possible ambiguity of his words. She never thought of it at all, but was immediately and unquestioningly interested. He picked up an item of tableware which was almost the duplicate of an Earth-type spoon, cleared a space along one edge of the table, and commanded her to watch without interfering in any way. Then, poising himself, gauging distances carefully, he snapped his palm-edge down on the tip of the bowl. The spoon flew in a twinkling arc, and he caught it, deftly. She was not impressed.

"All right," he chuckled. "Let's see you do it." She came round the table readily enough, set the spoon, flicked her right hand negligently, and the spoon circled lazily, drifted down into her right palm. She raised her brows at him.

"That was just fine," he applauded. "Now let's see you do it again—but without personal power!" She looked at him again, with a new light in her eye. Then she stared at the spoon in her hand as if she had never seen it before.

"I think I am beginning to understand," she breathed, putting the spoon where it had been on the table. He caught his breath as he saw the green mist of her garment suddenly modulate into pale gray and cling close to her body like a furry pelt. It was obviously in tune with her thoughts and feelings. What a garment! No wonder she hadn't bothered to change from last night. She had a whole wardrobe, right there. But, as soon as she made a move to flick the spoon, the green flame-color flowed back, and the gauzy fronds lifted up. She tried three times, and stopped herself each time, shaking her head.

"It is difficult—to hold back," she confessed. "One does it from long habit, automatically. I will try it again." This time she set herself in pretty determination, chopped down with her hand, and winced as she caught the bowl too full. Frowning, she tried once more, and the spoon flew far beyond her reach. It fell almost to the carpet, then came swooping back, obediently, into her hand. She put it down on the table, ruefully.

"Don't worry about it," he consoled her. "It's natural for you to use what you have. As we might put it, why go blindfold, when you can see? But, you know, a child could learn to do that, and things like it, in no time at all, on Earth."

"It is important to you, Highness?"

"It might be, yes. But you can forget that 'highness' stuff. I answer very well to Mr. Spencer . . . or 'Gordon', if you could bring yourself to it." An urgent staccato chiming cut him short.

"It is the arrival warning," she said, unaccountably breathless. "You must rest, now, on your couch, until you hear a single plain tone. That will mean that we are secured. Then I will come for you, and arrange everything. Once we are berthed, you will be my guest, and my responsibility . . . Gordon!" and she was gone before he could find his tongue.

Stretched out on his bunk, he took time out to examine his chaotic personal feelings, and criticize them, severely. Get a grip on yourself, he warned. You're old enough to be her father, almost. All right, so this is the first time any woman ever made your heart stick in your throat, and your knees turn to water, so what? She's a princess, remember—a *real* somebody. And that light in her eyes could be just a reflection for your greatness. Right now it's fine. But what comes after? Back to the programming, the back-water—and forget all about this. You couldn't offer her anything, except yourself. Yes, you're an ethical wonder-boy, here—for what it may be worth. But what does it cut up for, on Earth? And what does it mean, anyway, except that you're just naturally honest? You can't help it. It's the way you're made, isn't it? So how about being honest with yourself, right now—with her? Also, don't forget, you're a defective, so far as she is concerned.

By the time the "secure" tone was sounded he had himself well in hand, and allowed himself to be collected, entrusted his one suitcase to a green-skinned servant, was led to the gangway, ushered into a purring float-chariot, there to sit beside Delyra—all with carefully controlled civility. He paid polite attention to the sights as she showed them to him, and by the time they had reached the outlying districts he had come to the not-very-original conclusion that all big cities look very much alike, give or take a few peculiarities. Then her silence became so pointed as to penetrate his reserve. He met her eye, and looked away, awkwardly.

"You are cold . . . different, somehow," she said, candidly. "I have done something to offend you?"

"No!" he said, almost angrily. Never had he felt the language barrier as strongly as now. He had no choice of delicate words at all. "Princess . . ." He hesitated, then, "Forgive me if my words are improper, but what I am to say must be said. As well as being a person of little importance, I am also old. Old, that is, to the point where a man should be mated and have children." She was quite still, now, only her eyes alive. "I have neither mate nor issue because I have little to offer a mate, and no great urge to exchange my freedom for . . ." he caught at that, hurriedly and substituted, ". . . I have not yet met the woman who would be right for me. And I am almost past the age when I could hope to meet such a woman. Again, excuse my clumsiness, and please see me, not as someone great, but as a very ordinary man, ill-versed in the ways of attractive women, afflicted with very ordinary feelings, and trying very hard to keep them under control."

For a moment longer, she sat quite still. Their car was now gliding down a long avenue of high trees. They had just passed through a very ornate gate, so this, presumably, was the beginning of the estate. Light and shade fled across her face and he saw that her dress was now glowing a dull golden color, rippling like a field of grain in a breeze. Then she spoke, softly.

"I understand, I think. Such things are different, with us, because we have no need for explaining. Words are difficult. But I can say this. I, too, am of an age for mating, but have not yet met the right one. But, when you ask that I set aside your greatness, this is impossible. See . . . you are of such a height, such a weight. Your eyes are this color. These things are. So, also, you are Ethical Absolute. It is all the same. How can it be set to one side? And, truly, I am complimented, as any woman would be, that you have thought thus of me, and have said so!" Her dress flared into pink for a moment, then dissolved into many-greens as her mood switched.

"We are arrived!" she announced, standing up as the car stopped. "I will show you my home, and the room that is to be yours."

He scrambled out, offering his arm. They had halted at the foot of a white stone stairway, leading up to a facade almost Greek in its massive simplicity. Delyra went ahead, a nymph in a cloud of green flame, to greet a huge and smiling yellow man, then a trio of women, two young, one elderly. Privileged servants, Spencer guessed, and hung back, discreetly. She turned to hail him, all aglow.

"Good news, Gordon! Another of the Five is already here, an hour since. Now you will have someone to talk with, to answer all your questions. Come . . ." and she led him through a magnificent doorway into a huge hall mosaic-floored, and to another flight of stairs, this time in darkly glossy wood. Catching up with her he protested, mildly.

"Am I so difficult to talk to?"

"It is not that," she laughed. "But Harly Thalog is a 'talker'. It is his function. You will see."

He was still trying to translate "talker" as she led him from his room along a picture-hung gallery, to a great oak door that had "committee room" built into its proportions. It swung open at their coming, and Spencer had a moment

of qualm. This was where he came unstuck. This was the
real thing. He went forward to meet the man who rose at
their entrance. A burly man, three inches shorter than
Spencer, clad simply in a blue velvet jerkin, leather-belted,
and caught at the waist with a curious copper buckle—like
an old-time huntsman. Dark leather sandals helped the illusion. But his complexion was glossy brown with blue shadows, and his scant hair, mustache and forked beard were all
gleaming silver. He put out a hand in greeting.

"Good afternoon, Mr. Spencer," he said, deep-voiced
and in flawless English. "I have looked forward to this moment. Welcome. Please take a seat."

Spencer met the handclasp automatically, swallowed his
surprise and remembered his manners. "You're Harly
Thalog, so Delyra told me. I'm honored, and a bit shaken
by your English. I hadn't expected that."

Thalog brushed it aside, chuckling. "You would like some
refreshment? Put my learning to the test . . ."

"I already know about coffee. That's out, isn't it?"

"I regret, it is quite true. No stimulants. But we do have
euphorics. Whisky, isn't it? And effervescence?"

"Make mine straight. With water. Please." Spencer found
a seat, and watched Thalog instruct Delyra. "You're some
linguist, sir," he commented, as he found the synonym for
"talker." "I feel even more of an imposter, now. I have no
comparable talent, at all."

"That has nothing to do with it," Thalog explained. "I am
a linguist, by function and training. Happily, when one
knows how a man speaks, one knows also how he thinks,
to a degree. Therefore I know that, to you, the ethical sense
is an uncomfortable thing. Hence your feeling of not-wor-
thiness, yes?"

"That's about it," Spencer nodded, thoughtfully. "With
us, ethical values are hardly definite enough to be workable.

Oh, we respect and admire an honest man . . . yes, but
the solid credits, somehow, seem to go to other things, to a
skill in some particular field, winning out in competition,
beating the next man to some goal, that kind of thing. That
must seem irrational to you. It does to me, sometimes."

"On the contrary," said Thalog, "this is a logical out-
come of the lack of genuine personal knowledge, and is
common in a culture like yours, where every man is an
island to himself. It is a stage which is left behind when the
personal barrier is broken down."

"As a culture, we must seem pretty primitive to you."

"Only in that sense," Thalog smiled. "Not offensively.
Ah, here come the drinkables."

Spencer accepted the tall glass offered him, watched
Delyra as she settled on a cushion close by, and waited for
Thalog to go on.

"A society, any society, must have a code," the burly
man murmured. "If the society is grouped on a sight and
sound level, the code must be one which can be put in
words, seen in actions, measured by material things. Having
no valid way of judging men as they are, it must go by what
they seem, and do. And such a code, perforce, is static.
But the society, like the individuals composing it, grows
and changes, the code becomes ill-fitting, breaks down. The
need for a code, however, is so urgent that another is
formed. And so-on. I have seen this process at work, in
your own histories, which I have studied. The result could
have been predicted. The code, now, is so refined that no
one can think of a better. Yet it is still irksome and restric-
tive. People chafe under it. But they dare not abandon it,
having nothing to put in its place. Am I being too elemen-
tary?"

"You're making it sound simple, anyway," Spencer
grinned. "Maybe I can go on from there. On your level,

with personal-power, every man can know his fellow man directly and positively—as he really is. So a stated, fixed code is no longer essential . . ."

"Now *you* are oversimplifying," Thalog chuckled. "But you have the general idea. The essential difference is that with us a man has no need for show, to amass great wealth, to perform great deeds—to demonstrate what he is. He just is, and we know." Spencer took a sip of his drink, which was excellent, and sighed, ruefully.

"Even that idea isn't new to us," he said. "We have had people, all down the ages, who felt that they could tell, somehow, whether a man was good, or not. Some of them, by all accounts, could actually do it. But we've never had it on any workable basis. It's difficult to imagine what it would be like, all at once. I take it you encounter . . . deficient races . . . like us . . . pretty often?"

"Ah, no. I didn't say that," Thalog leaned forward, interestedly. "We do run across undeveloped races. But all, so far, have had the power, in latent form. Where it is indicated, and appropriate, we admit them under supervision, and assist them to develop. It is a simple and quick process. But you"—he smiled, disarmingly—"you Solarians are unique. I know of no other culture, on record, which lacks the power altogether, like you. At this moment, for example, if I close my eyes, you are just 'not there,' at all. It is remarkable. And all the more remarkable, if you will forgive my being personal, that you should be Ethical Absolute."

"No more remarkable than it is to me," Spencer shrugged, wryly. "I have already gathered, from the princess, here, that I'm deformed to her way of thinking. Not offensively, of course!" He glanced to where she was sitting, and was suddenly apologetic. "This must be dull, for her, not understanding a word we are saying?"

"But she does know, through me. That, too, is my function. Now, I am curious about you. Tell me how it is that you, alone, of the Solarian worlds, bothered even to take the higher tests?"

"This is where I give myself away," Spencer muttered, and took a good pull at his glass. Then, "How do you know so much about the higher tests?"

"I set them," Thalog explained, simply, "and thus I can assure you there will be no giving away as you term it. Please go on."

So Spencer thought back, and told, wryly, of a certain day, four years ago, and of his colleague, Frank Wallis, who was forever amusing himself with tests, and quizzes, and crossword puzzles. Wallis, also, was a machine tutor, specializing in applied physics. Brain-wracking was just his way of beating monotony. Ethical quizzes, as soon as they began to appear, offered him something novel. Not that he ever took any of them seriously.

"It's an understood thing, with intelligent people at least, that such tests are worthless. These were of the 'What would you do if . . .' kind of thing. I kidded Frank about these latest ones. They were obvious questions, with obvious answers, I told him. And we had an argument. It ended with him handing me a paper—and a challenge. Put up or shut up. So I filled it out, sent it in—and forgot all about it." He put down his glass, and Delyra refilled it.

"Go on!" Thalog invited.

"Well, I had a slick letter from the secretary of what called itself 'The Ethical Association.' Would I care to try a really tough test. No prizes, and no obligation—just for interest. I couldn't see any harm in it, so I did. And it went on. There was one paper, I recall, where all the questions were loaded. Wide open, but loaded. 'Which is more important, the individual, or the society?' 'Should a person be free to take his own life?' That kind of thing. About twenty of them. I read right through, didn't mark one. There was a space for comment, at the bottom . . ."

"Where you wrote 'None of these questions can be answered as they stand, without additional data,'" Thalog interrupted, chuckling. "I saw a facsimile of that."

"But how do *you* come to be involved?"

"It is quite simple. When we of the galaxy make contact with a new culture, one of the things we seek to know is its ethical standard. This is to put flesh on the bones of its history. We have many methods, developed over a long time. In this case, because you already have an established interest in tests and quizzes, we were able to use those— plus a few 'hidden' tests. As a linguist, I had studied your languages. Those based on Indo-European roots, at any rate. It was natural, therefore, that I would be the person best able to set the tests. I must add, without wishing to give offense, that your all-over ethical level is much higher than I would have expected, from a blind culture." This gave Spencer a twinge of guilt. He realized he couldn't go on with the deception very much longer.

"That final test, on Ganymede," he said. "That was really something. I didn't think, even then, that it was a Galactic matter, just that some of our advanced fanatics must have borrowed some of your specialized equipment. It was like a polygraph run, with extras. My trouble is, I haven't the same all-embracing trust in gadgetry that you seem to have. I've seen things go wrong, or be misread . . ." then he caught his breath. "Look," he said, "would you put me right with the princess? I've just remembered that I told her this was my first trip off Earth. And it isn't. I'd forgotten that trip to the testing station, on Ganymede!" Thalog laughed, a big, round, rolling laugh.

"That is quite all right," he soothed, between chuckles. "I

will explain. But, you see, your concern for truth confirms
the diagnosis. The machine made no mistake."

"As you say," Spencer shrugged, still not liking the idea
that a machine would know him better than he knew himself, but admitting the possibility. "And, while you're at it,
would you explain to her what a science-historian does? It
comes out all wrong, in Galactalk."

"A trade language," Thalog made a face. "Everyone must
speak it, but no one speaks it well. A crude instrument."
He turned aside to speak to Delyra, and Spencer watched,
in fascination, the flow and change of the tints of her garment. Given a little time, he thought, he could learn to
"read" her by that alone. Then it occurred to him that he
could achieve the same thing with a simple flick of his
tongue, and he lost himself in a cloud of wondering why
he could accept one, but not the other. A mellow gong
boomed in the distance, and he roused himself to see
Delyra hurrying away.

"The others are here," Thalog explained. "They, too, will
be keen to meet you. Please make use of me for translation,
it is my function. But, tell me, did you understand the principle of the test machine, on Ganymede?"

"I think so. My reactions were recorded . . . physical
responses, chemical changes, brain rhythms . . . we know
about those. But the projections I was asked to watch—
they were really something. I wish some of that material
could be made available for Earth, for teaching purposes."

"But surely you have the techniques and the facilities
for making such reconstructions of your own sociology and
history?"

"Not like that." Spencer was suddenly enthusiastic. "They
were strictly honest and factual. No prejudice, bias, or

judgments passed, at all. Of course, it was easier for you,
being alien, to be objective."

"Of course," Thalog said, dryly, and Spencer had to grin.

"Lord knows what you must think of us. But, you know,
I was baffled by the whole thing. After the test—nothing!
Until, months later, I had a card. Would I agree to being
put on a waiting list, with the chance of taking part in a
group-decision, sometime? No compulsion, no encourage-
ment—just take it or leave it. Isn't that an odd way to go
about it?"

"Is it? You made your choice, didn't you?"

"That's true. And here I am, for what difference it may
make . . ."

The far door swung open, and Delyra came hurrying in.
Spencer got up, nervously. Thalog went past him a step
or two, held out a hand to indicate.

"Than Simnel." He nodded to a small blue-gray man in
a silver-white robe. "Fasla-en-Narsis." She might have
stepped down from a mountain village in Italy, were it not
for her gorgeous silks. She managed to look old, grim, lively,
and yet not unattractive. "And Rik Wiswood." He was as
tall as Spencer, bald, grave and ordinary-looking, close-
clad in black leather. "This is the Solarian, Gordon
Spencer." In a brief aside, he added: "A nod suffices. We
do not shake hands, here." They all found seats and settled,
in easy quiet. Then Thalog stood up, looked round.

"Some of us have met before. All of us save Spencer
have taken part in at least one major decision. But this is
the first time we have met as a Five. As the 'question' was
put to me, originally, with the request that I summon a
Five—and as it was my summons which brought you here,
I propose that I shall act as 'Leader' and have the casting
vote. Agreed?" Spencer nodded with the rest.

"Very well. Now, before stating the question formally, are there any minor matters to settle?"

"A point." Simnel's sharp voice matched his smallness, chopping his Galactalk into jerky phrases. "Make clear—for Spencer—difference between formality and detail. Long, or short."

"Of course." Thalog turned aside, explained. "Some questions can be settled at once, on inspection. Then the thing is over, very quickly. But, if there is reasonable doubt, then further data, further discussion, is called for. The vote should be 'withhold.' There follows a long and detailed session of investigation. You understand?" There was a tiny twinkle in his eye.

"Snap decisions are frowned on, eh?"

"Not really. You must speak as you find. All the same, it is not often that such as we can come together like this, and enjoy the exchange of ideas . . ." He let it hang there. Spencer hid a smile. Then he had a question of his own.

"Suppose," he said, "that one of us had refused the invitation, for any one of a number of reasons? Myself, for instance?"

"Another would have been asked, until a Five was achieved."

"So there was no special reason for asking me?"

"On the contrary. I would have been most disappointed had you not come. But it was just simple curiosity. I wanted to meet you."

Spencer digested that, silently. There were no more preliminary questions.

"Very well." Thalog nodded. "I will now put the formal 'question.' From the Supreme Overlord of the Sofam sector we are asked to decide whether or not a new culture, comprising a three-star system, seven inhabited planets and minor outposts, be admitted to that sector, and, if admitted, on what level?"

"Withhold!" Fasla-en-Narsis said, promptly. "What else, on *that* question?"

"How say the rest of you?" Thalog looked round, met a chorus of agreement. "That will do, then I will instruct the expository delegation to attend us, tomorrow." He sat, and the formal atmosphere snapped like a thread. "Now, would any of you care to sample a typical Solarian potion? It has merit, I assure you. And, friend Spencer, we will introduce you to some of ours."

Somehow, and Spencer was never quite sure just how, he found himself fitting into the group like one finger of a hand. Curiosity was never offensive, confidences were swapped freely, opinions offered and analyzed, subtleties were understood despite the language barriers, and the amount of unprejudiced information he absorbed was even more heady than the various exotic tipples he tried, on their advice. It was late before the group finally broke apart. Walking carefully, he made his way to his room, and went to sleep in a warm glow that was not all liquor-inspired. It had been enlarging just to be free, forthright and candid, knowing that the other fellow was being the same, with no holds barred, no offense offered or taken.

And he had learned that the galaxy had its bad ones, too. Personal-power, like any other natural force, was available for the crooks, the villains, the unethical as well as the ethical. Again, ethical standards had the defects of their virtues. You respected another man's privacy, for instance —and, if he was ill-intentioned, you gave him an advantage. It sounded very familiar, to Spencer. But the big difference, he had found, was the attitude, and the judgment. It was justice, here, not law. You didn't measure a man by some "code." He was known for what he was, and judged accordingly. And the verdict was seldom "punishment," but "restitution." That was strange, at first, but he liked it. This was the way things ought to be, he thought.

Thanks to good health and a clean constitution, he was reasonably clearheaded when a chime woke him, in the morning. Sitting up in bed, he frowned at the stranger who stood in the doorway. A lean, keen-eyed man, medium-tall, wisp-bearded and businesslike in dark-blue velvet—yet familiar, somehow.

"Excuse me," he said, in careful Galactalk, "I am Garnol Taynee. I came after you, on the next ship, and arrived but a few moments ago. I trust you have been made more comfortable here than on your journey."

Spencer added it all together, swiftly, and felt embarrassed. "You must be Delyra's father—my host!" he made a futile gesture. "I am sorry I did not have the chance to thank you for your kindness . . ." Taynee cut him short with a shake of the head, came to the bedside.

"That was nothing," he said. "My privilege. My concern is that you were attacked. I feel a responsibility. I have made inquiries and I think you should know, Great One, that the attack was indeed meant for you. This is hard to believe but my inquiries show no trace that I was the intended victim."

"I never thought otherwise," Spencer sat forward, hugging his knees. "But it wasn't for me to press it. Did you get any definite information . . . about the men . . . or the man behind it?"

"Almost nothing. The men were casuals, taken aboard at Hanlar. Beyond that, nothing at all!"

"Planet of origin?"

"They were Latvas—a minor race, in the Sofam sector, I think. Why, is that significant?"

"I wish I knew." Spencer scratched his chin. "Frankly, a Galactic sector is a pretty vague item, to me. And I can't imagine why somebody from that area should want me out of the way."

"It is a hard thing to believe," Taynee said, gravely. "But you will be quite safe here, at least. And welcome. It is a great honor."

Which was all very fine, Spencer mused, as he dressed and made his way back to the committee room, but if Latvas could ship in to Chaldun as casual ship-crew, there was no reason why a whole bunch of them might not already have come in the same way, and with the same lethal intent. He found Wiswood in the room already, and helping himself to the contents of a tray. Settling in a seat, Spencer put the question bluntly.

"What would be a good reason for anyone wanting to kill me?"

"I could think of reasons," Wiswood frowned, giving the question impartial weighing, "but not good ones. I'd need more data."

"These were Latvas, acting under orders."

Wiswood dropped his abstract air, and stared. "You mean, this has actually happened to *you?* Forgive me, I thought you were speaking theoretically. But this is fantastic. You are sure?"

"You can ask the princess, she was there. And Garnol Taynee has just told me . . ." Spencer gave him the details, keeping back only his own personal secret. Wiswood listened, wide-eyed. Fasla-en-Narsis came in, frankly, yawning, her hair drawn into severe plaits, but the sleep left her face as she got the account. Spencer told the tale a third time, to Simnel, and watched all their faces, keenly, but there was nothing but blank surprise.

"It must have been error," Fasla-en-Narsis spoke for all

of them. "No one would offer violence like this . . . to one of us. We are custodians"—she gave Spencer an odd, withdrawn look—"as is anyone who possesses a talent. It is not ours to buy or sell. It belongs to humanoid life. We are merely the carriers, the agents. When one of us dies, it is the galaxy's loss. To kill one of us in unthinkable!"

"But someone thought of it," Spencer insisted, "and, in the circumstances, the idea of accident is even more unlikely than the intention. There is one hypothesis that occurs to me, though. You say no one would think of offering violence to a Great One. But . . . how do you know that I am . . . one of you?"

"That is rubbish!" Thalog boomed, from the door. "We *know*. If by nothing else, the very fact that you put such a question speaks for itself!"

"All right," Spencer agreed, but persisted along his line of thought. *"You* know . . . but it might not be as clearcut for someone else. I recall a phrase the princess used—that everybody knows Solarians are defective."

"You insult yourself unnecessarily," Thalog smiled. "The princess was guilty of an understandable exaggeration. Great sections of the galaxy have never even heard of Solarians. See here . . ." he reached for a metallic plate which hung on the wall. Spencer had seen it without understanding its purpose. Now he saw Thalog pull out a slim stylus from the bottom edge, and use it to scrawl a large circle.

"The galaxy," he said, and drew radii from the center. "Crudely, these are sectors. This, here, is Ferl, where we are now. Next to it is Dorn. On the other side is Sofam. Then Gemeal . . ." and he had accounted for less than an eighth of the disk. "Those are the family names of the elder races, the Overlords. I am of Dorn. So is Fasla. Simnel is of Gemeal. Wiswood is a Ferl, and is on home ground, as it were. But this is merely a convenience. We are a trader culture, and travel is our cheapest commodity. I could stun your mind with numbers, but I will not. Frankly, they stun me, too. Yet, in all this great congress of peoples, no one would think of offering harm to a Great One. It must have been error that you were attacked."

Spencer realized that he was not going to get any further with his ideas, and sat back, letting the conversation run between them. He couldn't escape his own thought, though. He kept seeing a strong analogy between his adventure and the familiar "home" tactics of bringing bias to bear on a jury. It looked as if somebody badly wanted him out of the way, and it could be for no other reason than to swing the verdict on this coming "question." If only he could find out who, and which way, he might offer to co-operate . . . He caught that thought back, ruefully. Being what he was, he would speak as he found, come what may, and no sort of pressure would change that.

"Your expression indicates a bad taste in the mouth, friend Spencer," Thalog broke in on his musings. "Do not let this thing worry you overmuch."

"I'm not . . . not the way you mean," Spencer smiled, wryly. "I'm just beginning to appreciate, all over again, that I am what I am, and I'm stuck with it. Tell me, suppose someone wanted to influence us, to put pressure on us, as a Five . . . ?" Thalog tightened his usually benevolent expression.

"You disappoint me, a little, my friend. I suppose it is natural for you to think in terms of your own culture, but you should try to realize that we do not think thus. We do not use force in that way."

Spencer was on the point of pressing the "suppose" just once more, when Delyra appeared. She was keen to show him round the estate, and he decided to accept her offer. There was a sudden woolliness, a feeling of thrusting at shadows, between him and the others. He felt the need to get away from them, for a while.

This morning, she was wearing what was almost a sweater, in white fleece, and snug-fitting breeches so Earth-like that he had a pang of homesickness. She led him to an outbuilding and made him known to a pair of overwhelming animals, more like overgrown St. Bernard dogs than anything else he could think of.

"I should have guessed that was riding kit," he commented, studiously trying to conceal his nervousness for the massive beasts.

"You approve this kind of dress?" she asked, anxiously. "Harly Thalog told me that your women dress thus when riding."

"Considerate of you . . . but I wish I felt happier about the animals."

"The droy? But they are quite harmless . . . watch!" and she got aboard hers by the simple expedient of commanding it to crouch, and walking along a paw to its shoulder. Then she watched while he did likewise.

He felt like a character from an old print as they shambled away round the angle of the outbuilding and into a long lane. There was no harness. You just caught hold of the knotty fur and hung on. They made for a low crest, about half a mile off, and by the time they had reached it he had learned something of the rhythm of movement of his mount. It was quite an experience. And quite an estate, too, as he could now see. She pointed out two orchards, a floral garden, a pool, and a large area, stretching back up the hill opposite, that was quite wild. Planned that way, he guessed. He also guessed, aloud, that it must take a small army of staff to run a place this size. But he was quite wrong. She explained.

One man, on his own, took care of all the "outside," so far as growing was concerned. Another took care of the livestock. Two women ran the huge house. One elderly woman supervised, and "mothered" Delyra in between times. And one more man, a major domo, was executive over all, responsible only to Garnol Taynee. Six people. He tried to explain to her that it would have taken possibly fifty, on Earth, to do the same job. Psionics made all the difference. And why not, he thought. But it made Garnol Taynee's assurances of safety seem thin and empty, suddenly. Then Delyra sat high on her mount, to point.

"There!" she cried. "It must be the delegation coming." He strained his eyes where she pointed, saw a distant blur on the white road, but could make nothing of it. But she was confident. "Yes, yes, they are coming!" she repeated, and put her droy into a lumbering gallop.

Spencer grabbed, and hung on as his own mount followed. This was a different rhythm, and for a few fast minutes he was all over that broad back, until he chanced on the right spot, just behind the shoulder blades. Then it wasn't so bad. As for Delyra, she might have been sitting in a glue-patch for all the concern she showed. They went down the hill, swung round the house, and into the long lane which led to the entrance gate. He didn't know whether to be glad or sorry by the time they lumbered to a stop just inside the great gates. Taynee stood there. He raised a hand in greeting, but there was concern in his smile.

"You are comfortable?" he asked. "I fear Delyra did not ask whether you had ridden a droy before."

"That's all right," Spencer grinned. "I managed, but I reckon I've had enough, for the moment."

"Of course," Taynee made a faint gesture and the great beast crouched so that Spencer could scramble down. He gave the woolly side a hearty pat, and Taynee came round, close by.

"I will mount, now," he said. "As master of the house, it is fitting for me to greet my guests so. A formality, you understand?"

"I see." Spencer nodded. "You want me to retire? I can conceal myself in the bushes, if you like?"

"Not at all. You may do as you please. Formality is not for you."

So Spencer moved to stand by the furry leg of Delyra's mount, and she slid to the ground to stand by him. The cavalcade drew near. In the lead floated a magnificent car, silent, and full of glitter.

"The representatives of the Great Overlord of Sofam," Delyra explained in a whisper. "The Chief Minister"—a weathered and wrinkled old man, seemingly shrunken inside his ornate robes—"and the supervisors of the new culture"—four more, not quite so brilliantly garbed. All stiff and dignified—and green.

Spencer was so caught by their color, and the offputting cast of their features, that he could not be sure—it was just an impression—that sight of him had startled one or two of the "supervisors" out of their poise. It was just a fleeting impression, but he tucked it away for future reference.

There followed, impressively, twelve droy of a different breed, smooth-haired and fast-looking, two by two. And a great heavily-built yellow man on each. Spencer forgot his poise enough to stare, for these might have been brothers to the two assassins who had set about him, on the ship. He watched them jog by, and strove to comfort himself with thoughts of coincidence. At their heels came two long floats, boxed in and inscrutable. These, he guessed, would contain the exposition materials. Then there came another silent floating car, not nearly as magnificent as the first, carrying six men. And this time, Spencer stared openly.

Bronzed, they were, and beak-nosed, with that combination of high-pitch alertness and complete ease which is the hallmark of one class of men, and one only. For looks, they could have doubled for typical Amerinds. Their dress was functional in a way that gave Spencer a pang of homesickness. Change the silver for drab, change a button or two, a fold here and there—and these men were a squad, were typical field-troops. A lieutenant and five, Spencer guessed, and would have staked his life on the rightness of the guess.

"Those will be the representative members of the culture," Delyra whispered, and Spencer nodded, thoughtfully. So much he had guessed, but something, very faintly, was beginning to smell all wrong to him. The tail of the cavalcade, yet another dozen hefty yellow men on droys, served only to make his inner uneasiness grow stronger. He had a query for Delyra.

"Those men?" she frowned. "They are just servants. Handlers. To help with the setting-up of the exposition. Why?"

"Would they be Latvas, d'you think?"

"You are associating them with the unfortunate business on the ship?" Taynee had overheard, and looked down, keenly. "They may be of that race but, I assure you, there can be no connection. Not here."

Spencer let it go, and, mounted behind Delyra, rode back to the house. At any other time he might have been embarrassed at snuggling so closely to her, but now his thoughts were such that he scarcely noticed she was there at all.

He knew, from experience, that there was such a thing as selective "blindness." When a man firmly believes that such-and-so a thing is not possible, he will refuse to see or hear it, no matter how obvious it may be. And he had no reason to doubt that the same was possible, even on a psionic level. The awkward part was that he had no way of finding out. In the very nature of the thing, it would be useless to ask a man, outright, if he was failing to "see" something.

The exposition was thorough, protracted, crammed with detail, and done with a high degree of expertise. The great hall had been commandeered for the purpose, and Spencer stuck close to Thalog, asking questions and studying the exhibits, alert for one or two themes. What he saw disturbed him—and what he did not see disturbed him even more.

The culture group in question, known as Kallone, dominated a three-sun system, each within a light-year of the other two, each with a planetary family. In all there were seven habitable planets and a scattering of outposts. The given figure for total population was big enough to be meaningless, until Spencer thought of it as Earth-times-seven. It was a frightening thought. He eyed the exhibits, the artifacts, the pictorial records, and the underlying motif was plain to see. In the equivalent of five hundred years, the Kallone had spread from a continent to a planet, had jumped to another planet, then another. The same drive was obvious, all through. Do it better, faster, bigger, expand, grow, push . . . then burst and leap . . . attack, subjugate, dominate . . . and do it all over again.

"You've seen this kind of thing often?" he asked Thalog, and the burly man shrugged.

"Not quite like this. All cultures have common factors, of course, but each has its own differences, too. The rate of spread, here, is faster than anything I have heard of. Also, as you can see, they have achieved integration and interstellar combination before making the breakthrough in atomic structure and power. That is highly unusual. Of course, their star system encouraged that. Also, as you can see here, this nebular dust cloud shuts them off, largely, from knowledge of the rest of the galaxy. That is why they have remained out of contact for so long. Surely, friend Spencer, they must remind you very much of your own culture?"

"They do," Spencer said, as flatly as he could manage. "They are so like us that the missing items seem to stand out."

"Missing items?"

"Right. Look, for instance, at the great dependence on physical power for almost everything—up to a point. But . . . well, such a culture should be very highly sophisticated as to weapons, and I have seen none, apart from a few primitive models, more symbols than anything else."

"What could be more natural?" Thalog made a gesture. "We have no great interest in weapons, of any kind. A maturing culture tends to leave such things to the past."

Spencer had his own opinions on that. He asked another question on the same theme, distracting Thalog, who was fingering a book. "Tell me," he said, "does the galaxy, or the Galactic Federation as a whole, or any sector of it, mount and operate a striking force . . . an army . . . a fleet . . . warships?"

Thalog sighed, meaningly. "Of course not," he said. "These things are, shall we say, common at a certain stage of development. It is a primitive thought-pattern, to think that anything can be settled by the use of force. With maturity there comes a sense of unity, of shared relationships and purposes, of co-operation. I am a little disappointed at your preoccupation with ideas of force, Spencer. Almost, you make me wonder if, after all, the test-machines have made an error in your case." He said it very gently, obviously trying to avoid being harsh.

But Spencer set his jaw. "That's a bit better," he said, grimly. "Now you're getting to know how I've been feeling all along. And now you can get an idea of how somebody else may be thinking, too!" Inwardly, he added "I'd like to know just who" and he shot a quick glance around, at the various faces watching.

The six Kallone stood in a bunch, in a clear space in the middle of the exhibits, deliberately aloof, giving nothing away. The Chief Minister had found a chair, at the far end of the hall and was deep in his own thoughts. Spencer glanced from him to the four who were responsible for the show, and shivered. All their eyes were on him, it seemed. He recalled that half-seen flicker of surprise, and tried to be objective about the sense of malevolence he felt. It was the unfortunate color of their faces, he told himself, and the strongly defined brow-ridges. They couldn't help the way they looked. Just the same, he hurried to join up with Thalog again. The burly man had his nose in another book, and was obviously managing to read it. Spencer caught his attention.

"If the verdict is favorable," he asked, "what then?"

"In detail, many things," Thalog nodded, thoughtfully. "In general, the Kallone culture will become the ward of the Sofam. The four you see . . . you would call them 'Protectors' . . . it will be their task to integrate the new culture and take charge of them, as quickly as is reasonably possible."

"How do you know it will be these four?"

"It is in the records," Thalog was patient. "These are the men who found and investigated the Kallone system. It is they who are making the request, who are putting the question."

"But I thought it was the Kallone people themselves who were doing that?"

"Of course . . . but through the Sofam representatives, who speak for them."

"Oh. Yes, I see . . ." A sudden light began to dawn in Spencer's mind, but he restrained it, cautiously, changed the line of questioning. "About the other thing, the personal powers?"

"We have a simple and efficient group-method for awakening the latent power, very quickly. The Kallone have the potential, in latent form."

"There's no doubt about that, then? That you will . . . I mean, their Overlords will . . . make them a present of full 'personal-power' capabilities? That is taken for granted?"

"But of course!" Thalog was having trouble, now, maintaining his calm patience. "Because these people have the latent power, it would be possible for us to dominate and manipulate them . . . to take an unfair advantage. That would violate every ethic we hold dear. It is our duty to bring them into full personal-power status, as quickly as possible."

"I see your point," Spencer nodded. He did, too. This was logic, and ethics, and selective blindness, all mingled in a web that he could see no way through. He had a sudden feeling of futility. "All right," he sighed. "Now . . . tell me how we cast our ballot." And watched as Thalog showed him the three signs—"For," "Against," and "Withhold."

He knew, now, how he was going to vote. This, he thought, could decide the fate of a culture. Never had he felt less competent, or more convinced. With the end of the exposition in sight, he saw one of the Protectors approach the Chief Minister and confer, in whispers, stiffly. Then the old man got up, made his way to where the Five were grouped. Spencer studied that old face, keenly, trying to

guess what thoughts were hidden under the mask. Then
Thalog went forward, and the two met at a distance from
the group. There was more hushed whispering. Now Spencer
could gather, from Thalog's back, that he was rejecting
something, vigorously. He wondered what. The burly man
came back, his face a study in careful control.

"The Chief Minister, Gal Horro, informs us that this con-
cludes the presentation of material evidence . . . and will
we decide now, or go on to examine further evidence?" He
looked at them, interrogatively. "We could try a decision,
now, if you wish? Simnel?" The little man made a gesture
in favor. Wiswood signed "Withhold." So did Fasla-en-
Narsis. Thalog's eye fell on Spencer, and he sagged, inwardly. Wishing himself anywhere but here, he made his
sign "Against"—and caught, again, that flash of malevolence
from one of the onlooking Protectors. Thalog nodded.

"Mine is the casting vote," he said, in a curious tone. "I
will cast with Spencer . . . but this is not final. Come, I
think we need a consultation." He led them away to the
committee room. When they had settled, he put the question to Spencer, flatly. "You voted against. I'm sure you had
good reasons. You will please explain them to me, and I
will convey the sense of it to the others."

"Your vote was 'Against,' also," Spencer reminded him.
"How about your reasons?" Thalog frowned, pursed his lips.

"Very well. That is just. I had many reasons. One, I
wanted to keep the question open a little while longer, because I am interested in various odd aspects of the Kallone
culture. Two, because I am bothered about you, friend
Spencer, and wish to hear more of how you think, in this
instance. Three, because, when Gal Horro approached me,
just now, it was to say that an objection has been raised,
against the validity of this Five!"

"Against me, you mean," Spencer put it, swiftly, while

the others were gasping their protest. "Did the Chief Minister say just who had raised the ban?"

"I gathered that it came from the Kallone," Thalog said, with a frown. "Where else?"

"That's what you were meant to think. But if you really think, it's nonsense. Isn't it? I never heard of the Kallone before today—"

"Must be the Kallone!" Simnel put in, excitedly. "No Galactic would dream of questioning the validity of a Five. It is unthinkable!"

"All right, it's unthinkable," Spencer stood up, and looked at the four pairs of eyes which looked back at him, curiously. "You people talk much more than I had anticipated. The idea of being able to read a man's mind is a hard one to shake. But it isn't like that, at all. You talk. A lot. And that's my only hope. I have to try to convince you that admitting the Kallone to full Galactic status would be just about the most insane thing you could do. And I can give you only some of my reasons."

"Why not all?" Thalog asked, quietly.

"Because I'm not able to give evidence on some of them, only my feelings, and you can't feel them. I'd like to ask a question, though, just to clear one point in my own mind. Can personal-power be used as a striking weapon? I don't mean as persuasion, but as a literal force?"

"Always this preoccupation with force, with weapons!" Thalog shook his head. Spencer eyed him, then looked at the rest.

"Won't somebody answer?"

"It is just . . . possible," Fasla-en-Narsis nodded. "Although my mind shrinks from the thought. But why do you want to know?"

"On the ship, coming here," Spencer said, evenly, "I was attacked, and the two men who made the attack were car-

rying knives. It has occurred to me that this was unnecessary. They could have strangled me, or killed me in any one
of many other ways, without laying a finger on me."

"But that would not have worked with you!" Simnel put
in, excitedly, "because you are . . ." and he stopped suddenly.

Spencer grinned, without humor, as he saw the change in
their faces, now. "I'm defective, yes. I'll say it for you. So
personal-power would not have affected me. Quite so. And
those two men knew that, beforehand. That is why they
were armed. They must have known who I was . . . yes?"
He let a tense moment go by, then added, softly, "Who's
going to be the first to say 'Unthinkable' . . . now? Or
blame it on the Kallone?"

"But . . ." Wiswood was obviously struggling with a new
idea, "you are trying to tell us that someone, deliberately,
wanted you removed, knowing who you were—simply in order to influence the decision of this Five!"

"That's right. That is what I have been saying, all along,
but, to you, it was 'Unthinkable.' Thalog, you accuse me of
being preoccupied with thoughts of force, and weapons. I
will not argue. I will accuse you, all four of you, in your
turn, of being stuck with the idea that certain things, even
though they happen right before your eyes, are unthinkable. This is a blind attitude. If you persist in it, I can do
nothing to convince you of my other points."

"You are asking us to set aside the values of centuries,"
Thalog rumbled. "It is not easy."

"It isn't exactly simple for me, either," Spencer snapped,
and was immediately apologetic. "I'm sorry, but I'm the
target, here, and it isn't easy. Look, let's leave my personal
problems, for the moment. I want you to face something
which is even more unthinkable than what you've already

met. I want you to get out of your heads the idea that the Kallone are primitive, or inferior in any way. I want you to make an effort, and try to see them as the equals of any Galactic culture. Can you?"

"Why should we?" Fasla-en-Narsis asked, curiously. "In our terms they are a primitive culture. They lack the personal-power . . ."

"And that's *all* they lack!" Spencer interrupted, pointedly. "This is a race which has, in five hundred years, dominated first a planet, then a system, then two more nearby systems— some fifteen billion people—and all by the skilled and efficient use of force and physical power. You will admit that, I think, Thalog? You saw enough to detect the pattern?"

"It is true enough, yes. But what are you trying to say?"

"A blind man learns to use his ears far more efficiently than a man who can see. He does not have better hearing. He just uses what he has, better. I can see and hear, reasonably well. So can most of my fellow men of Earth. But if it becomes necessary to follow a scent trail, we have to use an animal—just because we have neglected our sense of smell, in favor of other senses. In the same way, you have personal-power. You are born and grow up with it. You use it continuously. Consequently, you have neglected other things . . . the speed of thought and action that a 'deficient' race takes for granted. Where you automatically think in terms of reason and argument, and appeal to ethic the man of force thinks in terms of strongest and fastest. I am of such a culture, and know whereof I speak. We have sayings: 'May the best man win,' 'The first with the most,' 'The best form of defense is attack'—and many more. May I say, here, that these are not my personal beliefs—but they are common in my culture. The Kallone culture is almost the twin of my own, therefore the same, or similar, values will hold, there."

"But, don't you see, Spencer," Thalog was very patient, "this is exactly why they are inferior. Such is not the thinking of a truly mature culture."

"Thinking! I'm not talking about thinking, but action. These people, in action, are not in any way inferior to you. What they lack in one thing, they more than make up in others. A full-blown Galactic might be able to keep control over a Kallone, by personal-power. . . ."

"But that would be unethical . . ." Wiswood put in, and then stopped.

"Unthinkable?" Spencer demanded, sharply. "Are you beginning to get it? Are you, at last, beginning to see that the one superiority you have over the Kallone is the one thing you insist on giving away to them?"

"We must give them equal status," Thalog insisted, puzzledly. "What else can we do?"

Spencer sighed. This was even harder than he had imagined. "Scales!" he said, spreading his hands apart. "Equal balance . . . right? Now, take one item from this pan, put it in that . . . is it still equal?"

"What does that mean?" Fasla-en-Narsis snapped.

"Just that you are inferior, in many ways, to the Kallone. Your personal-power maintains the balance. Change that, and the balance is lost, in their favor, in favor of a culture which excels in force. I tell you, give the Kallone full status, give them personal-power, and they will explode. On Earth we have a saying about putting a lethal weapon in the hands of a child. You are about to make a present of just such a weapon to a culture which has as its ethic the expert and ruthless use of force."

"I object," Simnel said, suddenly, "to the suggestion that I am slow, feeble and physically inferior. I am not large, as you see, but I claim to be as physically fit as any person my size!"

Spencer put out his hand to take up a small bronze bowl. It fitted comfortably into his palm. He had had his eye on it for some time. Now, with no warning, he tossed it across the long table to Simnel. The bowl glinted, slowed in its flight, and slid down to be gripped in the little man's palm. Simnel grinned, shook it.

"You see? I was quick!"

"Toss it back," Spencer asked, quietly. Catching the thing, he gave the little man a square stare. "Let's try that again, *without* personal-power?"

Simnel's eyes widened. Then, shrugging, he said, "Very well. I will try."

Some seconds later, the bowl clattered to the floor. He missed it several more times. So did all the rest. Spencer was pleased, in an oblique way, to see that they were becoming irritable. He put the bowl aside, reached for the drawing plate on the wall, eyed Simnel once more. Then he drew, quickly two horizontal lines, crossed them with two verticals, and beckoned the little man.

"This is the diagram," he said, "of a very simple problem game that we know, on Earth, as ticktactoe, noughts and crosses, and other names. It is the most simple form of battle strategy I can think of." He went on to explain the rules.

Simnel lost the first five games in a row, in growing irritation. Then he caught on to the technique, and forced a stalemate. Then two more, and Spencer called a halt. "That will do," he decided. "Just remember the figures. Now, let's go and talk to the Kallone." He led the way out of the committee room, and Thalog fell in beside him. The burly man was his calm self again.

"There are other things on your mind," he said, quietly. "Your argument is a good one, but thin. Something else bothers you, I think?"

"That's good guessing," Spencer admitted. "There are

quite a few other things on my mind, but I can't talk about them, not without getting into deep water. I'll say this, though. I'm not against the Kallone. I just don't want to see them smashed up. I have a pretty shrewd idea what it would do to my own people if they were to be given personal-power, just like that. Translation from the ethic of force to the ethic of reason is not something to be done in one breath. The wiser men of my own culture have debated this for many years, and without any simple answers forthcoming."

"Your people have debated personal-power?" Thalog asked, wonderingly. "But . . . there was nothing of this, in your literature. How—?"

"Don't ask," Spencer hushed him. "That's one of the things I have no business talking about. Point is, right now . . . can you speak Kallone?"

"I'm a linguist, not a magician," Thalog protested. "I can follow their script fairly well . . . but one of the Sofam will act as interpreter for us, I imagine."

They had reached the main hall, but none of the Sofam were in sight, apart from the old Chief Minister. Nor were any of the yellow men visible. The six Kallone stood, alertly at ease, in the midst of the exhibits, impassive but watching the Five. Thalog called the Chief Minister with a gesture, and the old man came close, his uniform glittering oddly against his withered form. Spencer took time to study him, deciding that it was, indeed, his unfortunate color that gave the impression of dislike. The man himself appeared sensible enough. But regretful. Thalog shook his head.

"Gal Horro explains that he has had no contact with the Kallone. This was all done by the four Protectors. I will call them."

"No!" Spencer stopped him. "It's just as well they're not here. You can manage with this . . ." and he held out the drawing plate. Thalog shrugged.

"If you insist. I wish I knew what was in your mind, Spencer."

"I hope you will, soon enough," Spencer said, eyed the Kallone, and made a gesture to indicate that he wanted them to spread out in a semicircle round him. They did so, with every indication that they carried some sort of resentment for him. That was another little datum that he tucked away for a future consideration. For now, once they were to his liking, he said, over his shoulder to the rest of the Five, "Please watch, and note." He tossed the little bowl, without warning, to the man directly in front of him. The Kallone picked it out of the air without visible effort, and, at Spencer's invitation, tossed it back. As it met his palm, Spencer twisted his wrist, sent it spinning to the man at his left. As it was returned, he threw it again. And again.

"I hope that made you think," he said, turning to the rest of them, after the little demonstration had included each of the six men. "Please note their expressions. They are amused, and a little contemptuous, don't you think? Now, bring the plate, and let's try this man." He advanced, with Thalog, to the man on the right. It took a moment or two to communicate the basic elements of the game. It took the Kallone just one defeat to learn the strategy, such as it was. The next five games were stalemate. The look of contempt had become quite pronounced, now.

"You've made your point," Wiswood said, frankly, "but I don't see that it is very important. They are fit. Their reflexes, physical and mental, are better than ours. But what has that to do with personal-power?"

"Just this. These people have an ethic, and a very strong one, already. They have their own ideas on honesty and fair play, within the framework of what they know. They fight fair. At least, I am assuming so. Please note the phrase 'fight fair.' Assuming, again, a parallel between this culture and my own, to affect a man's mind is *not* fair—in their terms. It is something quite new, and will automatically be regarded as a new weapon."

"The idea of fighting fair," Fasla-en-Narsis interrupted, "is quite without meaning to us, however familiar it may be to you. Could you meet one of these men, in a fight?" Spencer sighed. He had half-foreseen this.

"I suspect," he said, "that any one of these men could make a fool of me in a fight. They are all professionals."

"Yet you overcame two assassins, did you not?"

"That was a different matter altogether. Still, it is a reasonable point, and I am prepared to make a spectacle of myself, if it will help."

He cast his eye over the six Kallone, and picked out, by guess, the leader, that one he had classed as "lieutenant" in his own mind. Calling Thalog to help, he approached the man. "Explain to him," he said, "as carefully as you can, that I would like to engage him in a friendly trial of skill. Please be sure to stress 'friendly.' This floor is hard, and I have no wish to have my skull split."

He let the burly man busy himself with the drawing plate and gestures, while he stripped off his suitcoat and shirt. He was not looking forward to this, at all, nor was he in any way hopeful that the tussle would convince anybody. The idea of force as a way of life was too much for these Galactics to grasp, all at once.

Within minutes, the Kallone leader had grasped the idea, and peeled off his tunic. Studying the flat-muscled hardness opposing him, Spencer calculated that he had a slight advantage in height, reach, and weight. And he had been attentive in Judo classes. He was going to need all that.

Spencer managed a friendly grin, struck out a feint, and the Kallone brushed it aside, armed him off, jabbed a return, and swayed as his thrust was parried. They circled, cautiously. Spencer tried again, got an armlock and was jolted out of it by a hard elbow to the ribs. He went back, came in again, and met the Kallone face to face, in a bear-hug. Then, despite his straining, he was swept off his feet and put down, none too gently, on his back. The Kallone sneered, fell back, let him get up. Then he darted in again, and was thrown, clean and solid, over Spencer's knee. It was Spencer's turn to stand back and let him get up.

Looking puzzled, and wary, the Kallone came back in. There was a quick flurry of arms, and the knee-throw didn't work at all, this time. Instead, it was Spencer who went down, on his face, in a shoulder-cracking armlock. Once more, the Kallone let go and danced back, but he was grinning, now.

Spencer grinned, too, ruefully, and worked his arm. "Play you one more," he said, and was certain that his meaning was taken, even if the words weren't. They came together solidly, grunting and twisting, feeling for holds. Then the Kallone went over and down, flat on his back, to a hip-throw. Spencer stood back, working hard for breath, to let him get up. Then he stuck out a hand, shook his head.

In Galactalk, he said, "Enough. You are too good for me. Too quick."

To his surprise, the Kallone nodded, grinning, and said, in the same tongue, "That was well done. A fair fight. You, too, are a warrior?"

"Not me," Spencer shook his head. "I am just an ordinary person. I wish it had been known that you understand this talk. Much trouble might have been saved, and many questions could have been answered. It is said, for instance, that your people . . . here . . . object to my presence, in this decision."

The Kallone's friendly grin slipped, suddenly, and he

stepped back to join his comrades. "You are Solarian?" he demanded. Spencer surprised, nodded. "We have been told," the grim-faced soldier went on, "that Solarians are strange people, that they reject fellowship with the rest of the galaxy. We were told that you, as one of them, would be opposed to our application in this 'decision.' And we saw you make the sign of rejection." There was a hard note of accusation in his voice. Spencer struggled to conceal his bafflement. There was something here that didn't add up. He felt the rest of the Five come near, around him. He caught a glimpse of Gal Horro's splendor, but the old man's face showed that he, too, was puzzled.

"Then," Spencer said, carefully, "it was you who asked that I be put out of this decision group. You objected to my presence?" He saw the nods, and shrugged. There was a slight hiss of indignant breath around him and he put up his hand, quickly. "No, let me handle this," he said, quietly. To the stiff-faced warriors he said, "You may choose whether you believe or not, but I had already told these others that I did not consider myself a proper person to take part in this great question. It is true, also, that I am opposed to their decision. I am quite ready, now or at any time, to withdraw."

"Spencer!" Thalog boomed, "you must not say this."

"I've just said it. And I will stand by it. But I would like to ask some questions of these men. You"—he indicated the man he had fought—"I do not know your name."

"I am Dana Krell. I lead this group."

"I had guessed as much. I am Gordon Spencer. Tell me, who has told you these things about me, and Solarians? Where did you learn this?"

"The Ambassadors of the Sofam told us, when we were coming here." The look on Gal Horro's face was enough to show that this was news to him. And Spencer seized at the word "Ambassador," as a clue to something that had irked him for a long while.

"The Sofam Overlords told you this," he nodded. "Thus they must have known, long ago, that I was to be here, and to take part in this decision." That was for the benefit of the rest of the Five. He hoped they would draw the obvious conclusions. He went on to the thing that was really bothering him.

"It is true," he said, "that my people rejected association with the rest of the galaxy. We are, in the main, a proud people, counting our freedom of more value than the offer of a subordinate place within the Galactic Federation, under the control of an Overlord. This was, perhaps, foolish of us. I am glad to see that you, although so like us in many ways, are prepared to surrender your self-determination and your warlike ways, in order to live under the rule of the Sofam." He watched the proud faces opposite him, and knew, before they spoke, that his wild guess had been accurate.

"Surrender!" Krell snapped. "Who talks of surrender? We, the Kallone, talk not of surrender, or of subordinate positions. We are an honorable race. This application we make is to be accorded full equality within the Great Federation."

"This you were told, by the Overlords?" Spencer said, quickly, before Gal Horro could voice the indignation that was purpling his aged features.

"This we were told," Krell confirmed. "We were told that the galaxy is great, with many planets for the taking, great wealth and unlimited prospects; that we, with the Sofam, would share in this . . ." his voice faltered as he saw the expressions opposite him. "It is not like this?" he asked.

"It's not a bit like that," Spencer said, quietly. "The whole of the galaxy is united . . . many millions of planetary

systems, beyond counting . . . all united, on a friendly
basis, of trade, business, reason and understanding. It is not
warlike. There are no conquests to make. There is no place,
here, for a warlike people. That, partly, is why my people
chose to remain apart. Do you understand? The values are
different, here."

"A trading culture? Merchants?" Krell said it with contempt, but Spencer was patient. This was something he
knew well enough.

"The Kallone are great warriors," he said. "They rule their
system, and two other suns. What of the other races who
were there?"

"We defeated them!" Krell said, simply.

"Of course. In any battle, one wins . . . and the other
loses. Remember . . . one loses, always. If, for instance, I
have more food than I can eat, and you have more clothes
than you can wear . . . and we fight . . . one must lose.
The winner will have more clothes than he can wear and
more food than he can eat . . . and the other one . . . loses.
In trade, both gain, no one loses. It is as simple as that."

Krell looked his bewilderment. It was no easier for him
to switch values than it had been for the Ethical Absolutes.

"I do not understand this talk," he said. "We have been
deceived."

"That's the big point," Spencer cut in, quickly. "You have
been fooled, deliberately and to some purpose. Somebody
has been trying to make use of you. Somebody with dreams
of conquest, I'd say."

"Spencer," it was Thalog again. "I can follow what you
are getting at, but what you are suggesting is monstrous."

"Yes. I know. It's unthinkable . . . again." His weary
tone hit the burly man like a slap in the face, but before he

could retort, a harsh voice crackled across the hall, from the great entrance.

"Solarian!"

Spencer swung round, and saw his last suspicions confirmed, right up to the hilt. There, three feet inside the doorway, stood one of the Sofam Protectors. In his hand was something so nearly like a pistol that it could not be anything else. The fat barrel was aimed directly between the stiff shoulder blades of Garnol Taynee, who stood, steady but pale, two paces in front of his captor. To the left of the door, stolid and silent, were three yellow men, each clumsily clutching long-barrelled weapons. Spencer took it all in, in one lightning glance. This was it . . . the naked face of violence. "Don't anybody do anything rash," he muttered, to those around him. "Those things are lethal, no matter who holds them."

Then Taynee was speaking, shakily. "I am to tell you, Great One Spencer, that you are to surrender yourself to these men, peacefully. If you attempt to resist, they will kill me. If they fail to return to their companions within a reasonable time, then my daughter will die, also. They have her captive."

For one blinding moment, Spencer fought the rage that flared inside him. Then he thrust emotion aside, became cold. He had wanted proof to show the others. Now he had it—and it was his responsibility, all the way.

Thalog rumbled, in his ear, "You cannot submit to this, Spencer. It is obvious that they mean to kill you, unbelievable as it seems."

"I know it." He lifted his hands wide, to shoulder height, turned on the little group at his back. To the rest of the Five, and Horro, he said, softly. "Don't try anything, anything at all. This is right outside your experience. Let me handle it." Then, to Krell, and his alert colleagues, he added, "This is what force does to weak men. Is this how you fight . . . against helpless men, and girls?" And then, "Think what this will do to your honor, to the name of the Kallone, throughout the galaxy!"

"What can we do?" Krell demanded. "We have no weapons. We were ordered to leave them behind, on the ship."

"They were not left behind, as you can see. Be alert, perhaps you can get them back again."

"Solarian!" the harsh voice came again. "You have heard the Prince Taynee. Do you surrender?"

Spencer gave Krell a hard look, turned again, and went, steadily, down the length of the hall, still with his arms spread. He drew near to Taynee, saw the beads of sweat on the tense man's face. As if from the casual need to speak, he moved between Taynee and the Sofam, and turned. Gently, and in a quite level voice, he said:

"When I say 'Now,' fall flat on your face, fast, and stay there. All right? *Now!*" and without waiting to see if he had been obeyed, he swung the edge of his hand in a slashing blow across the Sofam's face, catching him on the bridge of the nose. In the same movement, and with the swing of his body, he launched a kick to the crotch, and snatched the weapon as it fell. Still in the same swoop, he went forward, put his foot on the Sofam's neck, spun round, leveled the weapon at the three yellow men.

"Drop those things!" he snapped, waving the pistol meaningly, hoping they would not notice his fingers feeling the unfamiliar grip. His thumb felt a stud where a pistol would have had a hammer, and he pressed it. The kick, and the slam of the explosion came together—and there were only two yellow men, now. The third was a shattered mess that made Spencer fight to control his heaves. Contact-explosive bullets, he thought, and winced as the long-barrels clattered to the floor. Then the Kallone came up, on the run, to seize the weapons and stand ready. Spencer held out the pistol, shakily, to Krell.

"You'd better have this," he muttered. "More in your line."

"What now?" Krell demanded. "There is still the girl."

Thalog came up, heavily, followed by the rest. "You must not risk yourself any further, Spencer," he panted. "They are counting on the affection between yourself and Delyra. You will be trapped."

"I know that, too!" Spencer snapped. "What I need, most, is information. And this man has it. He'll have to talk. No . . . not your way." He waved Thalog back. "I don't want him thinking himself to death. Let me do it. I'll make him talk fast enough." He went down on his knees by the writhing Sofam, took a rough grip on one arm, twisted it up behind his shoulders so that the green man went flat on his face, groaning. Applying leverage, he took hold of the little finger, and bent it, hard. The green man screamed. Spencer didn't like what he was doing, but he liked the thought of Delyra in the clutches of power-crazy Sofam even less. He put on the pressure. And the Sofam talked.

"All right." Spencer stood up, when it was obvious that he had all there was to be known. "Can you take charge of this lot?" he indicated the sweating Overlord and the two stupefied yellow men.

"That we can do," Thalog said, grimly. "But why do you ask? What are you going to do?"

"I think you know. I'm going after Delyra, now that I know where she is. I'll need a droy—" he turned to Taynee, who nodded, reluctantly.

"If you wish," he said. "I know what you feel . . . but, you will be in danger, possibly killed. These men are insane!"

"Drunk with power," Spencer said, grimly. "It's strong

stuff for those who aren't used to it. As for being killed, that's a chance I have to take."

"You have no right to take it," Thalog growled. "If you are what you are, then your life is worth more than hers, however unpleasant it may seem."

"I'll leave you to figure out the niceties of it," Spencer shrugged. "I haven't the time to argue, right now. This has to be done quickly." He turned to find Krell barring his way.

"What talk is this?" the Kallone snapped. "They will let you go, alone, to rescue the girl?"

"They don't want me to go at all," Spencer said, carefully. "They count me a Great One in wisdom, and this is more value to them than the life of one girl. This is how reason works, against force."

"But the girl will be killed!"

"Possibly. The Sofam Overlords may carry out their threat, in their great need to have the Kallone as their private warriors. This is what they need you for, to bring force against the peaceful peoples of the galaxy."

"Then the honorable name of the Kallone will stink, throughout the whole of the galaxy . . ."

"And you will never be admitted to the Federation, on any kind of status. Yes, I'm afraid that is so. It is a pity, because there is another way, a much better way. With honor. But it may be too late, now."

"You will not go alone!" Krell said, harshly. "You shall not risk your life in defense of our honor while we stand idly by. We will come with you."

Within minutes the little party were mounted and thundering away, round the corner of the building and into the lane which led back to the wilderness up the hill. In the lead, Krell and Spencer manufactured hasty strategy. In front of them they could count on fifteen yellow men and the other three of the renegade Sofam—the whole armed with three of the long-barrels and five short-arms. The Kallone had carried one of each, as habit. Spencer's party had only the one short-arm and the three long-barrels taken from the yellow men. All they had to gamble on, and it wasn't much, was that this outbreak by the Sofam was a hasty move, undertaken in crazy desperation by amateurs at violence.

"If we can come at them quickly," Spencer explained, "before they have had time to realize how mad they have been, then we have a chance. In that state of mind, they will not harm the princess at all. They are assuming that their show of force will be enough to terrify the rest into rejecting me. And they would be counting, perhaps, on your support, having prepared you to dislike me, anyway."

"This is difficult thinking, for me," Krell admitted. "You say there are no warrior races in the Galactic Federation, at all—none?"

"Not one. There is no armed might of any kind. There is no need for it, when all are peaceful brothers. This is why, when the Sofam discovered your worlds, and saw force in action, for the first time, they were infected with the idea, like a disease. With your peoples to do their fighting for them, they would rule the whole galaxy, in time."

"But that is fool talk. It is one thing to conquer. It is another thing to hold that which has been taken. Besides, one does not war on helpless people. You have saved us from a great evil, Spencer."

"Not yet, I haven't," Spencer grinned, as they broke from the open path into thick scrub. "I think we had better take it easy, now. Don't want to scare them into anything foolish. You know what to do—surround me as if I'm your prisoner, and ride right up to the senior Sofam."

The tangled scrub made heavy going for the droy, and even heavier for the riders, who were forced to hang on like

grim death against hooking thorns and knotted branches.
Spencer refused to let his mind dwell on anything ahead of
the immediate future. Problems were swelling up, but they
would have to wait. Right now, a lot was going to depend
on speed and surprise. He made a last, urgent appeal to
the squad to mind their thoughts, to think as if they were a
victory party. This, he had found with relief, was not a new
concept to them, at all.

"We know of some who can sense what another is thinking," Krell had explained. "It is a great gift, though rare. I
have often thought what a useful art it would be, to a warrior, to know what his enemy is thinking."

Spencer wished, vainly, that Thalog, and the rest, could
have been present to hear that simple opinion. Then, suddenly, the thick scrub gave way to a great circular clearing,
and there they were, all of them.

He saw Delyra first, and not until that moment had he
permitted himself to think how much her safety meant to
him. She sat dejectedly on the grass in the focal point of a
semicircle, with the three Sofam standing behind her, and
the stolid yellow men gathered round. Like so many
zombies, Spencer thought, in one brief flash of anger. Then
he had scrambled down from his droy, and went running
across the grass to her, to slide into a kneel by her side.

"Princess!" he muttered. "Are you all right? Not hurt?"

"Gordon!" her garment which had been drab gray flared
into green-blue, "You? But you should not have come.
They mean to . . . to kill you!"

"That's something I have my own ideas about," he re-
torted. "Just so long as you're all right. Now, listen. When
I yell out, you drop flat on your face, and stay still." From
the corner of his eye he saw the glossy boots of one of the
Sofam coming close, and bunched himself, ready. "Understand me, now?" She blinked, and then nodded. He gave

her a quick grin, gathered his legs under him, and then, with a harsh shout, launched himself up and at the standing green man. One step, a swinging kick to the knee, a flailing hand to the wrist which held the pistol, a quick snatch with the other hand, and he had the weapon. Gripping it, he swept that hand up and back, smashing the Sofam across the face with the hard metal barrel.

Without pause, and only dimly aware that the quiet glade had suddenly erupted into cursing action, he leaped across the wilting form of the first Sofam, straight at the second, who had not yet managed to draw his pistol from its carrier. Up and down went his right hand, the shock of metal on skull a joyous jar up his arm. The third Sofam, teeth bared, lifted his weapon, and Spencer lashed out, frantically, with his. The two met, clashingly, and he cringed, expecting to be annihilated in an explosion. But there was only the exquisite agony of a crushed fingertip, and the sight of the two pistols flying in opposite directions. Biting on the pain, he flung out his left hand in a punch, felt it go home, saw the Sofam totter away. A flicker of movement to his left made him spin, in time to hoist his arm to fend off a grim-faced yellow man with a knife. A knife! The incongruity of it touched the back of his consciousness even as the blade burned him, laying his arm open from wrist to elbow. His perspective seemed to shift, suddenly, so that the real Spencer became remote and impersonal, standing afar off watching this vicious and bloodstained self, seeing it swing and grasp and heave, sending the lumbering yellow man flying through the air, to thud into the grass and lie still.

Off to his right, somewhere, there was an ear-aching explosion, and a scream. To his left, as he turned his head unsteadily, he saw the third Sofam, one hand tucked under his armpit, groping in the grass with his other hand, trying to retrieve one of the pistols. Spencer took an unsure step forward—it had grown dark, or foggy, or something—so he measured his aim very carefully, swung, and kicked the crouching officer full in the face. Staggering from the effort, he swung round again, and went down as a great yellow man met him, with a roundhouse swipe. His body saved him, even as his mind was in the act of saying "This is it!" By blind instinct, he clutched a shoulder, got his foot into the belly of the mass that fell on him, and thrust upwards. For a moment, he lay still, debating whether or not he should get up again. It hardly seemed worth it, and the little voice that kept screaming at him to get up didn't make sense, at all.

Then, amazingly, he realized that the glade was quiet. He struggled to his feet, looked round, blearily, pumping for breath. Krell's face showed up, split by a broad grin, and enhanced by an angry red bruise across a cheekbone.

"All over, finished!" he cried. "They were fools, indeed, to pile the long-barrels at a distance like that. Come, we will take them back to the house. And we must see to your hurt."

"I'm all right," Spencer tried a grin, and could feel it coming out silly with his exhaustion. But his head was clear enough, and things had slipped into focus, again. "The princess," he said, "is she still all right?"

His answer came from Delyra herself, as she rushed forward to take his arm. The relief of seeing that she was unhurt, not even frightened, but more concerned for him than anything else, was like the letting go of whatever had been holding him up. The surroundings became badly blurred for him, after that. He heard voices that were weak and distant, knew that someone was binding his arm—had a silly moment of wondering just how she was going to rip off a piece of her skirt, when she wasn't wearing one—and then there was just haze. And then a slow, rhythmic, jogging motion. He came to, realizing that he was astride a droy, that the unconscious bulk of a Sofam lay across the beast's broad shoulders in front of him, and that gentle arms clutched him round the waist.

Riding by him, knee to knee, he saw Krell, also with a Sofam captive. A touch to those arms told him that it was Delyra, riding behind him, holding him up. He took a deep breath, touched those arms again, and saw that his own right arm was bound in uniform cloth, Sofam uniform.

"Too old for this game," he mumbled, to Krell. "Should have left it to professionals, like you."

"Not so!" Krell denied, grinning. "You did well. And they were fools, anyway. We have a saying, 'It takes a man to bend a bow, but any fool can loose the arrow!' We have much to thank you for, Spencer."

"Eh?" Spencer shook his head, dimly. "This is a change I do not understand."

Krell laughed, harshly. "We have them all, alive, as you advised, except one. That was unfortunate, but it could not be helped. Now we are going back to the Great Ones, and they will know that this folly was not of the Kallone. You will speak for us, I think, Spencer. Yes?"

"What do you want me to say?"

"Just that we of the Kallone do not murder, or fight against unarmed people. We understand this trading that you spoke of, but it is our way to trade from strength, with those we respect and with power to back our agreements. This is our way, and we will not give it up."

"Suppose," Spencer said, and his ideas were dreamily clear, now, "there was a way in which you could be certain of the binding honor of a trading agreement, without force . . . if it was possible for you to know, at all times, how the other man was thinking . . . what then?"

Krell frowned, in hard thought. "It is a difficult thing to think," he admitted. "This is how the rest of the Galactic peoples are?"

"That's right."

"I think, if my people could be like this, then there would be no more need for force, truly. But it would take a long time. When a man has grown up with power in his arm it does not fade easily from his thinking. It will take a long time."

"You don't need me to speak for you," Spencer said, quietly. "You can say all that is necessary, yourself. You have said, just now, what I will say to the Great Ones myself, about my own people, who are very like yours. It will take us a long time, also."

And then the moment of lucidity passed and he felt the environment slipping away, so that he was thankful for the slim arms that held him safe. He had vague memories of stopping, of a distant voice saying, "He has lost much blood . . . needs rest." Then there was a very comfortable, warm, blackness, and a thankful letting-go.

The gentle ebb-and-flow of voices had been going on for some time. He had been hearing them, in growing irritation, wishing they would speak louder. He couldn't make out what they were saying. Then a phrase came clear.

". . . Can't see, now, how you can argue that the test-devices are not capable of error. Surely this proves it?" and that was Rik Wiswood's voice.

"Suspicions are not evidence," Thalog's voice was grimly dogmatic. "You know as well as I do that the devices are used only in the final stages, to give precise readings."

"Then how else do you explain it?" That was Simnel.

"There are three possible reasons. First, the Solarians have a long experience of testing methods and devices, and are, presumably, familiar with them. Second, there may be some inherent difference in the Solarian physical structure, which would falsify the readings . . ."

"But isn't that what we were just saying?"

"Not at all. The devices are not wrong, if used properly. But they can not give right answers from wrong data. This is just a guess, of course."

"A strong possibility, I would say," Fasla-en-Narsis spoke decisively. "There must be *some* difference in them. They are defective, remember?"

"The third possibility," Thalog said, strongly, "is one we must always keep in mind. That we may be mistaken."

Spencer thought it was time he came alive. He pushed his eyes open, cautiously, and found himself in his bed, in the Taynee mansion, with the rest of the Five sitting round him. All their eyes were on him, at once.

"Ah!" Thalog said, gently. "You are with us again. May I set your mind at rest on the main points, first?" Spencer nodded, guessing what he meant. "Very well. The princess is safe and well. The renegade Sofam are in safe custody. Their servants likewise. The Kallone await news of your well-being, have withdrawn their application to be accepted into the Federation, and are ready to depart for their home system as soon as they know you are well. Is this enough?"

"It will do," Spencer said, quietly. "I gather there is a matter of much greater importance on your minds, right now. I imagine I'm on trial!"

"In a sense, yes. But what is really on trial is our whole system of selection. It appears to have broken down, in your case."

"In fact, you consider I have been guilty of unethical behavior."

"That is what it looks like." Thalog was obviously uncomfortable. "We can judge only as we see, in your case. We await your explanation, anxiously."

"All right!" Spencer sat up. "Just let's get one thing straight, before you tell me what I did wrong. It's this. I don't care, one way or the other, about my so-called standing as an Ethical Absolute. I just did what I knew to be the best thing, in the circumstances. If I have to explain, or to defend that, all right."

"Of course. What else could you do?" Thalog shot a "What-do-you-think-of-that?" look at the rest. Then, settling himself, he said, "You will understand, I am sure, that there is no such thing as an 'absolute,' in ethics. We dislike the term commonly used to describe such as we are, but it is too well accepted, now, to be changed. There are no ethical absolutes. But there are certain basic essentials, such as the true value of a person as against that of a principle. The ethical person is he who can maintain the delicate but crucial balance between self-interest, and self-sacrifice, between individual and group values, between short-term and long-term effects. Balance is the essence; extremes are wrong. I am being vague, here, deliberately"—he cast another glance at his colleagues—"because I have the feeling we are making a mistake. Again!" He paused to think, shutting his eyes. Then,

"This 'decision,' for example, would not have been important. It was a major thing, but not difficult. Ordinarily, it would have gone through without question. But you have shown us, beyond doubt, that it would have been an error to admit the Kallone. More, you have been able to persuade them to withdraw their application. This is a good result. You are proven right. This makes us cautious. But . . . we saw you risk your personal safety, your life, for the sake of an urge, and we cannot consider this the act of a balanced person. You will understand, we do not condemn this act. It was brave, noble, inspiring . . . but unbalanced. This is what we saw. We await your explanation."

"You're isolating one point out of the whole," Spencer said, steadily. "That gives a wrong impression, to begin with. Also there is the fact that I had to make guesses in the absence of solid data. I was, in part, gambling on guesswork. Is that wrong, in itself?"

"Not at all. One must make the best use of what one has."

"All right. Now, somebody tried to put me out of the way. Somebody was thinking in terms of force, and weapons. The logical people to look at would be the Kallone. They were that kind of culture. But there was no link between them and myself, except that they wanted membership, and I was one of those who would decide. How could they know that I would be against them? It didn't add up. Then, when I saw that they had brought no weapons with them, that did not add up, either. From what I know of my own culture, it is second nature to carry weapons, just in case. Why, even our first interstellar ship, under John Field—a purely exploratory venture—carried weapons. The crew would not have felt comfortable without them. Please realize that for a culture without personal-power, this is axiomatic. Weapons, just in case!"

"Ah!" Thalog nodded, suddenly. "Know this . . . that the leader of the misguided Sofam four, one Tar Marras, was on the ship which met your John Field."

"That's it!" Spencer snapped his fingers. "That's the missing piece. He saw weapons. He also saw weapons, when studying the Kallone. Being no fool, he would see other parallels, and he would know that I would see them, also. *That* was the part that had me guessing. How the Sofam could know my reactions. Anyway, what with the Kallone weaponless . . . with all records of weapons cut out of the exhibition, it was obvious that someone was trying to give a false impression. Also, I could not see a culture like the Kallone seeking a subordinate role. My own culture would not consider it, either. Just these factors, alone, were enough to make me reject the Kallone application. But I had to know more, because it was quite possible that such an application would be made again, to a different Five, and would succeed." He looked at the faces watching him, saw only intent waiting. He wondered what they were thinking.

"I had to know, one way or the other, whether the pressure was being put on by the Kallone, or by somebody else. So, as you saw, I took the whole argument to the Kallone themselves. If they were trying to eliminate me, then that was their chance. But, although they did voice an objection, it was because of what they had been told. Which could mean, only, the Sofam. But, to you, that was 'unthinkable.' So I had to make it thinkable for you. It meant risking my life, which I did not like"—he kept his voice flat—"but it was for the sake of the Kallone culture . . . and for the rest of the galaxy, in the long view. But, I did not expect, nor foresee, that my host, or his daughter, would be put in danger, on my account. My purpose was achieved, otherwise, and my life was already in jeopardy, so I cannot see that it was unethical to take it further, and attempt to rescue the princess."

"Would you have gone, alone?"

"I think so. That part of the business was mine, anyway. But I would have been disappointed in the Kallone, had they not been eager to help. It was in keeping with their character, as I saw it."

Thalog's face was a study. So were the others. It was Fasla-en-Narsis who at last broke the silence.

"We owe you much," she said, quietly. "We have made things very difficult for you, and you have managed to keep a balance despite everything. Our only excuses are two. One, that we were ignorant of such things as force, and, two, that there was a barrier between us—between ourselves and you."

"That's another thing," Spencer sat forward, bracing himself. "I want to reopen this Kallone question, in another way. They must not be allowed to go back to their own system under the wrong impression—that there is no place for them in the galaxy. Because it is not true. This, again, is where your ignorance is upsetting your judgment. You class a culture as primitive just because it does not have personal-power. You"—he turned to Thalog—"expressed surprise at the high ethical standards of Solarians, who are 'defectives.' I have talked with the Kallone. I advise that you do the same. You will find that they have a very high ethical standard, also. It is perfectly possible to develop such standards, on the basis of force. It is a mistake, in other words, to class a culture as primitive, just because it does not have this one thing."

"This we are beginning to realize," Thalog said. "We will have to change many of our values."

"Not so many," Spencer grinned. "You need to change one, though. You must not expect a proud, highly developed culture to accept the word 'primitive.' And you cannot expect such a culture to change its way of thinking, overnight. That is what I wanted to get at. The Kallone must now be rejected. Instead, why not let them find their own way to developing personal-power—with a bit of judicious help?"

"Spencer!" Thalog was suddenly suspicious. "You are concealing something from us. You talk too freely of what can be done with personal-power, as if you were familiar with it. How can you know all this?"

"That is another thing you'll have to change," Spencer

said, keeping his voice as steady as possible over the butterflies in his belly. "Solarians are not defective, at all. I am not defective."

"How can this be?" Wiswood demanded. "I see you . . . yet, to my mind, you are not there, at all!"

"I have deceived you," he said. "This was unethical, possibly, but the secret was not mine to release, until now, until it had to be done. John Field and all his crew, every Solarian you have ever met, myself included is shielded. Protected."

"What may that mean?" Thalog snorted.

"Just this!" Spencer whispered, and moved his toothswitch to zero, flicking away his protection.

Now he was stripped naked in their sight. Now he would know, and they would know, beyond question, what manner of person he was.

Thalog turned away from him, deliberately, to Wiswood. "Now!" he boomed. "Now do you doubt the efficiency of the tests?"

"You mean . . . it's all right? It's true?" Spencer gasped.

"It is true. Did you ever doubt it? But you are as one who stands outside, waiting to enter. If you want to be with us, wholly, you have only to push, just a little."

And there was no need for him to speak. There was a pain that was not a pain, a twisting, struggling, breaking free, and he opened his eyes to a world that was different, in a way that he had never suspected it could be. It was a world in which everything was alive and had significance. By comparison, his old world had been a dull, gray place. He looked at Thalog, seeing him as a warm, strong flame, Fasla-en-Narsis as a keen blade, Simnel as a dancing spark of fire, Wiswood a clear glow—and all steady and serene. He shut his eyes, and they were still there.

"Now tell us," Thalog beamed on him, "what manner of device is this, that can blot out a man?" Spencer explained what he could of the gadget, and the immense difference between this channeled function and the real thing he could now perceive.

"We have known of this for a long while," he said. "We call it psionics, and we know what a disaster such a thing could be, if it were released all at once, into a culture like ours. But, you see, we do have the ethical stature to know this, and control it. Some of us. And, by degrees, it will spread. The Kallone, as I know, are very like us in this. If the know-how for a device like this could be 'leaked' to them, carefully, then they could follow the same path, by themselves. You agree?" He could see that they did.

"That's it, then," he said. "The party is over. As soon as I'm fit, I suppose it's me for home."

Fasla-en-Narsis snorted, in a most unladylike way, and there was a wave of fellow-feeling, engulfing him like a firm handshake.

"Home?" she said. "You are home now. Here, or anywhere else in the galaxy. And you are forgetting someone else—" He followed her brief gesture, to see Delyra standing in the doorway. What he saw there, with his new senses, told him that he was, indeed, home. To stay.

PHILOSOPHER'S STONE

by Christopher Anvil

Dave Blackmer was an interstellar courier, paid to deliver the almost microscopically-reduced electronic message banks which, on arrival at the branch offices of Terran corporations, yielded up confidential instructions and technical data from the home offices and giant laboratories back on Earth. Since the banks were theoretically stealable, certain key messages were given to Dave in deep hypnosis, and passed on by him in the same state when he reached the planet of destination. For Dave, the job itself was routine. Most of the travel was done in fast commercial spacers, the monotony varied by rare moments when hair-trigger reflexes and hidden weapons made a shambles of a highjacker's attempt at the message banks. Between such moments, he had time to consider a peculiar effect of his job that the company recruiter had warned him about before he took the job.

"Now, don't ask me to explain it," the recruiter had said, "but Einstein's theory predicts it, and our experience proves it. The faster you go, the slower the passage of time. At the speeds you'll be traveling, you've got to take this into account. Are you willing to do it?"

"What's it involve?"

"Well, suppose you're married. You go out on the fastest ship available, make two or three sub-space jumps, travel at top velocities, deliver the banks, load up for return, and in six weeks total you're back to report to the head office. The calendar in the office says one year and two months have elapsed since you left."

"You mean I'm a year two months older than when I left, and it only seemed like six weeks to me?"

"No, you're only six weeks older. The people *here* are a year two months older. They've lived that long while you were away for six weeks of *your* time."

Dave shrugged. "What does it matter when I live the rest of the fourteen months? I haven't lost anything."

"No, but remember, we said, 'Suppose you're married.' You've been away six weeks, as far as you're concerned. But that was a year and two months on Earth. You're married, and the little woman is conscious of having cooled her heels in solitary neglect for four hundred and twenty-five days and nights. You see what I mean?"

Dave nodded. "That's not so good."

The recruiter said, "In this business, marriage isn't worth it, believe me. But there are compensations, if you're interested in making money."

"High pay?"

"The pay is terrible. You'd do a lot better running a desk in an automatic factory."

"How much?"

"Five thousand a year, to start."

Dave turned as if to leave.

"Of course," added the recruiter, "you collect that five thousand at least half-a-dozen times a year."

Dave turned back and stared at him. The recruiter grinned. "We call it the 'accordion effect.' On Earth, time is stretched out like an accordion pulled wide. At high velocity, time is shortened like an accordion squeezed shut. On the company's books, you get paid by the calendar year.

But throughout most of the calendar year, you're making subspace jumps and traveling at ultrahigh velocity in the course of your work. You experience the passage of, say, five to six weeks, between the time you leave and the time you get back. Meanwhile, on Earth, the calendar year has elapsed, because of the higher rate of flow of time on a slow-moving object. So after five to six weeks' work, you get a year's pay. Nice, huh?"

And that had been Dave's introduction to the "accordion effect." Other delightful aspects had shown up later. Though Dave was earning at least thirty thousand a year, from his viewpoint, the government saw this as a mere five thousand a year, repeated six times; the government was thus content to go after his paychecks with a moderately loose net, rather than with the harpoons, axes, and big knives they would otherwise have used. Conversely, though from Dave's viewpoint only a year had passed on the job, from the viewpoint of his bank, the interest on his money had been compounding, piling up, and reproducing itself for half-a-dozen years.

At first, Dave's only worry was that some technological development would eliminate his job. Then he began to notice other results of the accordion effect: the apparently accelerated aging of Earthbound acquaintances; the stepping up, from Dave's viewpoint, of social and technological changes; the perceptible shift of position and power among the peaceable but still strenuously competing nations on the home planet. These, and the sudden emergence of totally unexpected developments, kept Dave constantly aware of the difference in viewpoint that his job brought about.

And now there was a new change. For the first few years —from his viewpoint—Dave had traveled in the fastest American and Soviet ships. Of late, however, his trips more and more often were made in spacers like the *Imperial Banner,* the *Unicorn,* the *Lion,* and the *Duke of Richmond.* He was currently aboard the *Queen of Space,* which was hurtling him from Transpluto Terminal to Aurora Shuttle-Drop with a time-lead of twelve hours fifty-seven minutes over the next fastest transportation. Some idea of life on the *Queen* could be deduced in advance from the first lines of the shipping company's brochure:

"With three grades of accommodation: magnate class, luxury class, and first class, the new liner *Queen of Space* fulfills your fondest expectations . . ."

But Dave had been unable to foresee all of it. With one hand behind him on the silver doorknob of the first-class lounge, he stepped into the corridor and glanced to his left to see, strolling toward him down the corridor, two elegantly-dressed young men, a little above medium height. They were spare, well-knit, and groomed to perfection. Dave, who seldom noticed clothes, became oppressively aware of their perfectly-tailored jackets, knife-creased trousers, and black shoes polished to mirror brightness. They favored Dave with a brief flick of a glance as they passed, leaving him conscious of his improperly-knotted tie, unsuitable tan sport jacket and slacks, and too thick-soled shoes. Dave bore up under it grimly, conscious that the trip would not last forever and that after seven or eight more trips, the accordion effect would probably present him with some new phenomenon.

A good-natured middle-aged man, carrying a thing like a small riding crop with a silver handle, moved out beside Dave at the doorway, cast a cool glance after the elegant pair, nodded to Dave, and walked down the corridor, carrying the crop turned up inconspicuously against the cloth of his sleeve. From the opposite direction, a beautifully-

dressed fop strolled by with a swagger stick. Then two men
went past deep in conversation.

"No, no," one was saying earnestly. "I'd have been
stuck there for life. A stinking baronet. But I found Carter.
He was nobody, then. Nobody. But I saw a possibility.
Nothing more, mind you. Just a possibility. And I—"

They disappeared around the corner. From their direction came a thickset man with beet-red cheeks carrying a
swagger stick. No, Dave saw, a gold-encrusted baton of
some kind—and everyone else in the corridor bowed and
stood aside till he passed, whereupon the conversation, respectfully subdued, sprang up again, and the traffic in the
hall got moving.

Dave noted that the courtesy was more elaborate than it
had been on previous trips. The social phenomenon, whatever it was, must be coming to full bloom. He watched the
hustling crowd go past, and became aware of a feeling of
loneliness.

Someone banged into Dave, muttered an apology in a
strained, suffering voice, and started past into the crowded
entrance of the first-class lounge. Dave muttered an automatic acceptance of the apology, started out into the corridor, then hastily changed direction as some grandee came
around the corner and they all stood against the wall for
him.

Growling under his breath, Dave shoved back out of the
way into the lounge, banged somebody, apologized, heard
a muttered, "Sure. Sure. That's all right. Never mind,"
whirled and caught sight of a man in a dark business suit
with a thick stubble of beard and horn-rimmed glasses. Dave
immediately grabbed him by the arm. The man whirled
around, a grim long-suffering look on his face.

From the corridor and all around them came snatches of greetings and conversation:

". . . Beg pardon, your Grace . . ."

". . . Be delighted, Sir Philip. I'm much indebted to you . . ."

". . . Lot of plebian rot, my lord. Hogwash. Income tax, indeed . . ."

". . . Well, that put me one step up the ladder, but I never hoped to lay hold on the swagger stick till—"

". . . No, no. What a bore. I wouldn't dream of it . . ."

". . . Best be up and doing, eh, your Grace? One day a commoner, next a baron, and pretty soon . . ."

"'. . . Tongue, you insolent dog,' I said. 'Your rank was bequeathed. It's no greater than mine, and it's on the slide. Your children will be commoners . . .'"

The man Dave had by the arm was staring at him as at some friend temporarily forgotten, but whose features were agonizingly familiar.

Dave said in a low voice, "You're Anatoly Dovrenin. A courier for Sovcom. Right?"

The man nodded. He said suddenly, "I've seen you. Wait—You're David Blackmer? Interstellar Communications Corporation?"

"Correct."

Dovrenin thrust out his hand. Dave grabbed it. They shook hands with the sincerity of two nineteenth-century midwesterners in a Boston drawing room. The instant they paused the bits and fragments of conversation washed over them again.

". . . Reconversion dynamometer. Well, I thought, that's good for a step up if I can twist it around a bit, so . . ."

". . . Incredible callousness. The chap was only a rung above me, you know. It wasn't the snub, it was the way he did it. So offhand. As if I didn't *exist* . . ."

". . . Of course, my dear fellow. Yes, yes. I assuredly will remember you. Now if you'll excuse me . . . Pardon, gentlemen . . ."

". . . Lord Essenden, you've met Sir Dene Swope? . . . Splendid . . . Now, if we can find a quiet seat in a corner somewhere . . ."

Dovrenin glanced around and muttered, "It's getting crowded in here."

Dave nodded, "I know exactly what you mean. My room's just down the hall. If you can spare a minute—"

Dovrenin brightened. "I've got a big collection of cheeses they gave me at home for a going-away present. Also, naturally, I have some Vodka. How about—"

"Good idea."

"But, I haven't got any crackers. There was a little slip in the five-year plan, and ah . . ."

Dave nodded knowingly. "I'll go down to the commissary and pick up a couple of boxes. Incidentally, I'm in 226."

"I'll be there. My room is 280, so it will take me a few minutes."

They parted, Dovrenin going up the corridor, and Dave down it toward the gravity drop to the commissary. A few minutes later he was carrying the crackers and on his way back, meditating on the effect of the change in the exchange rate from six dollars a pound to seven twenty-eight a pound.

Thus preoccupied, Dave failed to notice a sudden hush in the corridor as everyone stood back respectfully against the walls. Dave walked past unaware. An elaborately-dressed fop drew his breath in with a hiss, grabbed Dave's arm with one hand, and slapped him across the face with the other.

Dave instinctively grabbed the man by the shirt front and

knocked his unconscious form fifteen feet down the corridor.

There was a dead silence.

Dave picked up the crackers.

Coming toward him down the hall was the man with the riding crop that Dave had seen earlier. He smiled at Dave. Dave smiled at him. Dave walked down the hall with the accumulated gaze of many eyes focused on the back of his neck.

As he approached his room, he could see Anatoly Dovrenin coming down the hall from the opposite direction, carrying a box so large that he could see only by looking around one side of it. Behind Dovrenin, a door opened. People jumped to right and left to stand courteously waiting against the wall as a skinny individual carrying a silver-and-gold-encrusted baton emerged from a room behind Dovrenin, to walk behind him in deep conversation with a short fat man who was obviously paralyzed by greatness, and able only to bob his head and say, "Yes, Yes."

Dovrenin, peering around one side of the box, clearly had no idea what was behind him, till a gorgeously-dressed young man indignantly slammed him to the wall, knocking the box to the floor. Dovrenin waited with downcast gaze as the baton-bearing celebrity went past. There was a blur of motion as people began to move, then the magnificently-dressed young man appeared carrying the box, his expression blank, and Dovrenin right behind him with his hand holding something bulky in a side pocket.

Dave opened the door. The big box was carried in and set on the bed. Dovrenin's companion favored Anatoly and Dave with a hard look, and left the room.

Dave shut the door. Dovrenin carried over a chair and jammed it under the door's silver knob.

"I'm not very popular here right now."

Dave nodded. "My own circle of friends is strictly limited."

Dovrenin went to the box, and glanced around. Dave followed his glance:

The room, done in an exotic combination of silver and New Venus mahogany, had a bed, a chest of drawers, a table, three straight chairs, a large mirror, a plush armchair, and a thing like a wide-screen TV set. Another door, partly open, gave a view into a luxuriously-fitted bathroom.

Dovrenin glanced around, saw the two big boxes of crackers, and beamed. "You had no trouble?"

"No. I'd hardly touched my travel allowance. But if that exchange rate keeps going up—"

"It will," said Dovrenin grimly. "We have information that the next jump would put it at about $8.40 a pound. It may be higher yet when we get back."

Dave winced, then shrugged. "No need to worry about that now." He pulled a couple of boxes out from under his bed, Dovrenin in turn began to unload his own huge box. The table was soon laden with a variety of edible delicacies, and an assortment of liquids in different sizes and shapes of bottles. Various packets, cartons, and little boxes appeared, packed with delicate white cigarettes, and big brown cigars. Dave and Anatoly stepped back, grinned and eyed the table. The room promptly filled with the sounds of pouring liquids, tearing cellophane, and can openers at work. For a time, the conversation was strictly limited:

"Pretty good cheese. What do you call this?"

". . . And of course, there isn't anything in the world like American whisky. However, try some of our . . ."

". . . Stuff really has a sting, doesn't it? But hm-m-m now suppose we mixed in a little of this . . ."

There was enough food and drink on the table to last

most of the trip, but there were only two to consume it, and something in the atmosphere impeded the development of really spontaneous joy. The two men glanced around from time to time, unaware that they had the puzzled looks of couriers just home from a long trip, and still unaccustomed to the changes that happened while they were away.

"Eight-forty a pound," murmured Dave, lowering his glass.

Dovrenin put down a bottle of clear brown liquid. His expression clouded. "You should see what is happening to the ruble. And the fools at home try to pass it off as if it didn't mean anything—"

Dave shook his head. "I guess it's because we see things speeded up. They jar us more."

"Oh, of course," said Dovrenin. "But let me just show you." He got out a piece of paper, and wrote rapidly.

He slid the paper over, and Dave noted that it was headed "Overall Industrial Index." Dave read:

I	
U.S.	.98
U.S.S.R.	.86
Gr.Britain	.42
II	
U.S.	.99
U.S.S.R.	.89
Gr.Britain	.42
III	
U.S.	1.01
U.S.S.R.	.92
Gr.Britain	.47
IV	
U.S.	1.00

| U.S.S.R. | .95 |
| Gr.Britain | .55 |

V

U.S.	1.02
U.S.S.R.	.97
Gr.Britain	.69

VI

U.S.	1.01
U.S.S.R.	.99
Gr.Britain	.91

VII

U.S.	1.03
U.S.S.R.	1.01
Gr.Britain	1.26

Dave looked up. "This is accurate?"

"No, it's a summary of our official past estimates. Therefore, it's somewhat biased in our favor. But that can't hide the trend."

"No wonder the exchange rate's going up."

"Yes, and no wonder their ships are beating ours. But *why?*"

Dave shook his head. "All I heard of it at home was an article I read, headed, 'Boom in Free World Economy. Britain Profits from Westward Economic Shift,' whatever that means. The article didn't make sense."

Dovrenin nodded gloomily, and picked up the big glass in which Dave had mixed several drinks together. Dovrenin eyed it suspiciously, took a cautious sip, shrugged, said, "This is certainly innocuous," and drank it down like water.

Dave sat up.

Dovrenin swallowed several times, and looked around

vaguely. He cleared his throat. He opened his mouth, and no sound came out. Dave glanced uneasily at the empty glass. Dovrenin tried again, and now words came out clearly, "I will show you what I mean."

Dave eased his chair back, so as to have freedom of action, just in case.

Dovrenin came to his feet, and glowered around as if looking over a large assemblage, made up entirely of his inferiors.

"Comrades," he growled, his voice threatening, "unhealthy rumors have come to my ears." He looked around, and said in a different voice, "No, we'll skip that part." He cleared his throat, glowered, and said in a deep, authoritative voice, "The present situation in steel production proves the futility of inexpert analysis. Hasty generalizations drawn from overall figures lead to fantastic conclusions. Steel production is not one monolithic development, but is the resultant of three totally unrelated factors: land-based production, sea-based production, space-based production.

"Water covers seventy-five per cent of the Earth's surface. Do you suppose there is no iron in the water, and no iron under the water? To think so would be an absurdity. But it is the kind of absurdity into which the inexpert falls, to bruise himself severely.

"Clear-headed analysis shows that in *land-based production,* we are breathing fire down the necks of the imperialists, and will soon *forge unshakably into the lead.* Only by desperate attempts at sea-based and space-based production are the capitalists able to stave off for a while their day of ruin. The sea- and space-based production figures are in direct proportion to their desperation at overcoming us in land-based production, and are thus a *source of grim satisfaction* to every one of us capable of a true understanding."

Dovrenin leaned across the table and said moodily to Dave, "You understand that before we came to this part, everyone had been already psychologically beaten into a jelly, so that the reasoning seemed very good."

Dave nodded sympathetically. Dovrenin picked up the empty glass and held it in the air, turning it slowly around and looking at it. "I have had it explained to me that this revolution in productive capacity is purely and simply the result of chance inventions. Little things like innovation in dynamic drift, resonant screening, ionic immobilization, linear-directed pseudo-molecular forces, stress-mold patterns, and so on. Mere inventions. No connection with the usual socio-economic factors." He gripped the glass suddenly, and Dave, expecting to see it smashed against the wall, braced himself to duck the flying fragments. Instead, Dovrenin abruptly sat down, pulled over his paper, and did some figuring on the back of it. Then he wrote on the face of the paper, and slid it across to Dave, who read:

VIII	
Gr.Britain	1.83
U.S.	1.04
U.S.S.R.	1.03

"That," said Dovrenin, "is what we can expect to see very shortly."

Dave checked the figures. "Seems perfectly accurate, if the trend holds."

Dovrenin swore. "Dukes and earls all over the place! The verminous nobility are taking over the universe! What an experience for a loyal Party member."

Dave bit back the automatic comment, "Well, at least, that's better than if the Communists should take over." He observed the expression of suffering on Dovrenin's face, finished off his glass, and looked at the figures again. The room was now traveling in slow circles, so that it was with some difficulty that he worked out the next stage of the progression:

IX	
Gr.Britain	2.60
U.S.	1.05
U.S.S.R.	1.05

Dovrenin checked the figures, and nodded. "That is exactly it. My friend, I am so glad you came on this ship. Otherwise, I would have been all alone with these rabid imperialists." He poured out two generous glasses of something that had a rocket on the label. After the exchange of several toasts, the room picked up considerable speed.

Dovrenin held to the table with one hand, while Dave braced it from the other side, and the paper traveled back and forth. In time, Dave squinted at something reading:

XIV	
Gr.Britain	11.90
U.S.S.R.	1.15
U.S.	1.10

There was another lapse of time while Dave worked out a mixture to reverse the polarity and cut back the excessive rotational inertia the room was building up, and this somehow introduced an eccentric motion that landed them both on the floor, where they shared a fresh piece of paper bearing extended calculations on one side, and on the other an untidy scrawl reading:

Gr.Britain	3,162.4
U.S.	.1136
U.S.S.R.	1.149

"Well, well," said Dave, focusing his mind with some difficulty, "blood is thicker than water, and all that, but we can't let this happen."

Dovrenin nodded emphatically, and speaking carefully, said, "Together we will smash the filthy cap . . . er . . . imperialists."

Dave shook his head, and struggled to sit up. "Thing to do is get their secret, strain the dukes and earls out of it, and use it ourselves, see?" The beauty of this idea almost blinded him.

Dovrenin considered this, and a light seemed to burst on him, too. He beamed approval, then said, "How?"

"Have to get that first paper," said Dave. He managed to get up, and tried to step over to the table, but owing to the powerful Coriolis force operating in the room this proved to be impossible. He tried again on hands and knees, succeeded, located the paper, but found that the dizzying motion of the room impeded his concentration. He decided that something would have to be done, located a small brown bottle on the table, and after many patient tries managed to get hold of it. He unscrewed the cap and with great care swallowed the faintest taste. His nostrils immediately filled with bitter fumes, and he experienced the sensation of being slammed headlong into a brick wall.

The room had stopped spinning.

Dave set down the bottle, which was labeled "Snap-Out: The One Minute Drunk Cure. By appointment to His Majesty . . ."

"*Whew,*" said Dave. He fervently hoped he hadn't taken too much. When the room began to revolve again gently, he sighed with relief, and carefully poured out a sparing dose for Dovrenin, who was lying on his back counting the revolutions of the ceiling.

Dovrenin choked, gagged, and sat up. After a moment, he sighed with relief. "That's better."

Dave, without too much difficulty from the free-wheeling action of the room, rummaged through his chest of drawers, and got out a glossy brochure. "Listen to this," he said. "'Passengers desiring information on any subject have at their disposal a most complete reference library, which may be consulted by dialing "L" on any of the ship's viewers'."

Dovrenin looked doubtful. "Would it be that easy?"

"Maybe not, but we ought to get a few leads."

Dovrenin nodded. "Worth a try."

Both men looked not quite convinced, but as the alcohol they had absorbed overpowered the sparing dosage of Snap-Out, they appeared more confident.

Dave bent at the viewer, and dialed "L". A set of instructions jumped onto the screen, followed by a list of general topics. Dovrenin pulled up a chair and sat down nearby. Thirty minutes passed in plowing through a welter of information neither man was interested in. Then the heading "H.R.I.M. Government, Under Act of Revision, A Summary," sprang onto the screen.

Dave scanned the text, then hit the spacer button for the next page. The two men leaned forward, to read:

"Peerage. The House of Lords more drastically affected by the Revision.

"Two basic factors were taken into consideration. First was the unquestioned importance of technological innovation. One basic change of technique can revolutionize an industry. Second was the ingrained national characteristic of respect for titled nobility, a respect for rank and title apart from any immediate political power.

"At the moment of Commission's report, the foreign trade situation was extremely bad, with broadly-based competition

holding an accumulating advantage in resources and production capacity. A feeling of desperation had grown up,
and this may explain the speed with which the Commission's report was acted upon.

"Two measures were adopted. The principle of *decay of
inherited title* provided that the eldest son of a nobleman
assumed upon his father's death a rank and privilege lowered by two degrees. The son of a duke became an earl. The
son of an earl became a baron. The second principle, that of
acquisition of merit, provided that noble rank might be
acquired only by merit, and *principally by the bringing to
use of new technological innovations.* The patent of nobility
was awarded, not to the inventor, who was seldom interested, in any case, but to the individual *who brought the
useful invention to prominence.* The inventor was rewarded
by prize money and a percentage of profits, but received a
patent of nobility only if he himself brought the invention to
prominence.

"The result of these two measures was to create overnight
an interest in inventors and inventions which had not existed for the previous two centuries. The energies of those
who wished to rise socially, or who were moved to maintain
their ancient rank, were at once mobilized in the search for
useful innovations. Ingenious technical persons who had in
vain pleaded for at least a hearing suddenly found the
drawing rooms of the nation flung open to them.

"The effects were not slow in coming. A scheme for
ocean-mining which had been kicked around in a desultory
way for twenty years was seized upon at once and given a
trial. Serious difficulties developed, but the backer was determined upon a peerage. After a heroic struggle, the process was made economically feasible. The result was a
dramatic easing in the raw materials problem. New develop-

ments followed swiftly as a favorable climate was created for men of inventive minds.

"There were, of course, and still are, certain shortcomings. Fortunes have been lost on worthless devices. The wild scramble for position disgusts many. The bumptious self-importance of some newly-titled knights and baronets is a continuing offense. The lordly mannerisms of the degenerate scions of once-great families is an irritation which must be experienced to be appreciated.

"The main defense of the system is that it works. The social process it has set in motion is the unquestioned cause of the accelerating rise in Imperial power, dominion, and prosperity. This alliance of genius and worldly society is the hallmark that today distinguishes the Empire from the backward nations of the home world.

"One might wish to confer the blessings of our systems upon these nations foundering in the backwash of history. But repeated missionary efforts have failed, rousing savage passions where enlightenment was intended.

"We must not despair. The inevitable march of history will sweep the doubters along with the procession, if not at the van, yet somewhere in the dusty trail of the column, and at last all will issue out of the abyss and the confusion into the broad royal grandeur of space.

"In the end, all will be one mighty Empire."

Dave snapped off the viewer, and the two men looked at each other.

"All right," said Dovrenin. "Now we see how it works. *How do we adapt it?*"

Dinner time was approaching as, symbolic riding crop in hand, Richard, Prince of the Realm, strode briskly down the hall that ran past Room 226, where Dave and Anatoly still wrestled with their problem. From somewhere up the corridor, the stirring strains of "Rule, Brittania" came faintly to Richard's ears, the word "waves" replaced by "stars," destroying the rhyme but not injuring the meaning. Richard was in a good mood, and slapped his leg lightly with the riding crop every few steps, an outward sign of his satisfaction.

Word had just reached him that young Smythe had cracked the self-repair problem for gravitors in actual use. The silver-handled crop that Richard carried, modest symbol of his position as First Peer of the Empire was his for a time longer. Moreover, this discovery was bound to be so widely useful as to add another few years to his tenure as a prince of quasi-royal blood.

Even if, he thought, eyes narrowed, even if he should lose the first rank—which heaven forbid, but such things did happen—still it was no small matter to be a Prince of the Realm. Damn the accelerated decay on that rank. A fellow could never rest, without getting slammed back to a dukedom.

He rounded a corner, telling himself that it had taken three generations to work up to this position, and he didn't intend to lose it without a struggle. There were those—petty fellows, sweaty upstart barons, backslid sons of earls, and the like—who complained that a dynasty like that of his family was unfair to the others. The beautiful answer to that was, "The system exists for the benefit of the Realm and of the innovators, not for the benefit of the nobility." That left the croakers helplessly grinding their teeth. Good for them. Let them shut up and produce.

His family knew how to produce, how to keep the inventors happy and working. Hunt them out, keep them going, doubt them when doubt will stimulate, believe in them when they doubt themselves. After a time it became an instinct. He could walk past a tenement, with the smell of decaying orange peels in his nostrils, and detect an inventive mind at work in the basement across the street. There must, he supposed, be some outward sign that he wasn't consciously aware of, a flash of light and movement, a fleeting glimpse of apparatus, seen but not—

"Hullo," he said suddenly. "What's this?"

He'd come to an abrupt stop outside a blank-faced door numbered 226. There was a peculiar something in the air, like the almost palpable absence of sound a man is aware of in an intensely quiet room.

"Something doing," said Richard, his instincts alert. He glanced up and down the hall, then stepped to the door, his hand raised as if to knock, and paused, listening.

"So then," came the voice of Anatoly Dovrenin, "each Party member must sponsor one good invention every five years, or he loses his Party card. What do you think of that?"

"It's a good idea," came the voice of Dave Blackmer, muffled by the door, "but probably it still needs to have some more work done on it. Now *my* idea is to have two major leagues of half-a-dozen teams each, see? Each region's got its own team. The New York Bombers, Boston Gnats, Philadelphia Phillies. The 'players' get on the team because they sponsor inventors. Cash prizes, pennants, and gold, silver and bronze cups are given out every six months for the leading team, with special mention and smaller cups for the leading players on each team. What scores points is useful inventions brought to prominence."

Dovrenin's voice came through the door. "This will work? Or did this idea come out of the whisky bottle? Who will be interested? Where will your 'fans' come from?"

"Where do you think? What gets people interested in a little ball batted around the park? It's the *contest* that counts. It's regional pride. Once it gets going, it picks up speed. Listen, they'll have special scouts going around to spot inventors. The newspapers will feature a running coverage—"

Outside the door, Richard frowned, gauging the potential merit of the innovations with practiced instinct. "They've got hold of something," he told himself. "Haven't got it worked into proper form yet, but—"

Habit brought his hand up, to rap once eagerly on the door.

"Just a minute," said a voice, "I'll get the door."

Horrified, Richard realized what he had been about to do.

Some inventors were best left alone, like that fellow who had the plan to turn the polar regions into tropical gardens, and which would, just incidentally, immerse London under the melted ice.

Firmly, the First Peer of the Realm stepped back, said, "Sorry, I misread the number," and strode swiftly down the hall.

The door opened, and Dave and Anatoly stared after him.

"Now," said Dave, "what do you suppose *he* wanted?"

Dovrenin shrugged. "Who knows what goes on in the minds of these grasping imperialists? Let us get back to work."

The door closed.

The ship sped on, carrying twenty-eight assorted dandies, fops, and ne'er-do-wells, thirty crewmen, four hundred and seventy-eight status-conscious noblemen, sixteen inventors and assistants in specially outfitted workshops, one proletarian, and one free-enterpriser.

Not one of these travelers was aware that, between them, they had the long-sought, supposedly-mythical entity to turn dross into wealth. But they went on using it just the same.

THE CIRCUIT RIDERS

by R. C. FitzPatrick

He was an old man and very drunk. Very drunk or very
sick. It was the middle of the day and the day was hot, but
the old man had on a suit, and a sweater under the suit. He
stopped walking and stood still, swaying gently on wide-
spread legs, and tried to focus his eyes. He lived here . . .
around here . . . somewhere around here. He continued on,
stumbling up the street.

He finally made it home. He lived on the second floor
and he dragged himself up the narrow staircase with both
hands clutching the railing. But he was still very careful of
the paper bag under his arm. The bag was full of beer.

Once in the room, he managed to take off his coat before
he sank down on the bed. He just sat there, vacant and lost
and empty, and drank his beer.

It was a hot, muggy, August afternoon—Wednesday in
Pittsburgh. The broad rivers put moisture in the air, and
the high hills kept it there. Light breezes were broken-up
and diverted by the hills before they could bring more than
a breath of relief.

In the East Liberty precinct station the doors and windows were opened wide to snare the vagrant breezes. There
were eight men in the room; the desk sergeant, two beat cops
waiting to go on duty, the audio controller, the deAngelis

operator, two reporters, and a local book . . . businessman.
From the back of the building, the jail proper, the voice of a
prisoner asking for a match floated out to the men in the
room, and a few minutes later they heard the slow, exasper-
ated steps of the turnkey as he walked over to give his prisoner a light.

At 3:32 pm, the deAngelis board came alive as half-a-
dozen lights flashed red, and the needles on the dials below
them trembled in the seventies and eighties. Every other
light on the board showed varying shades of pink, register-
ing in the sixties. The operator glanced at the board, started
to note the times and intensities of two of the dials in his log,
scratched them out, then went on with his conversation with
the audio controller. The younger reporter got up and came
over to the board. The controller and the operator looked
up at him.

"Nothing," said the operator shaking his head in a negative. "Bad call at the ball game, probably." He nodded his
head towards the lights on the deAngelis, "They'll be gone
in five, ten minutes."

The controller reached over and turned up the volume
on his radio. The radio should not have been there, but
as long as everyone did his job and kept the volume low, the
Captain looked the other way. The set belonged to the
precinct.

The announcer's voice came on, ". . . ning up, he's
fuming. Doak is holding Sterrett back. What a beef!
Brutaugh's got his nose not two inches from Frascoli's
face, and Brother! is he letting him have it. Oh! Oh! Here
comes Gilbert off the mound; he's stalking over. When
Gil puts up a holler, you know he thinks it's a good one.
Brutaugh keeps pointing at the foul line—you can see from
here the chalk's been wiped away—he's insisting the run-
ner slid out of the base path. Frascoli's walking away, but

Danny's going right aft . . ." The controller turned the volume down again.

The lights on the deAngelis board kept flickering, but by 3:37 all but two had gone out, one by one. These two showed readings in the high sixties; one flared briefly to 78.2 then went out. Brutaugh was no longer in the ball game. By 3:41 only one light still glowed, and it was steadily fading.

Throughout the long, hot, humid afternoon the board held its reddish, irritated overtones, and occasional readings flashed in and out of the seventies. At four o'clock the new duty section came on; the deAngelis operator, whose name was Chuck Matesic, was replaced by an operator named Charlie Blaney.

"Nothing to report," Chuck told Charlie. "Rhubarb down at the point at the Forbes Municipal Field, but that's about all."

The new operator scarcely glanced at the mottled board, it was that kind of a day. He noted an occasional high in his log book, but most signals were ignored. At 5:14 he noted a severe reading of 87 which stayed on the board; at 5:16 another light came on, climbed slowly through the sixties, then soared to 77 where it held steady. Neither light was an honest red, their angry overtones chased each other rapidly.

The deAngelis operator called over to the audio controller, "Got us a case of crinkle fender, I think."

"Where?" the controller asked.

"Can't tell yet," Blaney said. "A hot-head and a citizen with righteous indignation. They're clear enough, but not too sharp." He swiveled in his chair and adjusted knobs before a large circular screen. Pale streaks of light glowed briefly as the sweep passed over them. There were milky dots everywhere. A soft light in the lower left hand corner of the screen cut an uncertain path across the grid, and two indeterminate splotches in the upper half of the scope flared out to the margin.

"Morningside," the operator said.

The splashes of light separated; one moved quickly off the screen, the other held stationary for several minutes, then contracted and began a steady, jagged advance toward the center of the grid. One inch down, half an inch over, two inches down, then four inches on a diagonal line.

"Like I said," said Blaney. "An accident."

Eight minutes later, at 5:32, a slightly pompous and thoroughly outraged young salesman marched through the doors of the station house and over to the desk sergeant.

"Some clown just hit me . . ." he began.

"With his fist?" asked the sergeant.

"With his car," said the salesman. "My car . . . with his car . . . he hit my car with his car."

The sergeant raised his hand. "Simmer down, young feller. Let me see your driver's license." He reached over the desk for the man's cards with one hand, and with the other he sorted out an accident form. "Just give it to me slowly." He started filling out the form.

The deAngelis operator leaned back in his chair and winked at the controller. "I'm a whiz," he said to the young reporter, "I'm a pheenom. I never miss." The reporter smiled and walked back to his colleague who was playing gin with the book . . . businessman.

The lights glowed on and off all evening, but only once had they called for action. At 10:34 two sharp readings of 92.2 and 94 even, had sent Blaney back to his dials and screen. He'd narrowed it down to a four block area when the telephone rang to report a fight at the Red Antler Grill. The controller dispatched a beat cop already in the area.

Twenty minutes later, two very large—and very obedient young toughs stumbled in, followed by an angry officer. In addition to the marks of the fight, both had a lumbering, off-balance walk that showed that the policeman had been prodding them with his riot club. It was called an "electronic persuader"; it also doubled as a carbine. Police no longer carried sidearms.

He pointed to the one on the left, "This one hit me." He pointed to the one on the right, "This one kicked me."

The one on the left was certain he would never hit another cop. The one on the right knew he would never kick another cop.

"Book 'em," the sergeant said. He looked at the two youths. "You're going in the can . . . you want to argue." The youths looked down. No one else said anything. The younger reporter came over and took down the information as the cop and the two toughs gave it to the sergeant. Then he went back to his seat at the card table and took a minityper from his pocket. He started sending to the paper.

"You ought to send that stuff direct," the card player said.

"I scribble too bad," the reporter answered.

"Bat crap," said the older man, "that little jewel can transcribe chicken scratches."

The cub scrunched over his minityper. A few minutes later he looked up at his partner, "What's a good word for hoodlum?"

The other reporter was irritated. He was also losing at gin. "What are you, a Steinbeck?" He laid down his cards. "Look kid, just send it, just the way you get it. That's why they pay re-write men. We're reporters. We report. O.K.?" He went back to his cards.

At 11:40 a light at the end of the second row turned pinkish but no reading showed on the dial below. It was only one of a dozen bulbs showing red. It was still pinkish when the watch was changed. Blaney was replaced by King.

"Watch this one," Blaney said to King, indicating an entry in the log. It was numbered 8:20:18:3059:78:4a. "I've had it on four times now, all in the high seventies. I got a feeling." The number indicated date, estimated area and relation to previous alerts in the month, estimated intent, and frequency of report. The "a" meant intermittent. Only the last three digits would change. "If it comes on again I think I'd lock a circuit on it right away." The rules called for any continuous reading over 75 to be contacted and connected after its sixth appearance.

"What about that one?" King said, pointing to a 70.4 that was unblinking in its intensity.

"Some drunk," said Blaney. "Or a baby with a head cold. Been on there for twenty minutes. You can watch for it if you like." His tone suggested that to be a waste of time.

"I'll watch it," said King. His tone suggested that he knew how to read a circuit, and if Blaney had any suggestions he could keep them to himself.

Joe Millsop finally staggered home, exhausted. He was half-drunk, and worn out from being on his feet all day, but the liquor had finally done its work. He could think about the incident without flushing hot all over. He was too tired, and too sorry for himself to be angry at anyone. And with his new-found alcoholic objectivity he could see now where he had been in the wrong. Old Bloomgarten shouldn't have chewed him out in front of a customer like that, but what the hell, he shouldn't have sassed the customer, even if she was just a dumb broad who didn't know what she wanted. He managed to get undressed before he stumbled into bed. His last coherent thought before he fell into a drugged sleep was that he'd better apologize in the morning.

8:20:18:3059:78:4a stayed off the board.

At 1:18 am, the deAngelis flared to a 98.4 then started inching down again. The young reporter sat up, alert, from where he had been dozing. The loud clang of a bell had brought him awake.

The older reporter glanced up from his cards and waved him down. "Forget it," he said, "some wife just opened the door and saw lipstick on her husband's neck."

"Oh Honey, how could you . . . fifty dollars . . ." She was crying.

"Don't, Mother . . . I thought I could make some money . . . some real money." The youngster looked sick. "I had four nines . . . four nines . . . how could I figure him for a straight flush, he didn't have a thing showing."

". . . How could you," sobbed the mother. ". . . Oh how could you."

The book . . . businessman dealt the cards. The reporter picked his up and arranged them in his hand, he discarded one; the businessman ignored it and drew from the deck, he discarded; the reporter picked the discard and threw away a card from his hand; the businessman drew from the deck and discarded the same card he'd drawn; the reporter picked it up, tapped it slowly in place with his elbow, placed his discard face down, and spread his hand.

"Gin," he said.

"Arrrgh," said the businessman. "Damn it, you play good. You play real good."

A light on the deAngelis flashed red and showed a reading of 65.4 on the dial.

"Can't beat skill," said the reporter. "Count!"

"Fifty-six," said the businessman. "That's counting gin," he added.

"Game," the reporter announced. "I'll figure the damage."

"You play good," said the businessman in disgust.

"You only say that 'cause it's true," the reporter said. "But it's sweet of you all the same."

"Shut up!" said the businessman.

The reporter looked up, concerned. "You stuck?" he asked solicitously. He seemed sincere.

"Certainly I'm stuck," the businessman snarled.

"Then stay stuck," said the reporter in a kindly tone. He patted the businessman on the cheek.

The same light on the deAngelis flashed red. This time the dial registered eighty-two. The operator chuckled and looked over at the gamblers, where the reporter was still adding up the score.

"How much you down, Bernie?" he asked the businessman.

"Four dollars and ninety-six cents," the reporter answered.

"You play good," Bernie said again.

The deAngelis went back to normal, and the operator went back to his magazine. The bulb at the end of the second row turned from a light pink to a soft rose, the needle on its dial finally flickered on to the scale. There were other lights on the board, but none called for action. It was still just a quiet night in the middle of the week.

The room was filthy. It had a natural filth that clings to a cheap room, and a man-made, careless filth that would disfigure a Taj Mahal. It wasn't so much that things were dirty, it was more that nothing was clean. Pittsburgh was no longer a smokey city. That problem had been solved long before the mills had stopped belching smoke. Now, with atomics and filters on every stack in every home, the city was clean. Clean as the works of man could make it, yet still filthy as only the minds of man could achieve. The city might be clean but there were people who were not, and the room was not. Overhead the ceiling light still burned, casting its harsh glare on the trashy room, and the trashy, huddled figure on the bed.

He was an old man, lying on the bed fully clothed, even to his shoes. He twisted fretfully in his sleep; the body tried to rise, anticipating nature even when the mind could not. The man gagged several times and finally made it up to a sitting position before the vomit came. He was still asleep, but his reaction was automatic; he grabbed the bottom of his sweater and pulled it out before him to form a bucket of sorts. When he finished being sick he sat still, swaying gently back and forth, and tried to open his eyes. He could not make it. Still asleep he ducked out of the fouled sweater, made an ineffectual dab at his mouth, wadded the sweater in a ball, and threw it over in front of the bathroom door.

He fell back on the bed, exhausted, and went on with his fitful sleep.

At 4:15 in the morning a man walked into the station house. His name was Henry Tilton. He was a reporter for the *Evening Press*. He waved a greeting to the desk sergeant and went over to kibitz the card game.

Both players looked up, startled. The reporter playing cards said, "Hello, Henry." He looked at his watch. "Whoosh! I didn't realize it was that late." He turned to the businessman. "Hurry up, finish the hand. Got to get my beauty sleep."

"Whaddaya mean, hurry up," said Bernie, "you're into me for fifteen bucks."

"Get it back from Hank here," the reporter said. He nodded at the newcomer, "Want this hand? You're fourteen points down. Lover boy's got sixty-eight on game, but you're a box up."

"Sure," said Tilton. He took the cards.

The morning news reporters left. The businessman dealt a new hand. Tilton waited four rounds, then knocked with ten.

Bernie slammed down his cards. "You lousy reporters are all alike! I'm going home." He got up to put on his coat. "I'll be back about ten, you still be here?"

"Sure," said Tilton, ". . . with the score." He folded the paper and put it in his pocket.

The businessman walked out and Tilton went over to the deAngelis board. "Anything?" he asked.

"Nah," said King. He pointed to the lights, "Just lovers' quarrels tonight; all pale pink and peaceful."

Tilton smiled and ambled back to the cell block. The operator put his feet up on his desk, then frowned and put them down again. He leaned toward the board and studied the light at the end of the second row. The needle registered sixty-six. The operator pursed his lips, then flicked a switch that opened the photo file. Every five minutes an automatic camera photographed the deAngelis board, developed the film, and filed the picture away in its storage vault.

King studied the photographs for quite awhile, then pulled his log book over and made an entry. He wrote: 8:20:19:3142:1x. The last three digits meant that he wasn't sure about the intensity, and the "x" signified a continuous reading.

King turned to the audio controller, "Do me a favor, Gus, but strictly unofficial. Contact everybody around us: Oakland, Squirrel Hill, Point Breeze, Lawrenceville, Bloomfield . . . everybody in this end of town. Find out if they've got one low intensity reading that's been on for hours. If they haven't had it since before midnight, I'm not interested."

"Something up?" the controller asked.

"Probably not," said the operator. "I'd just like to pin this one down as close as I can. On a night like this my screen shows nothing but milk."

"Give you a lift home?" the older reporter asked.

"Thanks," said the cub shaking his head, "but I live out by the Youghiogheny River."

"So?" the older man shrugged. "Half hour flight. Hop in."

"I don't understand," the cub said.

"What? Me offering you a lift."

"No," said the cub. "Back there in the station house. You know."

"You mean the deAngelis?"

"Not that exactly," said the cub. "I understand a deAngelis board; everybody broadcasts emotions, and if they're strong enough they can be received and interpreted. It's the cops I don't understand. I thought any reading over eighty was dangerous and had to be looked into, and anything over ninety was plain murder and had to be picked up. Here they had been ignoring eighties and nineties all night long."

"You remember that children's story you wrote last Christmas about an Irish imp named Sean O'Claus?" his companion asked him.

"Certainly," the cub said scowling. "I'll sell it some day."

"You remember the Fashion Editor killed it because she thought 'See-Ann' was a girl's name, and it might be sacrilegious."

"You're right I remember," the cub said, his voice rising.

"Like to bet you didn't register over ninety that day? As a matter of fact, I'll head for the nearest precinct and bet you five you're over eighty right now." He laughed aloud and the young man calmed down. "I had that same idea myself at first. About ninety being against the law. That's one of the main troubles, the law. Every damn state in the dominion has its own ideas on what's dangerous. The laws are all fouled up. But what most of them boil down to is this—a man has to have a continuous reading of over ninety before he can be arrested. Not arrested really, detained. Just a reading on the board doesn't prove a thing. Some people walk around boiling at ninety all their lives—like editors. But the sweet old lady down the block, who's never sworn in her life, she may hit sixty-five and reach for a knife. And that doesn't prove a thing. Ninety sometimes means murder, but usually not; up to a hundred and ten usually means murder, but sometimes not; and anything over one-twenty always means murder. And it still doesn't prove a thing. And then again, a psychotic or a professional gunsel may not register at all. They kill for fun, or for business—they're not angry at anybody."

"It's all up to the deAngelis operators. They're the kingpins, they make the system work. Not Simon deAngelis who invented it, or the technicians who install it, or the Police Commissioner who takes the results to City Hall. The operators make it or break it. Sure, they have rules to follow—if they want. But a good operator ignores the rules, and a bad operator goes by the book, and he's still no damn good. It's just like radar was sixty, seventy years ago. Some got the knack, some don't."

"Then the deAngelis doesn't do the job," said the cub.

"Certainly it does," the older man said. "Nothing's perfect. It gives the police the jump on a lot of crime. Premeditated murder for one. The average citizen can't kill anyone unless he's mad enough, and if he's mad enough, he registers on the deAngelis. And ordinary robbers get caught; their plans don't go just right, or they fight among themselves. Or, if they just don't like society—a good de-Angelis operator can tell quite a bit if he gets a reading at the wrong time of day or night, or in the wrong part of town."

"But what about the sweet old lady who registers sixty-five and then goes berserk?"

"That's where your operator really comes in. Usually that kind of a reading comes too late. Grandma's swinging the knife at the same time the light goes on in the station house. But if she waits to swing, or builds herself up to it, then she may be stopped.

"You know those poor operators are supposed to log any reading over sixty, and report downtown with anything over eighty. Sure they are! If they logged everything over sixty they'd have writer's cramp the first hour they were on watch. And believe me, Sonny, any operator who reported downtown on every reading over eighty would be back pounding a beat before the end of his first day. They just do the best they can, and you'd be surprised at how good that can be."

The old man woke up, but kept his eyes closed. He was afraid. It was too quiet, and the room was clammy with an early morning chill. He opened his eyelids a crack and looked at the window. Still dark outside. He lay there trembling and brought his elbows in tight to his body. He was going to have the shakes; he knew he'd have the shakes and it was still too early. Too early. He looked at the clock. It was only a quarter after five. Too early for the bars to be open. He covered his eyes with his hands and tried to think.

It was no use; he couldn't think. He sobbed. He was afraid to move. He knew he had to have a drink, and he knew if he got up he'd be sick. "Oh Lord!" he breathed.

The trembling became worse. He tried to press it away by hugging his body with his arms. It didn't help. He looked wildly around and tried to concentrate. He thought about the bureau . . . no. The dresser . . . no. His clothes . . . he felt feverishly about his body . . . no. Under the . . . bed . . . no . . . wait . . . maybe. He'd brought some beer home. Now he remembered. Maybe there was some left.

He rolled over on his stomach and groped under the bed. His tremulous fingers found the paper bag and he dragged it out. It was full of empty cans; the carton inside was ripped. He tore the sack open . . . empty cans . . . no! there was a full one . . . two full ones—

He staggered to his feet and looked for an opener. There was one on the bureau. He stumbled over and opened his first beautiful, lovely can of beer. He put his mouth down close to the top so that none of the foam could escape him. He'd be all right 'til seven, now. The bars opened at seven. He'd be all right 'til seven.

He did not notice the knife lying beside the opener. He did not own a knife and had no recollection of buying one.

It was a hunting knife and he was not a hunter.

The light at the end of the second row was growing gradually brighter. The needle traveled slowly across the dial, 68.2, 68.4, 68.6. . . .

King called over to the audio controller. "They all report in yet?"

The controller nodded. "Squirrel Hill's got your signal on, same reading as you have. Bloomfield thinks they may have it. Oakland's not too sure. Everybody else is negative." The controller walked over. "Which one is it?"

King pointed to the end of the second row.

"Can't you get it on your screen?"

"Hell, yes, I've got him on my screen!" King swiveled in his chair and turned on the set. The scope was covered with pale dots. "Which one is he? There?" He pointed to the left. "That's a guy who didn't get the raise he wanted. There?" He pointed to the center. "That's a little girl with bad dreams. She has them every night. There? That's my brother! He's in the Veteran's Hospital and wanted to come home a week ago."

"So don't get excited," said the controller. "I only asked."

"I'm sorry, Gus," King apologized. "My fault. I'm a little edgy . . . probably nothing at all."

"Well you got it narrowed down anyway," Gus said. "If you got it, and Squirrel Hill's got it, then he's in Shadyside. If Oakland doesn't have him, then he's on this side of Aiken Avenue." The controller had caught King's fever; the "it" had become a "him". "And if Bloomfield doesn't have him, then he's on the other side of Baum Boulevard."

"Only Bloomfield might have him."

"Well what the hell, you've still got him located in the lower half of Shadyside. Tell you what, I'll send a man up Ellsworth, get Bloomfield to cruise Baum Boulevard in a scout car, and have Squirrel Hill put a patrol on Wilkens. We can triangulate."

"No," said King, "not yet. Thanks anyway, Gus, but there's no point in stirring up a tempest in a teapot. Just tell them to watch it. If it climbs over 75 we can narrow it down then."

"It's your show," said Gus.

The old man finished his second can of beer. The trembling was almost gone. He could stand and move without breaking out in a cold sweat. He ran his hand

through his hair and looked at the clock. 6:15. Too early.
He looked around the room for something to read. There
were magazines and newspapers scattered everywhere; the
papers all folded back to the sports section. He picked up a
paper, not even bothering about the date, and tried to
interest himself in the batting averages of the Interconti-
nental League. Yamamura was on top with .387; the old
man remembered when Yamamura came up as a rookie.
But right now he didn't care; the page trembled and the
type kept blurring. He threw the paper down. He had a
headache.

The old man got up and went over to the bathroom. He
steadied himself against the door jamb and kicked the
wadded sweater out of sight beneath the dresser. He went
into the bathroom and turned on the water. He ran his
hands over his face and thought about shaving, but he
couldn't face the work involved. He managed to run a
comb through his hair and rinse out his mouth.

He came back into the room. It was 6:30. Maybe Freddie's was open. If Freddie wasn't, then maybe the Grill.
He'd have to take his chances, he couldn't stand it here
any longer. He put on his coat and stumbled out.

At eight o'clock the watch was changed; Matesic replaced King.

"Anything?" asked Matesic.

"Just this one, Chuck," said King. "I may be a fool, but
this one bothers me." King was a diplomat where Blaney
was not.

King showed him the entry. The dial now stood at 72.8.
"It's been on there all night, since before I had the watch.
And it's been climbing, just slow and steady, but all the
time climbing. I locked a circuit on him, but I'll take it off
if you want me to."

"No," said Matesic, "leave it on. That don't smell right to me neither."

The old man was feeling better. He'd been in the bar two hours, and he'd had two pickled eggs, and the bartender didn't bother him. Beer was all right, but a man needed whiskey when he was sick. He'd have one, maybe two more, and then he'd eat some breakfast. He didn't know why, but he knew he mustn't get drunk.

At nine o'clock the needle on the dial climbed past seventy-five. Matesic asked for coverage. That meant that two patrolmen would be tied up, doing nothing but searching for an echo. And it might be a wild goose chase. He was explaining to the Captain, but the Captain wasn't listening. He was looking at the photographs in the de-Angelis file.

"You don't like this?" the Captain asked.

Matesic said he didn't like it.

"And King said he didn't like it?"

"King thinks the same way I do, he's been on there too damn long and too damn consistent."

"Pick him up," the Captain turned and ordered the audio controller. "If we can't hold him, we can at least get a look at him."

"It's not too clear yet," said Matesic, "it'll take a spread."

"I know what it'll take," the Captain roared. "Don't tell me my job! Put every available man on this, I want that guy brought in."

The old man walked back to his room. He was carrying a dozen cans of beer, but the load was light and he walked upright. He felt fine, like a million dollars. And he was beginning to remember.

When he entered the room he saw the knife and when he saw the knife he smiled. A man had to be smart and a man had to be prepared. They were smart . . . wicked and smart . . . but he was smarter. He'd bought the knife a long, long time ago, in a different world—they couldn't fool him that way. They were clever all right, they fooled the whole world.

He put his beer on the bureau, then walked into the bathroom and turned on the water in the tub. He came back out and started to undress. He was humming to himself. When he finished undressing he went over to the bureau and opened a can of beer. He carried it into the bathroom, put it beside the tub, and lowered himself into the water.

Ah . . . that was the ticket. Water and being clean. Clean and being water. Being water and being candy and being smart. They fooled the whole world, but not him. The whole, wide world, but they couldn't fool him. He was going to fool them. All pretty and innocent. Hah! Innocent! He knew. They were rotten, they were rotten all the way through. They fooled the whole world but they were rotten . . . rotten . . . and he was the only one who knew.

He finished the beer and stood up in the tub. The water ran off his body in greasy runlets. He didn't pull the plug. He stepped out of the tub and over to the bathroom mirror. His face looked fine, not puffy at all. He'd fool them. He sprinkled himself with lilac water, put the bottle to his lips, and swished some of it in his mouth. Oh yes, he'd fool them. A man couldn't be too clever, they were clever, so he had to be clever. He began to shave.

The Captain was on an audio circuit, talking to an Assistant Commissioner. "Yes, Sir, I know that—Yes, Sir, it could be, but it might be something else—Yes, Sir, I know Squirrel Hill has problems, but we need help—Yes, Commissioner, it's over ninety now (the Captain signaled wildly to Matesic; Matesic held up four fingers, then two); 94.2 and still going up—No, Sir, we don't know. Some guy gonna quit his job . . . or kill his boss. Maybe he found out his wife is cheating on him. We can't tell until we pick him up—Yes, Sir—Yes, Sir—Thank you, Sir."

The Captain hung up. "I hate politicians," he snarled.

"Watch it, Captain," said Matesic, "I'll get you on my board."

"Get me on it, Hell," the Captain said, "I've never been off."

The old man finished dressing. He knotted his tie and brushed off the front of his suit with his hand. He looked fine. He'd fool them, he looked just like anybody else. He crossed to the bureau and picked up the knife. It was still in the scabbard. He didn't take it out, he just put it in his pocket. Good. It didn't show.

He walked out on the street. The sun was shining brightly and heat waves were coming up from the sidewalk. Good. Good. This was the best time. People, the real people, would be working or lying down asleep. But they'd be out. They were always out. Out all sweet and innocent in the hot sun.

He turned down the street and ambled toward the drug store. He didn't want to hurry. He had lots of time. He had to get some candy first. That was the ticket, candy. Candy worked, candy always worked. Candy was good but candy was wicked. He was good but they were wicked. Oh, you had to be smart.

"That has to be him," Matesic said. The screen was blotched and milky, but a large splash of light in the lower left hand corner outshone everything else. "He's somewhere around Negley Avenue." He turned to the Captain. "Where do you have your men placed?"

"In a box," the Captain said. "Fifth and Negley, Aiken and Negley, Center and Aiken, and Center and Negley. And three scout cars overhead."

The old man walked up Ellsworth to the Liberty School. There were always lots of young ones around Liberty School. The young ones were the worst.

"I'm losing him."
"Where are you?"
"Center and Aiken."
"Anybody getting him stronger?"
"Yeah. Me. Negley and Fifth."
"Never mind. Never mind, we got him. We see him now."
"Where?"
"Bellefonte and Ivy. Liberty School."

She was a friendly little thing, and pretty. Maybe five, maybe six, and her Mommy had told her not to talk to strangers. But the funny old man wasn't talking, he was sitting on the curb, and he was eating candy, and he was offering some to her. He smiled at the little girl and she smiled back.

The scout car settled to earth on automatic. Two officers climbed out of the car and walked quietly over to the old man, one on either side. They each took an arm and lifted him gently to his feet.

"Hello there, Old Timer."

"Hi, little girl."

The old man looked around bewildered. He dropped his candy and tried to reach his knife. They mustn't interfere.

It was no use. The officers were very kind and gentle, and they were very, very firm. They led him off as though he were an old, old friend.

One of the officers called back over his shoulder, "Bye, bye, little girl."

The little girl dutifully waved 'bye.

She looked at the paper sack on the sidewalk. She didn't know what to do, but the nice old man was gone. She looked around, but no one was paying any attention, they were all watching the softball game. Suddenly she made a grab and clutched the paper bag to her body. Then she turned and ran back up the street to tell her Mommy how wonderful, wonderful lucky she was.